Rosamunde Pilcher has had a long and distinguished career as a novelist and short story writer, but it was her phenomenally successful novel, *The Shell Seekers*, that captured the hearts of all who read it, and won her international recognition as one of the best-loved storytellers of our time. Her bestselling novels, *September*, *Coming Home* and *Winter Solstice* were made into television films. She was awarded an O.B.E for services to literature in 2002 and an honorary Doctor of Laws degree from Dundee University in 2010.

Praise for Winter Solstice

'Rosamunde Pilcher's warm spell is charming and utterly convincing'

Daily Mail

'An entrancing tale of middle-aged love, broken hearts and teenage angst'

Daily Express

'Britain's most under-rated novelist'

Sunday Times

'Pilcher's strength is knowing what she can do well and writing about what she knows. She has a way of tapping into the emotional life of her readers and making them care about characters not unlike themselves'

Daily Telegraph

Praise for *The Shell Seekers*

'A deeply satisfying story written with love and confidence'

Maeve Binchy in *The New York Times Book Review*

'Her genius is to create characters you really care about'

Daily Express

'This is storytelling at its best: a long satisfying read which would enhance any holiday'

Today

'A long, beguiling saga, typically English . . . splendid'

Mail on Sunday

'A beautiful haunting story . . . that will tug at your heart strings'

Prima

'The quality family novel we have been waiting for. If you can only choose one book this summer, choose this one'

Hello!

Praise for *September*

'*September* has a classical sense of time and place. Elegantly unfolding, it's a novel to wallow in like a finely scented bath'

Today

'An alluring sense of the Scottish Highlands is at the very core of this book . . . There is a comfortable pleasure to be had in following the interlocked lives of Violet Aird and her family and friends, with their numerous scandals and conflicts . . . Character is at the heart of a story, and this fine tale has plenty of that'

Belva Plain in *The New York Times Book Review*

'A wonderful, not-to-be-missed novel that is destined to provide many hours of pleasurable reading'

Woman and Home

'With the same effortless charm which made *The Shell Seekers* an international success, Rosamunde Pilcher draws enchanting cameos of family life in her new novel'

Annabel

'*September* has been awaited with bated breath. Could she carry on in the bestselling tradition with another remarkable novel or was it a one-off? The answer to this question must be "Yes, it is a big novel, and will delight her readers"'

Books

ROSAMUNDE PILCHER

THE BLUE BEDROOM AND OTHER STORIES

This collection first published in the USA in 1985 by St Martin's Press

First published in Great Britain in 1990 by Hodder & Stoughton
An Hachette UK company
Stories in this collection – apart from 'Amita' – were previously published in
Woman's Weekly or *Woman & Home*

This edition 2013

1

A CIP catalogue record for this title is available from the British Library

ISBN 978 1 444 76194 8

Printed in Great Britain by Clays Ltd, St Ives plc

Hodder & Stoughton policy is to use papers that are natural, renewable
and recyclable products and made from wood grown in sustainable forests.
The logging and manufacturing processes are expected to conform to
the environmental regulations of the country of origin.

Hodder & Stoughton Ltd
338 Euston Road
London NW1 3BH

www.hodder.co.uk

Contents

Toby

On a cold spring day, just before Easter, Jemmy Todd, the postman, walked into the Hardings' kitchen, laid the morning's mail on their breakfast table, and told them that Mr Sawcombe, their neighbour, had died, early that morning, of a heart attack.

There were four Hardings sitting at the table. Toby, eight years old, was in the process of eating cornflakes. Now, hearing about Mr Sawcombe, he could feel the cornflakes in his mouth, soggy and crunchy all at once, but there was no way to get rid of the mouthful, because it seemed that he had forgotten how to chew, and as well a lump began to grow in his throat, making it impossible to swallow.

The only good thing was that the rest of his family seemed to be equally shocked and dumbfounded. His father, dressed for the office and just on the point of getting up from the table and leaving for work, laid down his coffee cup and sat back in his chair and stared at Jemmy.

'Bill Sawcombe? Dead? When did you hear?'

'Vicar told me first thing, just as I was starting my round. Met him coming out of the church.'

Toby looked at his mother and saw that her eyes were bright with tears. 'Oh, dear.' He could not bear her to cry. He had seen her cry once before, when her old dog had had to be put down, and the sensation that his world was falling to pieces had stayed with him for days. 'Poor Mrs Sawcombe. What a dreadful shock for her.'

9

'He had a heart attack a couple of years ago, remember,' said Jemmy.

'But he got over it. And he'd been keeping so well, enjoying his garden, and having a bit of time to himself after all those years of running his farm.'

Vicky, who was nineteen, suddenly found her voice. 'I can't *bear* it. I simply don't think I can bear it.'

Vicky was home for Easter from London, where she had a job and a flat that she shared with two other girls. When she was on holiday Vicky never dressed for breakfast, but came downstairs in her bathrobe, which was made of white towelling and had blue stripes. The blue stripes were the same blue as Vicky's eyes and she had long pale hair and sometimes looked very pretty and sometimes very plain. She looked plain now. Distress made her plain, pulling down the corners of her mouth as though she was about to burst into tears, accentuating the peaky contours of her bony little face. Their father was always telling Vicky that she was much too thin, but as she ate like a ploughman, nobody could accuse her of anything except, possibly, greed.

'He was such a nice man. We shall miss him.' His mother's eyes turned to Toby, still sitting there with his cheeks full of unchewed cornflakes. She knew – they all knew – that Mr Sawcombe had been Toby's best friend. She leaned across the table and laid a hand over his own. 'We'll all miss him, Toby.'

Toby did not reply. But with his mother's hand over his own he found that it was possible to swallow the last of the cornflakes. His mother, understanding, gently removed the half-empty bowl that stood on the table in front of him.

'One thing,' said Jemmy, 'there's Tom there to take on the farm. It's not as though Mrs Sawcombe's on her own.'

Tom was Mr Sawcombe's grandson. Tom was twenty-three. Toby and Vicky had known him all their lives. In the old days when they were much younger, Vicky and

10

Tom used to go to parties together, to Pony Club dances, and to gymkhana camps in the summer. But then Tom went away, to Agricultural College, and Vicky grew up too and learned how to be a secretary, and she went to London, and somehow, now, they didn't seem to have very much in common.

Toby thought this was a shame. Vicky made lots of new friends, and sometimes brought them home. But Toby didn't think any of them was as nice as Tom Sawcombe. There had been one, called Philip, who had come to spend New Year with the Hardings. He was very tall and fair, and drove around in a car that looked like a shiny black torpedo, but somehow he didn't fit properly into the fabric of ordinary family life, and, what was more disturbing, when he was there Vicky didn't fit in either. She talked in a different way; she laughed in a different way.

On New Year's Eve, they had a small party, and Tom was invited, but Vicky behaved in an offhand and casual way towards him, and Tom was obviously very hurt. Toby thought her behaviour sickening. He was very fond of Tom and could not bear to see him so cast down, and when the uncomfortable evening was over, he told his mother so.

'I know just how you feel,' his mother said, 'but we must let Vicky lead her own life and make her own decisions. She's grown up now, she can choose her own friends, make her own mistakes, go her own way. That's what being a family is all about.'

'I don't want to be a family with Vicky if she's going to be so horrid.'

'Perhaps that's how you feel just now, but she is your sister.'

'I don't like that Philip.'

The dreaded Philip, however, mercifully faded out of Vicky's life. She did not invite him home again, and gradually his name in her conversation was replaced by

11

other names. Vicky's family breathed a sigh of relief and things returned to normal, but not so with Tom. Since that evening, communications between himself and Vicky appeared to have broken down, and now, if she was home, Tom never came near the house.

'No, Mrs Sawcombe's certainly not on her own,' said Mr Harding. 'She's got a good boy there.' He looked at his watch and got up from the table. 'I must be off. Thank you for telling us, Jemmy.'

'Sorry to be the bearer of sad news,' Jemmy replied, and went away in his little red post van to spread the tidings around the rest of the parish. Toby's father departed in the big car for the office. Vicky went upstairs to get dressed. Toby and his mother were left alone, sitting at the table.

He looked at her and she smiled, and he said, 'I've never had a friend who died before.'

'It happens to everybody, sooner or later.'

'He was only sixty-two. He told me so, the day before yesterday. That's not old.'

'Heart attacks are funny things. And at least he wasn't very ill or infirm. He would have hated to be bedridden, or dependent on his family – a nuisance to anybody. When people die, Toby, you have to think of good things, remember good times. And be glad for them.'

'I'm not glad Mr Sawcombe's dead.'

'Death is part of life.'

'He was only sixty-two.'

'Why don't you have some bacon and eggs?'

'I don't want bacon and eggs.'

'Then what do you want to do?'

'I don't know.'

'Why don't you go down to the village and see if David would like to play with you?' David Harker was Toby's holiday friend. His father ran the village pub, and sometimes David was good for a free fizzy drink or a pack of crisps.

Toby considered this. It was, perhaps, better than

nothing. 'All right.' He pushed back his chair and stood up. There was a horrible clamped sort of feeling in his chest as though somebody had hurt his heart.

' . . . and don't be too sad about Mr Sawcombe. He wouldn't want you to be too sad.'

He went out of the house and down the lane. Between the lane and the cow pasture that was part of Mr Sawcombe's farm was a small paddock where Vicky used to keep her pony. But the pony had long since departed, and Toby's father had let the grazing to Mr Sawcombe for Mrs Sawcombe's four Jacob ewes. They were her pets, horned and spotted, and had old-fashioned names like Daisy and Emily. One cold morning at the end of October, Toby had come down to see the sheep and had found a mighty horned ram in with the girls. The ram had stayed for a bit, and then had been manhandled home by his owner, bundled ignominiously into the back of a ramshackle van.

But he had done his stuff. Already three pairs of twin lambs had arrived, and now only Daisy was awaiting her time. Toby leaned over the fence and called to her, and she came slowly and with dignity, to fondle his hand with her noble nose, to let him scratch the woolly poll between her proud, curved horns.

Toby eyed her professionally, as Tom eyed her. She was enormous, her bulk made more huge by her fleece of long, soft wool.

'Are you going to have your twins today?' he asked her.

Daisy has twins too, Mr Sawcombe had said, only a day or so ago, *and we'll have a two hundred percent lambing, Toby. Two hundred percent. That's the best any sheep farmer can ask for. I'd like that to happen. For Mrs Sawcombe's sake, I'd like that to happen.*

Impossible to accept that he would never speak to Mr Sawcombe again. Impossible to accept that he had gone; that he simply wasn't there. Other people had died, but

never a person so close to Toby as Mr Sawcombe. Toby's
grandfather had died, but so long ago that Toby didn't
even remember him. There was only a photograph beside Granny's bed, and stories that Granny told him.
After his grandfather had died, Granny had stayed on
in the old, empty house until it became too much for her
to cope with, and then Toby's father had turned the back
wing of the Hardings' house into a Granny flat. So now
Granny lived with them. And yet not with them, for the
flat was quite separate, and she had her own kitchen
and bathroom and cooked her own meals and you had
to knock on the dividing door before you could go and
see her. Toby's mother said it was important always
to knock, because bursting in on Granny, unheralded,
would be an invasion of her privacy.

He left Daisy and went on towards the village, still deep
in thought. He knew other people who had died. Mrs
Fletcher who kept the village shop and post office had
died, and Toby's moher had put on a black hat and gone
to Mrs Fletcher's funeral. But Mrs Fletcher had not been
a friend. In fact, Toby had always been rather afraid of
her, so old was she, so ugly, sitting, selling stamps like
a great black spider. By the time Mrs Fletcher had passed
on, her daughter Olive had taken over the running of
the shop, but right up to the end Mrs Fletcher was
there, a brooding presence, munching on her dentures,
knitting socks, and keeping a beady eye on everything
that took place. No, he had not loved Mrs Fletcher. He
had not missed Mrs Fletcher. But already he was missing
Mr Sawcombe.

He thought of David. Go and play with David, his
mother had suggested, but all at once Toby knew that
he was not in the mood for being an astronaut, or going
to look for fish in the muddy stream that ran along the
bottom of the garden at the back of the pub. He would
go and call on another of his friends, Willie Harrell, the
village carpenter. Willie was a gentle, slow-speaking

man who wore old-fashioned bib-and-brace overalls and a baggy tweed cap. Toby had first made friends with him when Willie came to the house to fit new cupboards in the kitchen, and after that one of his favourite ploys on empty holiday mornings was to walk down to the village and have a few words with Willie in his workshop.

The workshop itself was a magic place, sweet smelling and littered with ringlets of shaven wood. Here Willie constructed farm gates and barn doors as well as window frames and joists and beams. And here, too, from time to time, Willie made coffins, for he was the undertaker as well as the joiner. In this role, he became a totally different person, bowler-hatted and dark-suited, and assuming, with his sombre attire, a hushed and respectful voice and expression of pious gloom.

His workshop door, this morning, stood open. His little van was parked in the littered yard. Toby went to the door and looked inside. Willie was leaning against his workbench drinking a mug of tea from a thermos.

'Willie.'

He looked up. 'Hello there, young Toby.' He smiled. 'What are you up to, then?'

'I thought I'd just come and talk.' He wondered if Willie knew about Mr Sawcombe. He went over to Willie's side and leaned against the workbench and picked up a screwdriver and began to fiddle with it.

'Got nothing to do?'

'Nothing much.'

'Saw young David a moment ago, out on his bicycle, wearing a cowboy hat. Not much fun playing cowboys on your own.'

'I don't feel like playing cowboys.'

'Well, I can't stop and talk to you today. I've got a job to do. Got to get up Sawcombe's back of eleven o'clock.'

Toby did not say anything to this. But he knew what it was all about. Willie and Mr Sawcombe had been friends all their lives, partners in the bowling team, church wardens together on Sundays. Now Willie was going to have to . . . Toby's mind shied from what Willie was going to do.

'Willie.'

'What is it?'

'Mr Sawcombe's dead.'

'I thought you knew,' said Willie sympathetically. 'Could tell by your face, the moment you walked in.' He set down his tea mug and laid a hand on Toby's shoulder. 'You mustn't grieve. You'll miss him, I know, but you mustn't grieve. We'll all miss him, come to that,' he added, sounding suddenly forlorn.

'He was my best friend.'

'I know.' Willie shook his head. 'Funny thing, friendship. You a little chap, how old are you? Eight years old. And yet you and Bill Sawcombe got on like a house on fire. We always thought it was because you was so much on your own, being so much littler than Vicky. Like an afterthought. Little afterthought, Bill and I used to call you. Harding's little afterthought.'

'Willie . . . are you going to make a coffin for Mr Sawcombe?'

'I expect so.'

Toby thought of Willie making the coffin, choosing the wood, planing the surface, tucking his old friend up in its warm, scented interior, as though he were tucking him up in bed. It was an oddly comforting image.

'Willie?'

'What is it now?'

'I know that when a person dies, you put them in a coffin and carry them to the graveyard. And I know that when people are dead they go to Heaven to be with God. But what happens in between?'

'Ah,' said Willie. He took another draught of tea, emptying his mug. Then he laid his hand on Toby's head and gave it a little shake. 'Perhaps that's a secret between God and me.'

He still did not want to play with David. When Willie had departed for Sawcombe's in his little van, Toby set off for home because he couldn't think of anything else to do. He took a shortcut through the sheep paddock. The three ewes who had already lambed were out in the middle of the field, with their children about them. But Daisy had taken herself off into a corner, to the shade and privacy of a tall Scotch pine, where she was sheltered from the wind and the blinking spring sunshine. And beside her, teetering on wobbly legs, tiny as a puppy, stood a single lamb.

Toby knew better than to go near her. He watched her for a little, saw the baby nuzzling the huge woolly body for milk, heard Daisy's gentle voice as she spoke to her baby. He found that he was torn between pleasure and disappointment. Pleasure because the lamb had arrived safely, and disappointment because it was not twins and now Mrs Sawcombe would not have her two hundred percent lambing. Daisy, after a little, lay cumbrously down. The lamb collapsed beside her. Toby went on up the field, climbed the fence, and went into the house to tell his mother. 'Daisy's had her lamb. That's the last one.'

His mother was mashing potatoes for lunch. She turned from the stove to look at Toby. 'Not twins?'

'No, just one. It's sucking and it looks all right. Perhaps we'd better tell Tom.'

'Why don't you go and phone him?'

But Toby didn't want to ring Sawcombe's in case Mrs Sawcombe answered the telephone and he wouldn't know what to say.

'Can't *you* do it?'

'Oh, darling, I can't just now. Lunch is ready and after that I'm going down to see Mrs Sawcombe and take her some flowers. I'll leave a message for Tom.'

'I think he should know now. Mr Sawcombe always liked to know right away about the lambs arriving. Just in case, he said.'

17

'Well, if you feel so strongly about it, get Vicky to phone Tom.'

'*Vicky?*'

'It can't hurt to ask her. She's upstairs, ironing. And tell her lunch is ready.'

He went to find his sister. 'Vicky, lunch is ready, and Daisy's had her lamb, and we wondered if you'd ring Sawcombe's and tell Tom. He'll want to know.'

Vicky put down the iron with a thump. '*I'm* not going to ring Tom Sawcombe.'

'Why not?'

'Because I don't want to, that's why. You ring him.'

Toby knew why she didn't want to ring Tom. Because she had been so horrid to him at New Year, and because since that he hadn't spoken to her. 'You ring him,' she said again.

Toby wrinkled his nose. 'What will I say if Mrs Sawcombe answers the phone?'

'Well, get Mother to ring him.'

'She's too busy and in a hurry because she's going to see Mrs Sawcombe after lunch.'

'Why doesn't she leave a message for Tom?'

'That's what she said she'd do.'

'Oh, Toby,' said Vicky, in exasperation, 'then what's all the fuss about?'

He said, stubbornly, 'Mr Sawcombe always liked to know *right away.*'

Vicky frowned. 'There's nothing *wrong* with Daisy, is there?' She was as fond of Daisy as Toby was, and now she stopped sounding cross and snappy and spoke in her ordinary nice voice.

'I don't think so.'

'Then she'll be all right.' She turned off the switch of the iron and stood it up on its end on the board to cool. 'Let's go down and have lunch. I'm starving.'

The sparse clouds of the morning thickened and darkened and after lunch it started to rain. Toby's mother, wearing a mackintosh and carrying an immense bunch of daffodils, set off in her car to visit Mrs Sawcombe. Vicky said that she was going to wash her hair. Toby, at a loose end, trailed up to his room, lay on his bed, and started to read a new book he had got from the library. It was all about Arctic explorers, but he hadn't got beyond the first chapter when he was interrupted by the sound of a car coming up the lane and stopping with a rattle of gravel outside the front door. He laid down his book, got off the bed and went to the window, and saw Tom Sawcombe's old Land-Rover, and, getting out of it, Tom himself.

He opened the window, and leaned out. 'Hello.'

Tom stopped and looked upwards. Toby saw his fair curly head, beaded with raindrops; his face brown and his eyes so blue; his thick, rugger-playing shoulders beneath the patched khaki jacket that he wore for work. Beneath this was a pair of faded jeans, knee-length green rubber boots.

'Your mother told me about Daisy. Came up to have a look at her. Is Vicky about?'

This was surprising. 'She's washing her hair.'

'Go and get her, will you? I'm not sure there's not another lamb there, and I'll need help.'

'I'll help you.'

'I know, boy, but you're a bit little to hold an old ewe like Daisy. Better get Vicky.'

Toby pulled his head in from the window and went to do as he was told.

He found Vicky in the bathroom, with her head in the basin, rinsing her hair with a rubber shower.

'Vicky, Tom's here.'

Vicky turned off the taps and straightened up, her pale hair dripping all over her T-shirt. She pushed it out of her face, and her eyes were on Toby's face.

'Tom? What does he want?'

'He thinks maybe Daisy has another lamb inside her.

He says he needs help, and I'm not big enough to hold her.'

She grabbed a towel and wrapped it around her head. 'Where is he?'

'Downstairs.'

Already she was out of the bathroom, running down the landing, down the stairs. Tom was waiting for them, having let himself into the house, as he had always done in the old days before he and Vicky had had their quarrel.

'If there's another lamb,' said Vicky, 'won't it be dead by now?'

'We'll have to see. Get me a bucket of water, there's a good girl, and some soap. Bring it down to the field. Come on, Toby, you come with me.'

Outside, it was now pouring with rain. They went down the lane and crossed the long, wet grass by the rhododendrons, then climbed the fence. Through the downpour, Toby could see Daisy waiting for them. She was on her feet again, sheltering the single lamb, keeping her head towards them. As they approached she made a sound, deep in her chest, but it in no way resembled her usual healthy bleat.

'There, girl. There.' Tom spoke gently. 'There she is.' He went right up to her, and with no fuss took hold of her horns. She did not struggle as she usually did when someone did this. Perhaps she knew that she had to have help and that Tom and Toby had come to help her. 'There, girl, quietly now.' Tom passed a hand down her back, down the thick, rain-sodden fleece.

Toby watched. He could feel his heart beating, not so much with apprehension as excitement. He was not afraid, because Tom was there, just as he had never been afraid of anything if Mr Sawcombe stood beside him.

'But, Tom, if she's got another lamb inside her, why hasn't it come out?'

'Maybe a big fellow. Maybe hasn't got himself in the right position.' Tom looked towards the house, and Toby followed his gaze and saw Vicky, with her long spindly legs and her seal-wet hair, coming down across the field towards them, weighted sideways by a slopping bucket. When she reached their side and had dumped the bucket down, Tom said, 'Good girl. Now, you hold her, Vicky. Firmly, but quite gently. She won't struggle. Keep your fingers tight in her fleece. And Toby, you take her horns, and keep talking to her. Reassuring like. Then she'll know she's in good hands.'

Vicky looked as though she were about to burst into tears. She knelt, right there in the mud, and put her arms around Daisy and pressed her cheek against Daisy's woolly flank. 'Oh, poor Daisy. You've got to be very brave and it will be all right.'

Tom stripped off. His jacket, his shirt, his white T-shirt. Naked to the waist, he soaped his hands and arms.

'Now,' he said. 'Let's see what's going on.'

Toby, clinging to Daisy's horns, wanted to close his eyes. But he didn't. *Keep talking*, Tom had told him. *Reassuring like*. 'There, there,' said Toby to Daisy because that was what Tom had said and he could think of nothing else. 'There, there, Daisy dear.' This was birth. The eternal miracle, Mr Sawcombe used to call it. This was life starting, and he, Toby, was helping it to happen.

He heard Tom. 'There we go. There we go . . . take it easy, old girl.'

Daisy gave a single moan of discomfort and displeasure, and then Tom was saying, 'Here he is! What a whopper, and he's alive.'

And there it was, the little creature who had been the cause of all the trouble. A white ram with black spots, smeared with blood and lying flat on its side, but still a sizey, healthy lamb. Toby let go of Daisy's horns and Vicky eased her loving stranglehold. Released, Daisy turned to inspect the new arrival. She made a soft, maternal sound, and stooped to lick it. After a little, she nudged it gently with her nose, and before very long, it began to move, to raise its head, to struggle, amazingly,

21

to its long and unsteady legs. She licked it again, recognising it as her own, taking responsibility, loving and caring. The little lamb took a drunken step or two, and, before very long, with some encouragement from his mother, started to suck.

Long after Tom had dried himself off with his shirt and then pulled on his clothes, they stayed there, oblivious of the rain, watching Daisy and her twins; fascinated by the miracle, and yet delighted with themselves and their combined achievement. Vicky and Toby sat side by side on the ground beneath the old Scotch pine, and there was a smile on Vicky's face that Toby hadn't seen in ages.

She turned to look at Tom. 'How did you *know* there was another lamb there?'

'She was still pretty bulky and she didn't seem very comfortable. She was restless.'

Toby said, 'That's a two hundred percent lambing Mrs Sawcombe's got.'

Tom smiled. 'That's it, Toby.'

'But why didn't the lamb come of its own accord?'

'Just look at him! He's a big fellow, with a big head. He'll be all right now, though.' He looked down at Vicky. 'But you won't be all right if you sit there in the rain much longer. And you'll catch a cold with your hair so wet.' He stooped and picked up the bucket, then held out his other hand to Vicky. 'Come along now.'

She put her hand into his and he pulled her to her feet. They stood smiling into each other's faces.

He said, 'It's good we're talking.'

'Yes,' said Vicky. 'I'm sorry.'

'Just as much my fault.'

Vicky looked shy. She smiled again, ruefully, the smile turning down the corners of her mouth. 'Don't let's quarrel again, Tom.'

'My grandfather used to say life's too short for quarrels.'

'I haven't said how sorry I am . . . about him . . . we're all at a loss. I don't know how to say it properly.'

'I know,' said Tom. 'Some things don't have to be said. Come along now.'

They seemed to have forgotten about Toby. They walked away from him, up the field, with Tom's arm around Vicky, and Vicky's wet head on his shoulder.

He watched them, and felt satisfied. Mr Sawcombe would have been pleased. He would have been pleased about Daisy's twins, as well. The second lamb was indeed a handsome fellow, not simply a whopper as Tom had described him, but with beautiful even markings and a pair of horns, like buds, already visible, bedded in soft, curly wool. He wondered what Mrs Sawcombe would call this lamb. Perhaps she would call him Bill. He stayed until it grew too wet and cold to stand about any longer, so he turned his back on the sheep and started to walk home.

His mother returned from her visit to Mrs Sawcombe and gave him a splendid tea of fish fingers and chips and beans and plum cake and chocolate biscuits and cocoa. While he ploughed his way through this, he told her of the great adventure with Daisy. ' . . . and Tom and Vicky are friends again,' he told her.

'I know.' His mother smiled. 'He's taken her off in the Land-Rover. Vicky's having her supper at the Sawcombes'.'

After tea Toby's father came home from the office, and they watched football together on television, and then Toby went upstairs to have a bath. He lay in the hot, steaming water that smelt of pine essence on account of he had stolen some out of Vicky's bottle, and decided that, after all, it hadn't been too bad a day. And then he decided to go and pay a call on his Granny, whom he had not seen all day.

He got out of the bath, put on his pyjamas and dressing gown, and went down the passage that led to her flat. He knocked at the door and she called 'Come in,' and it was like going into another world, because her furniture and curtains and things were so different to those in the rest of the house. No other person had so many photographs and ornaments, and there was always a little coal fire burning in the grate, and by this, in her wide-lapped chair, he found his Granny, knitting. As well, she had a book on her knee. She had television but she didn't enjoy it too much. She preferred to read, and Toby always thought of her deep in some book or other. But whenever he interrupted her, she would place a leather bookmark between the pages, close the book, and lay it aside so as to give him her undivided attention.

'Hello, Toby.'

She was terribly old. (Other boys' grandmothers were often quite young, but Toby's was very old because, like Toby, his father, too, had been an afterthought.) She was thin, as well. So thin that she looked as if she might snap in two, and her hands were almost transparent, with big knuckles over which she could not get her rings, which meant that she wore them all the time, and very sparkly and dashing they looked.

'What have you been doing today?'

He pulled up a stool and sat down to tell her. He told her about Mr Sawcombe, but she already knew. He told her about Willie making a coffin for Mr Sawcombe. He told her about not playing cowboys with David, and he told her about Daisy's lamb. And then he told her about Vicky and Tom.

Granny looked delighted. 'That's the best. They've patched up that silly quarrel.'

'Do you think they'll fall in love and get married?'

'They might. They mightn't.'

'Were you in love when you married Grandpa?'

'I think I was. It's so long ago that sometimes I forget.'

'Did you . . . ' He hesitated, but he had to know, and Granny was a person who never minded awkward questions. 'When he died . . . did you miss him very much?'

24

'Why do you ask that? Are you missing Mr Saw-combe?'

'Yes. All day. All day I've been missing him.'

'It'll get better. The missing bit will get better and then you'll only remember the good times.'

'Is that how it was with you and Grandpa?'

'I think so. Yes.'

'Is it very frightening to die?'

'I don't know.' She smiled, her familiar smile, amused and gamine, that was so surprising in that old and wrinkled face. 'I've never done it.'

'But . . . ' He looked intently into her eyes. Nobody could live forever. 'But aren't you *frightened*?'

Granny leaned forward to take Toby's hand into her own. 'You know,' she said, 'I've always thought that each person's life is like a mountain. And each person has to climb that mountain alone. To begin with, you start in the valley, and it's warm and sunny, and there are lots of meadows and little streams, and buttercups and things. That's when you're a child. And then you start to climb. Slowly, the mountain becomes a little steeper and the going isn't so easy, but if you stop every now and then and look about you, then the wonderful views are worth every bit of effort. And the very top of the mountain, the peak, where the snow and the ice glitter in the sunshine and it is all beautiful beyond belief, why, that is the summit, the great achievement, the end of the long journey.'

She made it sound magnificent. He said, full of love for her, 'I don't want you to die.'

Granny laughed. 'Oh, my darling, don't worry about that. I'm going to be around, being a nuisance to you all, for a long time yet. And now, why don't we each have a peppermint cream, and then a game of clock patience? How nice that you came to see me. I was beginning to be a little tired of my own company . . . '

*   *   *

Later, he said goodnight and left her; went to clean his teeth, and then to his bedroom. He drew back the curtains. It had stopped raining and there was the beginnings of a moon climbing the sky in the east. In the half light, he could see the paddock and the dim shapes of the sheep and their lambs, gathered beneath the sheltering branches of the old pine. He took off his dressing gown and got into bed. His mother had put a hot-water bottle into it, which was a treat, and he pulled this up onto his stomach and lay wide-eyed in the soft darkness, feeling warm and thoughtful.

He decided that today, he had learned a lot. A lot about life. He had helped at a birth, and had seen, in Vicky and Tom, the start of a new relationship. Perhaps they would get married. Perhaps not. If they did get married, then they would have babies. (He already knew how babies started because once, in the course of a manly chat about cattle breeding, Mr Sawcombe had told him.) Which would make him, Toby, an uncle.

And as for death . . . *Death is a part of life*, his mother had told him. And Willie had said that death was a secret between God and himself. But Granny believed that death was the glittering, shining peak of each person's private mountain, and that perhaps was the best, the most comforting of all.

Mr Sawcombe had climbed his mountain and reached the peak. Toby imagined him, standing there triumphant. Wearing sun-goggles because of the brightness of the sky, and his best Sunday suit, and perhaps holding a flag.

He was suddenly very tired. He closed his eyes. A two hundred percent lambing. How satisfied Mr Sawcombe would have been, and what a pity that he had not lived long enough to know about Daisy's twins.

But as sleep crept up on him, he smiled to himself, because, for no particular reason, he was suddenly pretty certain that wherever he was now, his old friend already knew.

Home for the Day

After a European business trip that had taken in five capital cities, seven directors' lunches, and countless hours spent in airport lounges, James Harner flew into Heathrow from Brussels on a Wednesday afternoon in early April. It was, inevitably, raining. He had not got to bed until 2 a.m. the previous night, his bulging briefcase weighed heavy as lead, and he seemed as well to have caught a cold.

The smooth and shaven face of Roberts, the advertising agency's driver who had come to meet him off the plane, was the first cheerful thing that had happened to him all day. Roberts wore his peaked cap, and he moved forward to relieve James of his suitcase, and to say that he hoped he had had a pleasant trip.

They drove straight to the office, and James, after casting a cursory eye over his desk and presenting his secretary with the small bottle of duty-free scent that was no more than her due, took himself down the passage to call on his chairman.

'James! How splendid. Come along in, old boy. How did it go?'

Sir Osborne Baske was not only James's chairman, but, as well, an old and valued friend. There was, therefore, no need for formal pleasantries or polite small talk, and within half an hour James had him more or less briefed on what had been happening: which firm had shown interest, which had remained cagey. He kept the best till last – namely, the two valuable accounts that were already in the bag: a Swedish firm that made

27

prefabricated knock-down furniture, quality goods, but in the slightly lower price bracket, and an old-established Danish silversmiths which was expanding cautiously throughout all the market countries of the EEC.

Sir Osborne was gratifyingly delighted and could not wait to pass on the good news to the rest of the directors. 'There's a board meeting on Tuesday. Can you get a complete report out by then? Friday if possible. Monday morning at the latest.'

'If I get a clear day tomorrow, I should be able to get it typed on Friday morning, and circulated on Friday afternoon.'

'Splendid. Then they can pursue it during the week-end when they're not playing golf. And . . . ' But he paused tactfully while James, suddenly overcome by an agonizing sneeze, fumbled for his handkerchief, exploded enormously into it, and blew his nose. ' . . . got a cold, old boy?'

He sounded nervous, as though James might already have infected him. He did not approve of colds, any more than he approved of large waistlines, heavy business lunches, or heart attacks.

'I seem to have caught one,' James admitted.

'Hmm.' The chairman considered. 'Tell you what, why don't you have a day at home tomorrow? You look fairly washed out, and you'll have more chance of getting that report done in peace without endless interruptions. Let you see something of Louisa, too, after all this time away. What do you say?'

James said he thought it was a splendid idea, which he did.

'That's arranged then.' Sir Osborne stood up, ending the interview abruptly before any more germs could be released into the sterile air of his palatial office. 'If you start off now, you should be home before the worst of the rush-hour traffic. We'll see you on Friday morning. And if I were you, I'd take care of that cold. Whisky and lemon, hot, last thing at night. Nothing better.'

Fourteen years earlier, when James and Louisa had first been married, they had lived in London, in a basement flat in South Kensington, but when Louisa became pregnant with the first of their two children, they had made the decision to move out into the country. With some financial juggling, they had achieved this, and not for a single moment had James regretted it. The twice-daily hour-long journey to and from work seemed to him a small price to pay for the sanctuary of the old red brick house and the ample garden, and the simple joy, each evening, of coming home. Commuting, even on roads swollen with traffic, did not dismay him. On the contrary, the hour in the car by himself became his switching-off time, when he put behind him the problems of the day.

In midwinter, in darkness, he would turn into his own gateway and see, through the trees, the light burning over his own front door. In spring, the garden was awash with daffodils; in summer, there was the long drowsy evening to look forward to. A shower, and changing into an open-necked shirt and espadrilles, drinks on the terrace beneath the smoky-blue blossom of the wistaria, and the sound of wood pigeons coming from the beech wood at the bottom of the garden.

The children rode their bicycles around the lawn and swung on the rope ladder that hung from their tree-house, and at weekends the place was usually invaded by friends, either neighbours or refugees from London, bringing their families and their dogs, and everybody lazed in chairs with the Sunday newspapers, or indulged in friendly putting matches on the lawn.

And at the heart of all this was Louisa. Louisa, who never failed to amaze James, because when he had married her, he had done so without the remotest suspicion of the sort of person she had turned out to be. Gentle and undemanding, she had proved, over the years, to have an almost uncanny instinct for home-making. Asked to lay an exact finger on this, James

29

would have been defeated. He only knew that the house, although frequently strewn with children's toys, shoes, drawings, had about it an ambience of peace and welcome. There always seemed to be flowers about the place, and laughter, and enough food for the extra guests who decided to stay for supper.

But the real miracle was that all this was achieved so unobtrusively. James had stayed in other houses where the woman of the house spent her day looking careworn, always cleaning and tidying, shutting herself into her kitchen, only to emerge two minutes before the meal was served, and looking exhausted and cross to boot. It wasn't that Louisa never went into her kitchen, but people were inclined to drift in there after her, carrying their drinks or their knitting, and not minding when she gave them beans to slice or mayonnaise to stir. Children trailed in and out of the garden, and they too would remain, to help shell peas, or to make small pale biscuits out of the scraps of pastry from the apple pie.

Sometimes it occurred to James that Louisa's life, when compared to his own, must be very dull. 'What have you been doing today?' he would ask when he got home, but 'Nothing much' was all she ever told him.

It was still raining, the afternoon sliding into early dark. Now he had reached Henborough, the last small town on the main road before turning to their own village. The traffic lights showed red, and he stopped the car alongside a flower shop. Inside he saw pots of red tulips, freesia, narcissus. He thought of buying Louisa flowers, but then the lights turned green, and he forgot about the flowers and moved forward with the rest of the traffic.

It was still light as he came up the drive between the clumps of rhododendron. He eased the car into the garage, turned off the engine, collected his luggage from the boot, and let himself in through the kitchen door. Rufus, who was a spaniel and getting on in years, let out a warning 'woof' from his basket, and James's wife looked up from her seat at the kitchen table, where she was drinking a mug of tea.

'Darling!'

How wonderful to be so welcomed. 'Surprise, surprise.' He put down his case, and she got to her feet and they met in the middle of the floor and lost themselves in an enormous hug. He could feel the fragile bones of her ribs through her old blue pullover. She smelt delicious, vaguely of bonfires.

'You're early.'

'I escaped before the rush hour.'

'How was Europe?'

'Still there.' He held her off. 'Something is wrong.'

'What could be wrong?'

'You tell me. No bicycles abandoned in the middle of the garage, no chatter of highly pitched voices, no little gangs darting around the garden. No children.'

'They've gone down to Hamble to stay with Helen.' Helen was Louisa's sister. 'You knew they were going.'

He had known. He had simply forgotten.

'I thought you'd probably murdered them and buried them in the compost heap.'

She was frowning. 'Have you got a cold?'

'Yes. I found it lurking somewhere between Oslo and Brussels.'

'Oh, poor old thing.'

'Not poor old thing at all. It means that I'm not going to London tomorrow. I am going to stay here, in the bosom of my wife, and write my EEC report at the dining room table.' He kissed her again. 'I missed you. Do you know that? I really missed you. Incredible. What's for dinner?'

'Steaks.'

Better and better. He said it. 'Better and better.' He opened his briefcase and gave her the bottle of scent (a larger size than his secretary's), received her grateful

31

embrace, and then took himself upstairs to unpack, undress, and soak in a hot bath.

The next morning James awoke to pale sunshine and a marvellous silence broken only by the faint tweetings of bird song. He opened his eyes and saw that he was alone in his bed, and only the dent in the other pillow bore witness to the presence of Louisa. He realised, with some surprise, that he could not remember when he had ever taken a day off during the week. Revelling in idleness, he felt youthful, like a schoolboy with an unexpected holiday. He groped a hand under his pillow and pulled out his watch and saw that it was eight-thirty. Bliss. The hot whisky and lemon consumed the night before had done their work, and his cold was in retreat, vanquished. He got up, shaved and dressed and went downstairs, and found his wife in the kitchen sipping her coffee.

'How do you feel?' she asked.

'Like a man reborn. Cold's all gone.'

She went to the stove. 'Bacon and eggs?'

'Perfect.' He reached for the morning paper. Normally he read the morning paper when he got home in the evening. There was something almost obscenely luxurious about reading it at leisure at his own breakfast table. He scanned the stock market, the cricket, finally the headlines. Louisa began to stack the washing-up machine. James looked at her.

'Doesn't Mrs Brick stack the dishwasher?'

Mrs Brick was the plumber's wife from the village who helped Louisa with the housework. One of the good things about Saturday mornings was that Mrs Brick came, to race around behind the vacuum cleaner and fill the house with the good smell of floor polish.

'Mrs Brick doesn't come on Thursday. She doesn't come on Wednesdays or Mondays either.'

'Hasn't she ever?'

'No. Never.' Louisa put down his bacon and eggs in

front of him and poured him a large cup of black coffee. 'I'll turn the heater on in the dining room. It's icy in there.' She drifted off, presumably to see to this. Presently the sound of the vacuum cleaner disturbed the morning air. *Work*, it seemed to say. *Work, work.* James took the hint, collected his briefcase and his calculator, and made his way to the dining room. Morning sunshine streamed through the long windows. He opened his briefcase and spread its contents about him. This, he thought, putting on his spectacles, is what life is all about. No interruptions, no telephone.

Instantly the telephone rang. He raised his head and heard Louisa go to answer it. A long time later, it seemed, there was a single ring as the call was concluded. The vacuum cleaner started up its hum once more. James returned to work.

Presently there came a new sound to obtrude the morning hush. A churning and whirring came from some distant spot, which after consideration James identified as the washing machine. He wrote *North of England. Total Coverage.*

And then, in close succession, two more telephone calls. Louisa dealt with all of them, but the fourth time it rang, she did not answer it. James tried to ignore the insistent bell, but after a little while, exasperated, he pushed his chair back from the table and charged out across the hall to the sitting room.

'Yes?'

A timid voice said, 'Oh. Hello.'

'Who is it?' barked James.

'Well, I think perhaps I must have the wrong number. Are you Henborough 384?'

'Yes, that's right. James Harner here.'

'I wanted Mrs Harner.'

'I don't know where she is.'

'It's Miss Bell speaking. It's about the church flowers for next Sunday. Mrs Harner and I always do the flowers together, you see, and I thought perhaps that this

Sunday she wouldn't mind if I asked her to do them with Mrs Sheepfold, and then I could do them next week with the rector's wife. You see, it's my sister's daughter . . . '

It seemed time to stop the flow. 'Look, Miss Bell, if you just hold on I'll see if I can find Louisa. Don't ring off. I shan't be a moment . . . '

He laid down the receiver and went into the hall. 'Louisa!' No reply. Into the kitchen. 'Louisa!'

A faint cry came through to him from behind the back door. He went out and ran his wife to earth on the back lawn, pegging out what seemed to be a Chinese laundry-worth of washing. 'What is it?'

He said, 'Miss Bell is on the telephone.' Then, diverted, he grinned. 'Tell me, Mrs Harner, how do you get your washing so white?'

Louisa was bang on cue. 'Oh, I use Sploosh,' she replied in the faintly whining voice of the woman in the television commercial. 'It makes even my husband's undies shining clean, and everything smells so fresh. What does Miss Bell want?'

'Something about her sister's daughter and the vicar's wife. That telephone's never stopped ringing all morning.'

'I'm sorry.'

'Not at all. But I'm mad with curiosity to know why you're so popular.'

'Well, the first call was Helen to say the children were still alive. And then it was the vet to say it's time Rufus had another injection. And then it was Elizabeth Thomson wanting us to go to dinner next Tuesday week. Did you tell Miss Bell I'd ring her back?'

'No, I told her to hold on. She's holding on now.'

'Oh, James.' Louisa dried her hands on her apron. 'Why didn't you *say*?' She went indoors. James tried his hand at hanging out a sock or two, but it was dull and fiddly work, so he abandoned it and went back to his makeshift desk.

He wrote another heading and underlined it beautifully in red ink. It was nearly half-past ten, and he wondered whether Louisa would remember to bring him a cup of coffee.

By midday the need for refreshment would no longer be ignored. He laid down his pen, took off his spectacles, and leaned back in his chair. All was quiet. He got to his feet, went out into the hall, and stood at the foot of the stairs with his ear cocked, like a dog expecting to be taken for a walk. *'Louisa!'*

'I'm here.'

'Where's here?'

'In the nursery bathroom.'

James trod up the stairs in search of her. The nursery bathroom door was shut, and when he opened it her voice warned, 'Do be careful,' so he was, cautiously peering around the edge of the door. There were dust sheets on the floor and the step ladder had been set up, and on the top of it was his wife, engaged in painting the wooden pelmet at the top of the window. The window was open, but still the smell of paint was very strong. It was also extremely cold.

James shivered. 'What on earth are you doing now?'

'Painting the pelmet.'

'I can see that. But why? Wasn't it all right before?'

'You never saw it before because it was covered with a sort of frill with bobbles on.'

He remembered the sort of frill. He said, 'What's happened to it?'

'Well, with the children away, I decided it was a good time to wash the bathroom curtains, so I did, and I washed the pelmet too, but it had a sort of backing, and it went all gluey, and all the bobbles began to come off, so I've thrown it in the dustbin and now I'm painting the pelmet underneath to match the rest of the paintwork and then it won't show.'

James thought about this and then he said, 'I see.'

'Did you want something?' She was obviously longing to get on with the job.

'No, not really. I just thought a cup of coffee would be nice.'

'Oh, sorry. I never thought. I never make any for myself unless Mrs Brick is here.'

'Oh. Well, never mind. Anyway,' he added hopefully, 'it'll soon be lunchtime.' He was getting hungry. He went back to his report, helping himself to an apple from the bowl on the sideboard. Settling down once more to his slide rule and his calculator, he hoped that lunch would be something hot and meaty.

Soon Louisa could be heard coming back downstairs, cautiously, which meant that she was carrying the step-ladder and the paint can, which, in turn, meant that she had finished painting the pelmet. He heard kitchen drawers open and shut, saucepans clatter, a mixer drone. Presently a delicious smell permeated through to where James laboured: frying onions, the tang of green peppers, enough to make any man's juices run. He finished his paragraph, drew another neat line, and decided that he had earned himself a drink.

In the kitchen, he came up behind Louisa as she stood at the stove, put his arms around her waist, and peered over her shoulder at the delicious casserole she was stirring.

He said, 'That looks like an awful lot for two people.'

'Who said it was for two people? It's for twenty people.'

'You mean we're expecting eighteen guests for lunch?'

'No. I mean that we have twenty for Sunday lunch the weekend after next.'

'But you're cooking it now.'

'Yes, I know. It's a moussaka. And when I've finished it, I put it in the deep freeze, and then the day before the lunch party I take it out, and hey presto.'

'But what are we going to eat for lunch today?'

'You can have anything you like. Soup. Bread. Cheese. A boiled egg.'

'A boiled egg?'

'What did you expect?'

'Roast lamb. Chops. Apple pie.'

'James, we never have great big lunches like that.'

'Yes, we do. At weekends we do.'

'Weekends are different. At weekends we eat scrambled eggs for supper. On weekdays it's the other way around.'

'Why?'

'Why? So that you can have a good meal at night when you come struggling home from the office, careworn and fatigued. That's why.'

She had a point there. James sighed and watched while she seasoned the moussaka. Salt, pepper, a pinch of mixed herbs. His juices started to run again. He said, 'Couldn't I have a little of that for my lunch?'

Louisa said, 'No.' He thought she was being very mean. To cheer himself up he got ice out of the refrigerator and poured himself a restoring gin and tonic. With this in his hand he made his way to the sitting room, intending to sit by the fire and finish the morning paper until such time as his lunch should be ready.

But no fire burned in the sitting-room grate and the atmosphere was chill and cheerless.

'Louisa!'

'Yes?' Was it his imagination, or was she beginning to sound just the slightest bit impatient?

'Do you want me to light the fire for you?'

'Well, you can if you want to, but isn't it rather a waste if neither of us is going to be in there?'

'Aren't you going to come and sit down this afternoon?'

'I shouldn't think so,' said Louisa.

'What time do you usually light it?'

'About five o'clock, usually.' She said again, 'You can light it if you want to,' but perversely, he didn't, and took a sort of masochistic pleasure in settling himself down in a chair and self-consciously reading the leading article.

In the end, lunch was better than he had feared. Rich vegetable soup, crusty brown bread, farm butter, a little Stilton, a cup of coffee. He lit a small cigar, just to round it all off.

'How's it going?' asked Louisa.

'How's what going?'

'The report.'

'I'm about two-thirds of the way through.'

'What a clever old thing you are. Well, I'll leave you in peace, and then you can get on with it without any interruptions.'

'Leave me? For whom do you leave me? Tell me the name of your lover.'

'I haven't actually got a lover, but I do have to take Rufus for a walk, so we're going to call on the butcher and pick up the spring lamb he promised me.'

'When are we going to eat spring lamb? Next Christmas?'

'No, tonight. But if you're going to be sarcastic, I can easily put it in the deep freeze until such time as you feel better disposed.'

'Don't you dare. What else are we having?'

'New potatoes and frozen peas. Don't you ever think of anything except food?'

'I do sometimes think about drink.'

'You're a glutton.'

'I'm a gourmet.' He kissed her. He thought about this. He said, 'It's funny kissing you at meals. I don't often kiss you at table.'

'It's having no children here,' said Louisa.

'Let's do it more often. Get rid of them, I mean. If your sister Helen can't have them, we'll put them into kennels.'

*   *   *

The house that afternoon, without Louisa, without the dog, without children, guests, or any sort of activity, was totally dead. The silence was deafening, disconcerting as some continuous and unexplained sound. From where he sat working, James could hear only the muffled ticking of the clock in the hall. It occurred to him that this was how it was for Louisa most of the time, with himself in London and the children at school. No wonder she talked to the dog.

When she finally returned, the relief was so great that he had to restrain himself from going to greet her. Perhaps she sensed this, for a moment or so later she put her head around the door and said his name. He tried to look as though she had taken him unawares. 'What is it?'

'If you want me, I'm out in the garden.'

James had hoped she was going to light the fire, and sit beside it, doing her tapestry and waiting for him to join her. He felt cheated. 'What are you going out into the garden for?'

'I'm going to tidy the rose bed. It's the first day I've had a chance to get at it. But if someone arrives in a van and rings the bell, could you answer it, or come and let me know?'

'Are you expecting company?'

'Mrs Brick's brother-in-law said he'd come this afternoon if he could.'

Mrs Brick's brother-in-law was an unknown quantity to James. 'What do you intend doing with him?'

'Well, you see, he's got this chain saw.' James gazed at her, totally confused, and Louisa became impatient. 'Oh, James, I *told* you. One of the beech trees has come down in the wood, and the farmer said I could have the broken branches for firewood if I could get someone to cut them up. So Mrs Brick said her brother-in-law would come. I did tell you. The trouble is, you never listen to anything I say, and if you do listen, you don't hear.'

'You're making noises like a wife,' James told her.

'Well, what do you expect? Anyway, keep an ear open for me. It would be maddening if he came and went away again, thinking I wasn't here.'

James agreed that it would be maddening. Louisa duly shut the door and took herself away. A little later, she could be seen, rubber-booted, deep in the rose bed. Rufus sat by the wheelbarrow and gazed at her. *Stupid dog*, thought James. *He could at least help.*

The report claimed him once more. He could not remember anything having taken him so long to complete. But at last he had embarked on the final summing up, and was just struggling to achieve a particularly well-rounded phrase when his peace was shattered by the grinding approach of some ancient piece of machinery. It came up the drive from the road and stopped at the back of the house, where it continued to shudder while the driver – who obviously did not want to risk turning off the engine until he was sure he would be staying – rang the back door bell.

The well-turned phrase was lost forever. James got to his feet and went to answer the summons. On the doorstep he came face to face with a tall and handsome man, white-haired and ruddy-faced, dressed in corduroys and a tweed jacket. Behind him, droning and shaking on the tarmac, and issuing clouds of noxious exhaust, stood a battered blue truck, liberally coated with mud and manure.

The man had exceptionally bright and unblinking blue eyes. 'Mrs Harner?'

'No, I am not Mrs Harner. I am Mr Harner.'

'It's Mrs Harner I'm wanting.'

'Are you Mrs Brick's brother-in-law?'

'That's right. Redmay's the name. Josh Redmay.'

James felt disconcerted. This did not look like any relation of Mrs Brick. Rather, with his blue eyes and his quarter-deck manner, did he resemble some retired admiral, and moreover, not one accustomed to having to deal with lower-deck pen-pushers.

'Mrs Harner's round the front of the house, in the garden. If you . . . '

'I brought the chain saw.' Mr Redmay had no time for pleasantries. 'Where's the tree?'

It would have been splendid to tell him 'two points west of south-west.' But James could only say, 'I'm not quite sure, but my wife will show you.'

Mr Redmay gave James a long measuring look, which James, by squaring his shoulders and tilting his chin, managed to meet, eye to eye. Then Mr Redmay turned on his heel, went back to his mud-spattered vehicle, reached up into the cab, and switched off the ignition. Silence fell and the truck stopped shaking, but the smell of exhaust remained, painfully evident. From the back he lifted the chain saw and a can of petrol. At the sight of the blade, a shark's jaws filled with teeth, James was suddenly apprehensive, visited by nightmare visions of Louisa without any fingers.

'Mr Redmay . . . '

Mrs Brick's brother-in-law turned. James felt a fool, but didn't care. 'Don't let my wife get too near that thing, will you?'

Mr Redmay's expression did not change. But he ducked his head in James's direction, heaved the chain saw onto his shoulder, and disappeared around the corner of the house. *At least*, thought James, going back indoors, *he didn't actually spit at me.*

By a quarter to five the report was finished. Read and reread, corrected, squared off, and stapled. With some satisfaction, James slid it into his briefcase and snapped the lock shut. Tomorrow morning his secretary would type it. By the afternoon a fair copy would be in the in-tray of every director in the firm.

He was tired. He stretched and yawned. From the other end of the garden the chain saw continued to whine. He got up and went into the sitting room, took that box of matches off the mantelpiece and lit the fire, and then he went into the kitchen and filled a kettle and put it on to boil. He saw the basket of laundry on the table, clothes waiting to be ironed. He saw the bowl of peeled potatoes, and on the stove a saucepan simmered; when he lifted the lid, he was assailed by the fragrance of asparagus soup. His favourite.

The kettle boiled. He made tea, and filled a vacuum flask, found mugs, a bottle of milk, a packet of lump sugar. He went through the cake tins and found a huge fruit loaf. He cut three substantial slices, then put everything into a basket, pulled on an old jacket, and let himself out of the house.

The late afternoon was still and blue, the damp air smelt cool and fresh, of earth and things growing. He went down across the lawn, through the paddock, and over the fence into the beech wood. The scream of the saw grew louder and he found Louisa and Mr Redmay without difficulty. Mr Redmay had knocked up a make-shift saw horse with a tree stump, and the two of them were working together, Mr Redmay wielding the saw and Louisa feeding him with branches, to be reduced, in a matter of seconds, to piles of logs. The air was filled with the scent of sawdust.

James thought they looked both businesslike and com-panionable, and was assailed by a small pang of jealousy. Perhaps when he retired from the rat race of the advertis-ing world, he and Louisa would spend their twilight years together, cutting wood.

Louisa looked up and saw him coming. She spoke to Mr Redmay, and after a little the saw was switched off, the scream of its blade dying to silence. Mr Redmay straightened up and turned to observe James's approach.

He came up with his basket, feeling like the farmer's wife. He said, 'I thought it was time we all had a cup of tea.'

* * *

It was very companionable, sitting in the darkening wood, drinking tea and munching fruit loaf and listening to the pigeons flying in. Louisa seemed tired, but she leaned against James's shoulder and said with great satisfaction, 'Just look at it all. Could you believe we'd have got so many logs off just a few branches?'

'How are we going to get them all up to the house?' James asked.

'I've fixed it with your missus,' said Mr Redmay, puffing on his cigarette. 'I'll borrow a tractor and a trailer from the farmer and bring them up on that. Tomorrow maybe. It's getting dark now. We'd better call it a day.'

So they packed up the tea-things and made their way home. When they reached the house, Louisa went up to have a bath, but James asked Mr Redmay in for a drink, and Mr Redmay instantly accepted, so they sat by the sitting-room fire and each downed a couple of whiskies, and by the time Mr Redmay took himself home, they were the best of friends.

'Mind,' said Mr Redmay, 'that little wife of yours, she's one in a million.' He clambered up into the cab of his truck and slammed the door. 'Any time you want to get rid of her, you just let me know. I can always find a job for a hard worker.'

But James said that he didn't want to get rid of her. Not just yet.

When Mr Redmay had gone, he went into the house and upstairs, and Louisa was out of her bath, and had changed into her blue velvet housecoat with the sash tied tightly around her narrow waist. She was brushing her hair. She said, 'I never asked about the report. Is it done?'

'Yes. Finished.' He sat on the edge of the bed and loosened his tie. Louisa splashed on some scent and came to kiss the top of his head. 'How hard you've worked,' she told him, and went out of the room and downstairs. He sat there for a little, then he finished undressing and had a bath. By the time he got down-stairs, she had disposed of the basket of laundry, but he could smell, still, the fragrance of freshly ironed clothes. As he passed the dining room, he saw her through the open door, laying the table. He stopped to watch her. She looked up and saw him there and said, 'What is it? Is something wrong?'

'You must be tired.'

'Not specially.'

He said, as he said every evening, 'Do you want a drink?' and Louisa replied, as she did every evening, 'I'd love a glass of sherry.' They were back in their usual routine.

Nothing had changed. The next morning James went to London, spent the day in the office, ate a pub lunch with one of the young copy writers, and returned – in the usual solid river of rush-hour traffic – to the country in the evening. But he did not go straight home. He stopped the car in Henborough, got out and went into the flower shop and bought Louisa an armful of fragile yellow jonquils, pale pink tulips, violet-blue iris. The girl wrapped them up in tissue paper, and James paid for them and took them home and presented them to Louisa.

'James . . . ' She looked astonished, as well she might. He was not in the habit of bringing her home armfuls of flowers. 'Oh, they're beautiful.' She buried her face in them, drinking in the scent of the jonquils. Then she looked up. 'But why . . . ?'

Because you are my life. The mother of my children, the heart of my house. You are the fruit loaf in the tin, the clean shirts in the drawer, the logs in the basket, the roses in the garden. You are the flowers in the church and the smell of paint in the bathroom, and the apple of Mr Redmay's eye. And I love you.

He said, 'No reason in particular.'

She reached up to kiss him. 'What sort of day did you have?'

'All right,' said James. 'How about you? What have you been doing?'

'Oh,' said Louisa. 'Nothing much.'

Spanish Ladies

On a Wednesday at the beginning of July, old Admiral Colley died. He was buried the following Saturday, in the village church, and two weeks later his granddaughter Jane was married to Andrew Latham in the same little church. There were a few raised eyebrows in the village, and a few reproachful letters from distant and elderly relatives, but 'That was what he would have wanted,' the family said to each other, and dried their tears and went on with the arrangements. 'That was what he would have wanted.'

Because it was July and six-thirty in the morning, Laurie awoke to a bedroom filled with sunshine. It lay across her bed like a warm blanket. It conjured slivers of reflected light from the triple mirror on her dressing table, floodlit the faded pink carpet. Beyond the open window she could see the pale, cloudless sky, herald of a perfect day. A breeze blew in from the sea and stirred the daisy-patterned curtains. The curtains matched the wallpaper and the frills around the quilted bed, and had been chosen by Laurie's mother when Laurie was thirteen and away at boarding school. She remembered coming home to the totally redecorated bedroom and having to hide her dismay, because in her heart of hearts she yearned for a room as neat and austere as a ship's cabin, with whitewashed walls and space for all her books, and a bed like Grandfa's, with drawers underneath and a little ladder to climb when you wanted to get into it.

Happy the bride the sun shines on. She listened and from far beneath her, in the depth of the old house, she heard a door open and shut and one of the dogs start to bark. She knew that her mother was already up and about, probably making an early morning cup of tea and sitting at the kitchen table, composing what must surely be the last of her hundreds of lists of things to do.

Fetch Aunt Blanche from station.
Hairdresser. Will she need lunch?
Robert to florist for carnations.
Dogs' dinner. DON'T FORGET.

Happy the bride the sun shines on. Across the upstairs landing, in the other little attic bedroom, Jane presumably slumbered. Jane had never been an early riser, and the fact that this was her wedding morning was unlikely to break the lifelong habit of twenty-five years. Laurie pictured her, blonde and rosy, her hair tangled and the old eyeless teddy bear jammed under her chin. The teddy bear was a source of mild annoyance to their mother, who did not think that he should accompany Jane on her honeymoon. Laurie agreed that he did not go with pristine negligées and romance, but Jane had a way of sweetly agreeing with whatever was demanded of her and then doing the very opposite, so Laurie was fairly sure that this evening the bear would be right there, in the bridal suite of some expensive hotel.

Her imagination wandered on down through the house. To the double guest room where her elder brother and his wife slept. To the old nurseries where their children were tucked into inherited cots. She thought of her father, perhaps beginning to stir; to open his eyes, to give thanks for the fine weather, and then to start worrying. About the car park arrangements, the quality of the champagne, the fact that his morning suit trousers had had to be let out. The bills.

'We can't afford a big wedding,' he had stated firmly the moment the engagement was announced. And the others had chimed in in much the same vein, but perhaps for different reasons. 'We don't want a big wedding,' Jane had said. 'Perhaps a registry office and a little lunch afterwards.'

'We don't want a big wedding,' her mother had agreed weakly, 'but the village will expect it. I suppose we could have something very simple . . . '

Which left Laurie and Grandfa to make their contributions to the discussion. Laurie made no contribution at all, being at Oxford at the time of the engagement, and totally involved with tutorials and lectures, but Grandfa came down solidly on the side of what he called a bit of a splash. 'Only got two daughters,' he told Laurie's parents. 'What's the point of some hole-in-the-corner ceremony? No need to have a marquee. Clear the furniture out of the drawing room, and if it's a nice day, the guests can move out onto the lawn . . . '

She could hear him saying it. She turned over in bed and buried her face in the pillow and fought against the great surge of tearless grief that threatened to engulf her, because he had been, all her life, her favourite person, her wisest counsellor, her very best friend. Jane and Robert were close in age, but Laurie had come along six years later and had always been something of a loner, almost an only child. 'What a funny little thing she is,' her mother's friends would observe, thinking that Laurie was not listening. 'So self-contained. Doesn't she ever want another child to play with?' But Laurie did not need other children, because she had Grandfa.

Grandfa had been in the Navy all his life. After his retirement and the death of his wife, more than twenty years ago, he had bought a piece of land off his son, built himself a little house, and moved to Cornwall, leaving Portsmouth behind forever. It was a wooden house, a cedar house with a shingle roof and a wide verandah that jutted out over the old sea wall. At high tide the water lapped against the stones and reminded Grandfa of his days at sea. He had a telescope fixed to his verandah rail and this afforded him much pleasure. There were no boats to watch, because although there were a few ramshackle crabbers pulled up on the shingle below his house, nothing nowadays came in or out of the estuary except the sea, but he enjoyed watching the birds and counting the cars on the causeway that ran along the far side of the sands. In winter they were few and far between, but once the summer tourists started, they crowded bumper to bumper, the sun flashing on their windscreens and the endless drone of traffic steady as a distant hum of bees.

He had died on his verandah, on a warm evening, with his ritual pink gin in his hand and his gramophone playing in the room behind him. He was very fond of his gramophone. He never owned a television, but he had a great love of music. *Night of love, O lovely night, O, Night that's all divine.* 'The Barcarolle.' He had been playing 'The Barcarolle' when he died, because they had found it still on the gramophone, the finished disc still spinning, the needle grinding in the final groove.

He had an old upright piano, too, which he played with gusto but not a great deal of finesse. When Laurie was small he taught her songs and they had sung them together, with Grandfa providing the accompaniment. Mostly sturdy sea shanties with no-nonsense tunes. 'Whisky Johnny' and 'Rio Grande' and 'Shenandoah.' But his favourite was 'Spanish Ladies':

> *Goodbye and farewell to you, fair Spanish ladies,*
> *Goodbye and farewell to you, ladies of Spain,*
> *For we have received orders for to sail for old England . . .*

He would play it in slow march time, with great crashing chords, and Laurie would have to hold the long notes and she frequently ran out of breath.

'Wonderful slow march,' Grandfa would say, remembering Colours at Whale Island, with the Royal Marine band playing 'Spanish Ladies' while the Captain inspected the Guard, and the White Ensign fluttered high in the morning sky.

His stories were legion, of Hong Kong and Simonstown and Malta. He had fought the war in the Mediterranean and then moved to the Far East and Ceylon. He had survived bombings and sinkings and shattered ships, only to bob up again, joking, indestructible, surviving to become one of the best loved flag officers in the Service.

Indestructible. But he wasn't indestructible. No person was indestructible. At the end of it all he had keeled over in his chair, listening to 'The Barcarolle,' and the glass of pink gin had fallen to the floor and shattered into a thousand pieces. There was no saying how long he might have sat there, with nobody knowing that he had gone, but one of the local fishermen, working on his boat, had looked up and seen him and realised something was wrong, and had walked up to the house, his cap in his hand, to break the news.

Goodbye and farewell to you, fair Spanish Ladies . . .

At the funeral service they had sung 'Holy, Holy, Holy!' and then 'Eternal Father Strong to Save.' And Laurie had looked at the simple coffin draped in the White Ensign, and had broken into noisy, unstoppable tears and had to be discreetly ushered out of some side door by her mother. She had not been back into the church since the funeral; had made a lot of excuses for missing the wedding rehearsal yesterday. 'I'm the only bridesmaid, and I know what I have to do. There's no point in my coming, and there's so much to do here. I'll help move furniture, and vacuum the drawing-room carpet.'

But today – today was the wedding day and there could be no excuse.

And no excuse to stay in bed. Laurie got up, dressed, and brushed her hair, then went along to see Jane. Jane had been given breakfast in bed which, being lazy, she loved. Laurie hated breakfast in bed because she always ended up sitting on crumbs.

She said 'Good morning, how are you feeling?' and went to give Jane a kiss, and Jane said, 'I don't know. How should I be feeling?'

'Nervous?'

'Not nervous at all. Just cosy and comfortable and cossetted.'

'It's a super day,' said Laurie, and pulled Teddy out from under the pillow. 'Hi, Teddy,' she said to him. 'Your days are numbered.'

'Not at all,' said Jane, snatching him back. 'There's life in him yet. He's got to survive to be mauled by all our children. Have a bit of toast.'

'No, you eat it. You've got to keep your strength up.'

'You've got to keep your strength up, too. You've got to do all the right things, like catching the bouquet when I hurl it in your direction, and being charming to the best man.'

'Oh, *Jane.*'

'Well, come on, it's William Boscawan. Surely it isn't impossible to be charming to William? I know you usually snarl like a wounded animal if he so much as walks into the room, but that's your fault. He's never been anything but civil to you.'

'He's always treated me like a ten-year-old.'

William Boscawan was an old bone of contention. His father was the family lawyer and William had joined the firm some five years ago, and so had returned to live and work in the neighbourhood. And not only to live and work, but also to break the heart of every girl in the county. He had even had a small fling with Jane until he had lost her affections, permanently, to Andrew Latham, but this had made no different to his friendship with Andrew, and when the wedding arrangements were made, nobody was surprised when Andrew announced that William was to be his best man.

'I can't think why you don't like him.'

'I like him all right. There's nothing wrong with him. It's just that he's so smooth.'

'He's not a bit smooth. He's sweet.'

'I mean . . . oh, you know what I mean. That car, and that boat, and all those girls batting their eyelashes every time his glance swivels their way.'

'You're being very mean. He can't help it if girls fall in love with him.'

'I'd like him better if he wasn't quite so successful.'

'That's just a sort of inverted sour-grapery. Just because other people like him, there's no reason why you shouldn't like him too.'

'I've told you, I don't dislike him. I mean, there's nothing about him to dislike. I just wish sometimes he'd get spots on his face, or have a blow-out in that fast car of his, or fall in the water when he's sailing.'

'You're impossible. You'll end up with some old academic bore with glasses like the bottoms of bottles.'

'Yes, those are the sort of men I go round with all the time.'

They glared at each other, and then started to laugh. Jane said, 'I give up. Your aggressions have defeated me.'

'Just as well,' said Laurie. 'Now, I'm going down to have some breakfast.' She made for the door, but as she opened it, Jane said 'Laurie' in quite a different tone of voice, and Laurie turned with her hand on the knob.

'Laurie . . . you're going to be all right?'

Laurie stared at her. They had never been very close, had never exchanged confidences or shared secrets, and Laurie knew that for this reason, it had taken some effort for Jane to say that. She knew that, in return, she should let down her own barrier of reserve, but it was her only protection against the emptiness, the sense of aching loss. Without it, she would be lost, would probably burst into tears and be unable to stop crying for the rest of the day.

She could feel every nerve in her body drawing in on

itself, like a sea anemone suddenly touched. She said, 'What do you mean?' and even to herself she sounded cold.

'You know what I mean.' Poor Jane looked agonised. 'Grandfa . . . ' Laurie said nothing. 'We . . . we all know it's worse for you than for any of us,' Jane floundered on. 'You were always his special person. And now, today . . . I wouldn't have minded the wedding being put off. I wouldn't have minded being married in a registry office. Andrew feels the same way as I do. But Mother and Father . . . well, it simply wouldn't have been fair to them . . . '

'It's not your fault,' said Laurie.

'I don't want you to be unhappy. I don't want to feel we're making you more unhappy than you are.'

She said again, 'It's not your fault.' And after that there didn't seem to be anything else to say, so she went out of the room and closed the door behind her.

The morning progressed. The house, unfamiliar and stripped of furniture, was slowly taken over by strangers. The caterers arrived, vans appeared at the door, tables were erected, glasses set out, looking as the sun struck them like hundreds of soap bubbles. The florist's lady turned up in a little truck to put the finishing touches to the arrangements that she had spent most of yesterday concocting. Robert drove to the station to fetch Aunt Blanche. One of the children was sick. Laurie's father couldn't find his braces, and her mother all at once threw a fit of temperament and announced that she couldn't possibly wear the hat which had been made to go with her bride's mother's outfit. She came downstairs wearing it, to prove her point. It was a sort of baker's boy beret made of azalea pink silk. 'I look like nothing on earth in it,' she wailed, and Laurie knew that she was near to tears, but they all told her she looked smashing, and once she'd had her hair done and was wearing the bride's mother's outfit, she'd knock the rest of them into a cocked hat. She was still unpersuaded when the hairdresser arrived, but this new turn of events mercifully diverted her, and she allowed herself to be led upstairs.

'Good,' said Laurie's father. 'Nothing like a new hairdo for calming down the nerves. She'll be all right now.' He looked at Laurie as he ran a hand over his thinning hair. 'You all right?' he asked her. His voice was casual, but she knew that he was thinking about Grandfa, and she couldn't bear it. She said, deliberately misunderstanding, 'I haven't got a hat, I've only got a flower.' She saw her father's expression and hated herself, but before she could say anything more, he had made some excuse and taken himself off, and then it was too late.

The caterers provided a lunch for them all in the kitchen, and the entire family sat around the familiar table and ate unfamiliar food, like chicken in aspic and potato salad and trifle, when they usually had soup and bread and cheese. After lunch, they all went up to change, and Laurie brushed her silken hair, wound it up into a coronet on the top of her head, and fixed the single camellia into the coils. Then she dressed herself, finally slipping the long, pale dress over her petticoat and doing up the row of tiny buttons on the front. She fastened a rope of pearls around her neck, picked up her bridesmaid's posy, and went to stand in front of the long mirror that hung on the back of the door. She saw a girl, pale and unfamiliar, her neck exposed by the upswept hair, dark eyes shadowed, face empty of expression. She thought, *This is how I have looked ever since Grandfa died. Untouchable, unreachable. I want to talk about him, but I can't. Not yet. Once I get through today and it's all over, perhaps then I shall be able to talk. But not yet.*

She opened the door, went down the steep stairs, and knocked at the door of her mother's bedroom. She went in and her mother was sitting at the dressing table, putting on her mascara before finally dealing with the dreaded hat. Her hair, fresh from the stylist's hands, curled and fronded about her neck. She looked immensely pretty. Her eyes met Laurie's in the mirror. After a little, she turned on the stool to take a long look at her younger daughter. She said, with a small shake in her voice, 'Oh, my darling, you look quite lovely.'

Laurie smiled. 'Didn't you think I would?'

'Yes, of course. It's just that suddenly I feel all maternal and proud.'

Laurie went to kiss her. 'I'm early,' she said. She added, 'You look lovely too. And the hat's really pretty.'

Her mother caught her hand. 'Laurie . . . '

Laurie pulled her hand free. 'Don't ask me if I'm all right. Don't talk about Granfa.'

'Darling, I understand. We all miss him. We all have a great empty hole in our hearts. He should be here today and he isn't. But for Jane's sake, for Andrew's sake, for Grandfa's sake, we mustn't be sad. Life must go on, and he wouldn't have wanted anything to spoil this day.'

Laurie said, 'I won't spoil it.'

'It's worst for you. We all know that.'

She said, 'I don't want to talk about it.'

She went downstairs. Everything was ready for the wedding reception. Everything was unfamiliar, everything was strange. It wasn't just the house, the unrecognisable drawing room, the massive flowers and the caterer's tables. It was herself. The thin, light feeling of the dress, the delicate shoes, the chill around her neck without the usual heavy fall of hair over her shoulders. Nothing was the same. She knew that nothing would ever be the same again. Perhaps this was the beginning of growing old. Perhaps when she was really old, she would look back and think, *That was the beginning. That was the day when I stopped being a child, when I knew that good things couldn't go on forever.*

Still holding her posy, she went through the open French windows and sat on a chair on the terrace, looking out at the garden. Small tables and chairs had been set out on the lawn, sun umbrellas flowered, casting dark round shadows on the grass. Beyond, the garden sloped to the blue waters of the estuary. The masts of the fishing boats showed beyond the fuchsia hedge, and the high-pitched roof of Grandfa's house. She thought of magic and the vagaries of time; of being able to put back the clock. To be twelve years old again, in shorts and sneakers, running down the lawn with her swimming towel under her arm, to collect Grandfa and take him on their daily expedition to the beach. Or to catch the little train into the local town, where he would stock up on tobacco and razor blades and buy Laurie an ice cream cornet, an they would sit on the harbour wall in the sunshine and watch the men working on their boats.

A car drove up to the house from the road. Laurie heard the scrunch of gravel, a door slam, but took no notice, imagining that it was something to do with the wedding – a barman, recruited at the last moment, or the postman with greetings telegrams for the happy couple. But then the front door opened, and a man's voice called out, 'Anybody around?' and it was, unmistakably, the best man, William Boscawan.

He was the last person she wanted to see. Laurie froze, silent and still as a shadow. She heard him cross the hall and open the kitchen door. 'Anybody there?'

Still soundless, she walked down into the heat of the garden and crossed the lawn. The breeze caught her long, fragile skirts and blew the airy fabric against her legs, and the soles of the new sandals slipped a little on the dry grass. She reached the gate in the fuchsia hedge and nobody had called her back. She closed the gate and went on down the path to the cedar house.

The door was unlocked. It had never been locked. She went in and smelt the fragrance of the cedar panelling, and tobacco smoke, and a whiff of the bay rum that the old man had always used on his hair. The narrow hallway was hung with photographs of the ships he had commanded. She saw his huge Burmese temple gong, and the antlers of the wildebeeste he once shot in South Africa. She opened the door of his living room and went in, and there were the worn Persian rugs, the sagging leather chairs. It was very warm; a bluebottle buzzed against the closed windows on the opposite side of the room. She went across and undid the latch of the window and it slid aside. The stuffy abandoned room was filled with a great gust of air. Laurie stepped out onto the verandah, and the flood tide lapped at the sea wall below her feet, and the estuary was blue as the sky and dappled with sun pennies.

Laurie felt suddenly exhausted, as though, in order to get here, she had walked for miles. Grandfa's chair stood by the telescope. She sat in it, cautiously spreading the skirts of her dress so that they should not crush. She leaned back her head and closed her eyes.

Small sounds began impinging on her consciousness. Traffic sounds from the distant causeway, the slapping waters of the high tide, the scream of a solitary gull. She thought that if she could just sit here, alone, undisturbed, for the rest of the day . . . not go to the wedding, not talk to anybody . . .

Somewhere a door opened. The draught this caused through the house stirred Grandfa's heavy curtains. Laurie opened her eyes but did not move.

The door shut again, and then footsteps came through the house. The next moment William appeared at the open window. He stepped over the sill and stood looking down at Laurie. Even in that moment of dismay, she had time to admit to herself that in his morning suit with the best man's white carnation, he looked sensational. The stiff white collar accentuated his tan, his black hair matched the sombre coat, his shoes were gleaming. He wasn't good-looking. He wasn't even handsome, but his sheer masculinity, his smile, his blue and sparkling eyes added up to an attraction that was impossible to ignore.

He said, 'Hello, Laurie.'

'What are you doing here?' she asked him. 'Aren't you meant to be supporting Andrew and getting him to the church on time?'

William grinned. 'Andrew's as cool as a cucumber,' he told her. He went back indoors and returned with a chair which he set down and then sat in, facing Laurie, with his long legs stretched out in front of him and his hands in his trouser pockets. 'But a little anxious about confetti in the suitcases. So I came over to fetch Jane's luggage, and we're going to hide it in some unsuspected car. He says he doesn't mind about tin cans tied to the bumper, or even kippers hidden in the engine, but he does object to confetti being spread all over the hotel bedroom floor.'

'Did you see Jane?'

'No, but your father fetched her stuff down. It was then that he realised you were nowhere around, but one of the caterer's ladies had seen you come down the garden, so I came too. Just to make sure that everything was all right.'

Laurie said, 'I'm fine.'

'You're not ratting on the wedding?'

'Of course not,' she told him coolly. 'And hadn't you better go back to Andrew before panic sets in?'

William glanced at his watch. 'It's all right. We've got ten minutes to spare.' He stretched and looked about him. 'What a fantastic spot this is. Like being on the bridge of a ship.'

Laurie leaned back in her chair. 'Did you know,' she asked him, 'did you know that this wasn't always an estuary? Long, long ago, before it all got silted up with sand, it was a deep water channel that reached a mile or more inland. And the Phoenicians came, sailing their ships up on the flood tides, with cargoes of spice and damask, and all the treasures of the Mediterranean. And they would tie up and unload and barter, and finally start back again on their long and hazardous journeys, loaded to the gunwales with Cornish tin. About two thousand years ago, that happened. Just think. Two thousand years.' She looked at William. 'Did you know that?'

'Yes,' said William. 'But I liked hearing it again.'

'It's nice to think about, isn't it?'

'Yes. It keeps things in proportion.'

Laurie said, 'Grandfa told me.'

'I thought he probably had.'

Without thinking, she said it. 'I miss him so much.'

'I know you do. I think we all do. He was a great man. He had a great life.'

She had not thought of someone like William missing the Admiral. She looked at him in some curiosity and thought, *I don't really know him at all.* It wasn't like talking to a stranger on a train. Suddenly it was easy.

'It's not that I was with Grandfa all that much. I mean, lately I've been away from home more than I've been here. But when I was little, I was with him all the time. I can't even get used to knowing that he's never going to be here again.'

'I know.'

'It wasn't just his telling you things, like the Phoenician boats two thousand years ago. So much had happened in *his* lifetime. The whole world changed under his very eyes. He remembered it all. And he always had time to talk. He could answer questions and explain things. Like how a boat can sail against the wind, and the names of stars. And how to use a compass, and how to play Mah Jong and backgammon. Who's here now to tell Robert's little children all those marvellous things?'

'Perhaps that's up to us,' said William.

She met his eyes. His expression was sombre. She said, 'You think I'm being impossible, don't you?'

'No.'

'I know I'm being impossible, and everybody thinks I'm spoiling things for Jane. I don't mean to. It's just that if I could have had a little more time . . . But this wedding . . . ' Suddenly her eyes filled with tears. 'Oh, if only we could have put it off. Just for a little while. I can't bear the thought of having to go into the church. I can't bear the thought of having to smile and be nice to people. I can't bear any of it. Everybody says that Grandfa would have wanted us to go ahead, just the way the wedding was planned. But how does anybody *know* what he would have wanted? They couldn't ask him, because he wasn't here to ask. How can they *know* . . . ?'

She couldn't go on. The tears were spilling down her cheeks. She tried to wipe them away, but William took a handkerchief out of his trouser pocket and tossed it across to her, and Laurie accepted it wordlessly, wiped the tears with the soft cotton, then blew her nose. She said, hopelessly, 'I wish I could just sit here for the rest of my life.'

He smiled. He said, 'That wouldn't do anybody any good. And it wouldn't bring the Admiral back. And you know, you're mistaken. He did want the wedding to go ahead. He said as much. He went to see my father about two weeks before he died. I think he'd probably been feeling a little unwell, or perhaps he had some sort of a premonition, but they were talking about the wedding, and the Admiral told my father that if anything did happen to him, then he didn't want it, under any circumstances, to make any difference to Jane's wedding.'

Laurie wiped her eyes again. After a little: 'Is that *really* true?' she asked him.

'I give you my word, it's true. Isn't it typical of the old boy? He always liked everything cut and dried, shipshape and Bristol fashion. And I'll tell you something else, too, although I shouldn't jump the gun. It's a confidence, so you'll have to keep it to yourself.' Laurie frowned. 'He's left this house to you. He wanted you to have it. His favourite grandchild and his best friend. Now, don't start crying again, because if you do, your face will go all red and blotchy and you'll be a hideous

bridesmaid instead of a beautiful one. This is a very
happy day. Don't look back over your shoulder. Think
about Jane and Andrew. Keep your chin up. The Admiral
will be so proud of you.'

She said, 'I'm so afraid of making a fool of myself.'

'You won't,' William told her.

And now it was time. In the porch of the ancient church,
the bride and her father and the bridesmaid arranged
themselves. Above, the clangor of the wedding bells was
stilled. From inside the crowded nave came the small
whispers and rustles of an impatient and festive congregation. Laurie gave Jane a kiss, and stooped to arrange
the skirts of her dress. Jane's bouquet was heavy with
the scent of tuber roses.

The vicar, in his starched white surplice, waited to
lead the small procession. The church warden gave a
signal to Miss Treadwell, the village schoolmistress who
played the organ. The music started. Laurie took a deep
breath. They moved forward, through the doorway,
down the two wide shallow steps.

Inside, the church was dim, awash with flowers and
drowned in their scent. Sun shone through stained-glass
windows as the congregation, in all its finery, surged to
its feet. Laurie did not think about Grandfa's funeral,
but instead concentrated on her mother's pink hat, her
brother's broad shoulders, the sweetly brushed heads of
his children. *One day*, she thought, *when they're bigger,
I'll tell them about the Phoenicians. I'll tell them all the
marvellous things that Grandfa ever told me.*

It was a good thought to hold on to. It was looking
ahead. Suddenly, Laurie realised that the worst was
over. She had stopped feeling nervous and miserable.
She simply felt wonderfully calm, making her way down
the flagged aisle behind her sister, stepping in time to
the music.

The music. The music Miss Treadwell was playing.
It was resounding, triumphant, exactly right for a

wedding. It had probably never been played before on just such an occasion, but it bore them up towards the altar on a tide of glorious, joyous sound.

Spanish ladies

A lump swelled in Laurie's throat. *I never knew. I never knew they were going to use Grandfa's music for a wedding march.*

But how could she have known? She had refused to come to the wedding rehearsal, and probably none of her family had had the heart or could summon the nerve to tell her.

Goodbye and farewell to you, fair Spanish ladies . . .

Grandfa. He was here. He was in the church, revelling in the tradition, the ceremony, encouraging all of them. Still part of the family.

Goodbye and farewell to you, ladies of Spain

Andrew and William stood waiting at the end of the aisle. Both men had turned to watch as the little procession approached. Andrew's eyes were on Jane, and there was pride and wonder written all over his face. But William . . .

He was watching Laurie, his expression steadfast, concerned, reassuring. She realised that the lump in her throat had come to nothing, and that she wasn't going to cry. She wished there was some way of telling William about Grandfa, but then she caught his eye, and he smiled and sent her an unmistakable wink, and she knew that there was no need to tell him because he already knew.

Miss Cameron at Christmas

The little town, which was called Kilmoran, had many faces, and all of them, to Miss Cameron, were beautiful. In spring, the waters of the firth were blown blue as indigo; inland the fields were filled with lambs, and cottage gardens danced with daffodils. The summer brought the visitors; family parties camping on the beach, swimming in the shallow waves, the ice cream van parked by the breakwater, the old man with his donkey giving rides to the children. And then, around the middle of September, the visitors disappeared, the holiday houses were closed up, their shuttered windows staring blank-eyed across the water to the hills on the distant shore. The countryside hummed with combine harvesters, and as the leaves began to flutter from the trees and the stormy autumn tides brought the sea right up to the rim of the wall below Miss Cameron's garden, the first of the wild geese flew in from the north. After the geese, she always felt it was winter.

And perhaps, thought Miss Cameron privately, that was the most beautiful time of all. Her house faced south across the firth, and although she often woke to darkness and wind and the battering of rain, sometimes the sky was clear and cloudless, and on such mornings she would lie in her bed and watch the red sun edge its way over the horizon and flood her bedroom with rosy light. It winked on the brass rail of her bed and was reflected in the mirror over the dressing table.

*   *   *

Now, it was the twenty-fourth of December, and just such a morning. Christmas tomorrow. She was alone, and she would spend tomorrow alone. She did not mind. She and her house would keep each other company. She got up and went to close the window. There was an icing of snow on the distant Lammermuirs and a gull sat on the wall at the end of the garden, screaming over a piece of rotten fish. Suddenly it spread its wings and took off. The sunlight caught the spread of white feathers and transformed the gull into a magic, pink bird, so beautiful that Miss Cameron's heart lifted in pleasure and excitement. She watched the gull's flight until it dipped out of sight, then turned to find her slippers and go downstairs to put on a kettle for her cup of tea.

Miss Cameron was fifty-eight. Until two years ago she had lived in Edinburgh, in the tall, cold, north-facing house where she had been born and brought up. She had been an only child, the daughter of parents so much older than herself that by the time she was twenty, they were already well on the road to old age. This made leaving home and making a life for herself, if not impossible, then difficult. Somehow, she achieved a sort of compromise. She got herself to University, but it was Edinburgh University, and she lived at home. After that, she had taken a teaching job, but that, too, had been in a local school, and by the time she was thirty there could be no question of abandoning the two old people who – unbelievably, Miss Cameron often thought – were responsible for her very existence.

When she was forty, her mother, who had never been very robust, had a little heart attack, lay feebly in her bed for a month or so, and then died. After the funeral, Miss Cameron and her father returned to the tall and gloomy house. He went upstairs to sit morosely by the fire, and she went down to the kitchen and made him a cup of tea. The kitchen was in the basement, and the window had bars on it, to discourage possible intruders. Miss Cameron, waiting for the kettle to boil, looked out through the bars to the small stone area beyond. She had tried to grow geraniums there, but they had all died, and now there was nothing to be seen but a stubborn sprout of willow herb. The bars made the kitchen feel like a prison. She had never thought this before, but she thought it now, and knew that it was true. She would never get away.

Her father lived on for another fifteen years, and she went on teaching until he became too frail to leave, even for a day. So she dutifully retired from her job, where she had been not exactly happy, but at least fulfilled, and stayed at home, to devote her time to what remained of her father's life. She had little money of her own, and supposed that the old man had as little as herself, so frugal was the housekeeping allowance, so cautious was he with things like coal and central heating and even the most modest forms of enjoyment.

He owned an old car, which Miss Cameron could drive, and on warm days she used sometimes to bundle him into this, and he would sit beside her, in his grey tweed suit and the black hat that made him look like an undertaker, while she drove him to the seaside or the country, or even to Holyrood Park where he could take a little stumbling walk, or sit in the sun beneath the grassy slopes of Arthur's Seat. But then the price of petrol rocketed, and without consulting his daughter, Mr Cameron sold the car, and she did not have enough money of her own to buy another.

She had a friend, Dorothy Laurie, with whom she had been at University. Dorothy had married – as Miss Cameron had not – a young doctor, who was now an eminently successful neurologist, and with whose cooperation she had produced a family of satisfactory children, now all grown up. Dorothy was perpetually indignant about Miss Cameron's situation. She felt, and said, that Miss Cameron's parents had been selfish and thoughtless, and that the old man was getting worse as he was getting older. When the car was sold, she blew her top.

'It's ridiculous,' she said, over tea in her sunny, flower-filled drawing room. Miss Cameron had prevailed upon her daily help to stay over for the afternoon to give Mr Cameron his tea, and make sure that he didn't fall down the stairs on his way to the lavatory. 'He can't be as penurious as all that. Surey he can afford to run a car, for your sake, if not for his own?'

Miss Cameron did not like to point out that he had never thought of any person except himself. She said, 'I don't know.'

'Then you should find out. Speak to his accountant. Or his lawyer.'

'Dorothy, I couldn't. It would be so disloyal.'

Dorothy made a sound which sounded like 'Pshaw' and which is what people used to say in old-fashioned novels.

'I don't want to upset him,' Miss Cameron went on.

'Do him good to be upset. If he'd been upset once or twice in his life, he wouldn't be such a selfish old . . . ' She bit back what she had been going to say and substituted ' . . . man, now.'

'He's lonely.'

'Of course he's lonely. Selfish people are always lonely. That's nobody's fault but his own. For years, he's sat in a chair and felt sorry for himself.'

It was too true to argue with. 'Oh, well,' said Miss Cameron feebly, 'it can't be helped. He's nearly ninety now. It's too late to start trying to change him.'

'Yes, but it's not too late to change you. You mustn't let yourself grow old with him. You must keep some part of life for yourself.'

He died at last, painlessly and peacefully, falling asleep after a quiet evening and an excellent dinner cooked for him by his daughter, and never waking again. Miss Cameron was glad for him that the end had come so quietly. There was a funeral and a surprising number of people attended it. A day or so later, Miss Cameron was summoned to her father's lawyer's office. She went, in a black hat and a state of nervous apprehension. But as it happened, nothing turned out as she had thought it would. Mr Cameron, the canny old Scot that he was, had played his cards very close to his chest. The penny-pinching, the austerity of years, had been one huge, magnificent bluff. He left in his will, to his daughter, his house, his worldly possessions, and more money than she had ever dreamed of. Polite, and outwardly composed as ever, she left the lawyer's office and stepped out into the sunlight of Charlotte Square. There was a flag flying high over the ramparts of the castle and the air was cold and fresh. She walked down to Jenners and had a cup of coffee, and then she went to see Dorothy.

Dorothy, on hearing the news, was characteristically torn between fury at old Mr Cameron's meanness and duplicity and delight in her friend's good fortune. 'You can buy a car,' she told her. 'You can travel. You can have a fur coat, go on cruises. Anything. What are you going to do? What are you going to do with the rest of your life?'

'Well,' said Miss Cameron cautiously, 'I will buy myself a little car.' The idea of being free, mobile, with no person but herself to consider, took a bit of getting used to.

'And travel?'

But Miss Cameron had no great desire for travel, except that one day she would like to go to Oberammergau and see the Passion Play. And she didn't want to go on cruises. She really wanted only one thing. Had wanted only one thing in her life. And now she could have it.

She said, 'I shall sell the Edinburgh house. And I shall buy another.'

'Where?'

She knew exactly where. Kilmoran. She had gone there for a summer when she was ten, invited by the kindly parents of a school friend. It had been a holiday of such happiness that Miss Cameron had never forgotten it.

She said, 'I shall go and live in Kilmoran.'

'Kilmoran? But that's only just across the firth . . .'

Miss Cameron smiled at her. It was a smile that Dorothy had never seen before, and it silenced her. 'That is where I shall buy a house.'

And so she did. A house in a terrace, facing out over the sea. From the back, from the north, its aspect was both plain and dull, with square windows and a front door that led straight off the pavement. But inside, it was beautiful, a Georgian house in miniature, with a slate-flagged hallway and a curving staircase rising to the upper floor. The sitting room was upstairs, with a bay window, and in front of the house was a square garden, walled in from the sea winds. There was a tall gate in the wall, and if you opened this, a flight of stone steps led down the sea wall to the beach. In summer, children ran along the top of the sea wall and screamed and shouted at each other, but Miss Cameron minded this noise no more than she minded the noise of the waves, or the gulls, or the eternal winds.

There was much to be done to the house and much to be spent on it, but with a certain mouselike courage, she both did and spent. Central heating was installed, and double glazing. The kitchen was rebuilt, with pine cupboards, and new pale green bathroom fixtures took the place of the old white chipped ones. The prettiest and smallest articles of furniture were weeded out of the old Edinburgh house and transported, in an immense van, to Kilmoran, along with the china, the silver, the familiar pictures. But she bought new carpets and curtains, and had all the walls repapered and the woodwork painted a shining white.

As for the garden – she had never had a garden before. Now she bought books and studied them in bed at night, and she planted escallonia and veronica and thyme and sea-lavender, and bought a little lawnmower and cut the ragged, tufty grass herself.

It was through her garden that she met, inevitably, her neighbours. On the right-hand side lived the Mitchells, an elderly, retired couple. They chatted over the garden wall, and one day Mrs Mitchell invited Miss Cameron for supper and a game of bridge. Cautiously, they became Miss Cameron's friends, but they were old-fashioned and formal people, and did not suggest that Miss Cameron call them by their Christian names, and she was too reserved to suggest the idea herself. Thinking about it, she realised that now the only person who called her by her Christian name was Dorothy. It was sad when people stopped realising that you had a Christian name. It meant that you were growing old.

However, the neighbours on the left-hand side of Miss Cameron's house were a different kettle of fish altogether. In the first place, they did not live permanently in their house, but used it only at weekends and for holidays.

'They're called Ashley,' Mrs Mitchell had volunteered over the supper table, when Miss Cameron had made one or two discreet enquiries about the closed and shuttered house on the other side of her garden. 'He's an architect with a practice in Edinburgh. I'm surprised you've not heard of him, living there all your life, as you have. Ambrose Ashley. He married a girl much younger than himself . . . she was a painter, I think . . . and they have a daughter. She seems a nice little girl . . . Now have a little more quiche, Miss Cameron, or perhaps some salad?'

It was Easter when the Ashleys appeared. Good Friday was cold and bright, and when Miss Cameron went out into the garden, she heard the voices from over the wall, and she looked at the house and saw the shutters down and the windows open. A pink curtain fluttered in the breeze. Then a girl appeared at the upstairs window, and she and Miss Cameron, for a second, gazed into each other's faces. Miss Cameron was embarrassed. She turned and hurried indoors. How terrible if they thought she was prying.

But later in the day, while she was weeding, she heard her name being called, and there was the same girl, looking at her over the top of the wall. She had a round and freckled face, dark brown eyes, and reddish hair, abundant and thick and windblown.

Miss Cameron got up off her knees and crossed the lawn, pulling off her gardening gloves.

'I'm Frances Ashley . . . ' Over the wall, they shook hands. Close to, Miss Cameron realised that she was not as young as she had at first appeared. There were lines around her eyes and mouth, and perhaps that blaze of hair wasn't entirely natural, but her expression was so open, and she gave off such an aura of vitality, that Miss Cameron lost some of her shyness, and felt, almost at once, at ease.

The dark eyes travelled over Miss Cameron's garden. 'Goodness, how hard you must have worked. You've made it all so neat and pretty. Are you doing anything on Sunday? Easter Sunday? Because we're having a barbecue in the garden, provided it doesn't pour with rain. Do come, if you don't mind joining in a picnic.'

'Oh. How kind.' Miss Cameron had never been invited to a barbecue. 'I . . . think I'd like to come very much.'

'About a quarter to one. You can come by the sea wall.'

'I shall look forward to that very much.'

During the next couple of days, she realised that life with the Ashleys in residence next door was very different from life without them. For one thing, there was much more noise, but it was a pleasant noise. Voices calling and laughter and music that floated out through the open windows. Miss Cameron, steeling herself for 'hard rock,' or whatever it was called, recognised Vivaldi and was filled with pleasure. She caught glimpses of the remainder of the little family. The father, very tall and thin and distinguished, with a head of silver hair, and the daughter, who was as red-headed as her mother and had legs that looked endless in faded jeans. They had friends to stay as well (Miss Cameron wondered how they were packing them all in) and in the afternoons they would all surge down the garden and invade the beach, playing ridiculous ball games, the red-headed mother and daughter looking like sisters as they raced, bare-footed, across the sands.

Easter Sunday dawned bright and sunny, although the wind was keen and cold and there was still a scrap of snow to be seen, clinging to the crest of the Lammermuirs across the water. Miss Cameron went to church, then came home to change out of her Sunday coat and skirt and to put on something more suitable for a picnic. She had never owned a pair of trousers, but she found a comfortable skirt, a warm sweater, and a windproof anorak, then locked her front door and went out of the house, through the garden, along the sea wall, and in through the gate of the Ashleys' garden. Smoke was blowing from the newly lighted barbecue and the little lawn was already crowded with people of every age, some sitting on garden chairs or camped on rugs. Everybody seemed very jolly and as thogh they all knew one another very well, and for a second Miss Cameron was overcome with shyness and wished that she hadn't come. But then Ambrose Ashley materialised at her side, towering over her and holding a toasting fork with a burnt sausage skewered to its end.

'Miss Cameron. How splendid to meet you. And how good of you to come. Happy Easter. Now come and meet everybody. Frances! Here's Miss Cameron. We've invited the Mitchells, too, but they haven't arrived yet.

Frances, how do we stop the fire from smoking? I can't give this sausage to anyone but a dog.'

Frances laughed. 'Then find a dog and give it to him, and then start again . . . ' and suddenly Miss Cameron was laughing too, because he did look marvellously comic, with his straight face and his burnt sausage. Then somebody found her a chair and somebody else gave her a tumbler of wine. She was about to tell this person who she was and where she lived when she was interrupted by a plateful of food being handed to her. She looked up and into the face of the Ashley daughter. The dark eyes were her mother's, but the smile was her father's engaging grin. She could not have been more than twelve, but Miss Cameron, who had watched countless girls grow up during her years of teaching, knew at once that this child was going to be a beauty.

'Would you like something to eat?'

'I'd love something to eat.' She looked about her for somewhere to put her glass, then set it on the grass. She took the plate, the paper napkin, the knife and fork. 'Thank you. I don't think I know your name?'

'I'm Bryony. I hope you like steaks pink in the middle, because that's what this one is.'

'Delicious,' said Miss Cameron, who liked her steaks very well done.

'And there's butter on the baked potato. I put it there so that you wouldn't have to get up.' She smiled and moved away, back to help her mother.

Miss Cameron, trying to organise her knife and fork, turned back to her neighbour. 'What a pretty child.'

'Yes, she's a darling. Now I'm going to get you another glass of wine, and then you must go on telling me all about that fascinating house.'

It was a wonderful party and did not finish until six. When it was time to go, the tide was so high that Miss Cameron did not relish walking along the sea wall, and so returned to her own house the conventional way, via front doors and the pavement. Ambrose Ashley came with her. When she had opened her door, she turned to thank him.

'Such a lovely party. I did enjoy it. I feel quite Bohemian, drinking all that wine in the middle of the day. And I hope, when you next come, you will all come and have a meal with me. Luncheon, perhaps.'

'We'd love it, but we won't be coming back for a bit. I've got a teaching job at a university in Texas. We're going out in July, having a bit of a holiday first, and then I start work in the fall. It's a sort of sabbatical. Bryony's coming too. She'll have to go to shool in the States, but we don't want to leave her behind.'

'What a marvellous experience for you all!' He smiled down at her, and she said, with truth, 'You will be missed.'

The seasons passed. Spring turned to summer, to autumn, to winter. There were storms and the Ashleys' escallonia was blown from the wall, so Miss Cameron took herself next door with garden wire and cutters and tied it up. It was Easter again, it was summer, but still the Ashleys did not reappear. It was not until the end of August that they came back. Miss Cameron had been shopping and changing her library book. She came round the corner at the end of the street and saw their car parked by their door, and her heart gave a ridiculous leap. She let herself into her house, put her basket onto the kitchen table, and went straight out into the garden. And there, over the wall, was Mr Ashley, trying to cut down the ragged, overgrown grass with a scythe. He looked up and saw her, and stopped in the middle of a sweep. 'Miss Cameron.' He laid down the scythe and came over to shake her hand.

'You're back.' She could scarcely contain her pleasure.

'Yes. We stayed longer than we had intended. We made so many friends and there was so much to see, and so much to do. It was a wonderful experience for all of us. But now we're back in Edinburgh, and I'm back in harness.'

'How long are you staying here?'

'Just a couple of nights, I'm afraid. It's going to take me all that time to get rid of the grass . . . '

But Miss Cameron's attention had wandered. A movement from the house caught her eye. The door opened and Frances Ashley came out, and down the steps towards them. After a second's hesitation, Miss Cameron smiled, and said, 'Welcome back. I'm so pleased to see you both again.'

She hoped so much that they had not noticed the hesitation. She would not for all the world have wanted them to even guess at her shock and astonishment. For Frances Ashley had returned from America marvellously, obviously, pregnant.

'She's having another baby,' said Mrs Mitchell. 'After all this time. She's having another baby.'

'Well, there's no reason why she shouldn't have another baby,' said Miss Cameron faintly. 'I mean, if she wants to.'

'But Bryony must be fourteen.'

'That doesn't matter.'

'No, I know it doesn't matter . . . it's just . . . well, rather unusual.'

The two ladies were silent for a moment, agreeing on this.

After a little, 'It's not,' said Mrs Mitchell delicately, 'as though she was as young as she used to be.'

'She looks very young,' said Miss Cameron.

'Yes, she does look young, but she must be thirty-eight at least. I mean, I know that is young, when you're getting on in years like we are. But it's not young to have a baby.'

Miss Cameron had not realised that Mrs Ashley was thirty-eight. Sometimes, when she was out on the sands with her leggy daughter, they looked the same age. She said, 'I'm sure it will be all right,' but even to herself, she didn't sound sure.

'Yes, of course,' said Mrs Mitchell. They met each other's eyes, and then, quickly, both looked away.

And now it was midwinter, and Christmas again, and Miss Cameron was alone. If the Mitchells had been here, she might have asked them over for lunch tomorrow, but they had taken themselves off to spend Christmas in Dorset with a married daughter. So, their house stood empty. On the other hand, the Ashleys' house was occupied. They had arrived from Edinburgh a day or two ago, but Miss Cameron had not spoken to them. She felt that she should, but for some obscure reason it was more difficult to make contact in the wintertime. There could be no casual chat over the garden wall when people stayed indoors with fires lighted and curtains drawn. And she was too diffident to find some reason for contact and go knocking at their door. If she had known them better, she would have bought them Christmas presents, but if they then had nothing for her, it could be embarrassing. As well, there was the complication of Mrs Ashley's pregnancy. Yesterday Miss Cameron had spied her, hanging out a line of washing, and it appeared as if the baby might arrive at any moment.

In the afternoon Mrs Ashley and Bryony set out for a walk across the beach. They went slowly, not running and racing as they usually did. Mrs Ashley wore wellingtons and trod tiredly, heavily, as though weighed down not simply by the bulk of the baby, but by all the anxieties of the world. Even the bounce seemed to have gone from her russet hair. Bryony slowed her pace to match her mother's, and when they returned from their little excursion, she had her hand under her mother's elbow, helping her along.

I mustn't think about them, Miss Cameron told herself briskly. *I mustn't turn into the sort of meddling old lady who watches the neighbours and makes up stories about them. It is nothing to do with me.*

Christmas Eve. Determined to be festive, Miss Cameron arranged her cards on the mantelpiece and filled a bowl with holly; brought in logs and cleaned the house, and in the afternoon went for a long walk across the beach. By the time she got home, it was dark, a strange, cloudy evening with a blustery wind blowing from the west. She drew the curtains and made tea. She was just sitting down to this, her knees close to the blazing fire, when the telephone rang. She got up and went to answer it, and was amazed to hear a man's voice. It was Ambrose Ashley from next door.

He said, 'You're there.'

'Of course.'

'I'm coming round.'

He rang off. An instant later her front door bell pealed and she went to answer it. He stood on the pavement, looking ashen, fleshless as a skeleton.

She said at once, 'What's wrong?'

'I have to take Frances to Edinburgh, to the hospital.'

'Has the baby started?'

'I don't know. But she's been feeling unwell for a day or two. I'm scared. I've rung our doctor, and he says to bring her in right away.'

'What can I do to help?'

'That's why I'm here. Could you come across and stay with Bryony? She wants to come with us, but I'd rather not take her and I don't want to leave her on her own.'

'Of course.' Despite her anxiety, a warmth filled Miss Cameron. They needed her help. They had come to her. 'But I think it would be better if she came to me. It might be easier for her.'

'You're an angel.'

He went back to his own house. A moment later, he emerged, with his arm around his wife. They crossed the pavement, and he gently eased her into the car. Bryony followed with her mother's suitcase. She wore her jeans and a thick white pullover, and as she leaned into the car to hug her mother and give her a kiss, Miss Cameron felt a lump come into her throat. Fourteen, she knew of old, could be an impossible age. Old enough to understand, but not old enough to be of practical help. She had a mental picture of Bryony and her mother running off across the sands together, and her heart bled for the child.

The car doors were shut. Mr Ashley gave his daughter a quick kiss. 'I'll call you,' he told them both, and then got behind the driving wheel. Minutes later, the car had gone, the red rear light swallowed into the darkness. Miss Cameron and Bryony were left there, on the pavement, in the dark wind.

Bryony had grown. She was now nearly as tall as Miss Cameron, and it was she who spoke first. 'Do you mind me coming through to be with you?' Her voice was controlled and cool.

Miss Cameron decided to follow her example. 'Not at all,' she told her.

'I'll just lock up the house and put a guard on the fire.'

'You do that. I'll be waiting for you.'

When she came, Miss Cameron had put more logs on the fire, made a fresh pot of tea, found another cup and saucer, and a packet of chocolate biscuits. Bryony sat on the hearthrug with her thin knees drawn up to her chin, and held her teacup with her long fingers wrapped about it, as though hungry for warmth.

Miss Cameron said, 'You must try not to worry. I'm sure everything will be all right.'

Bryony said, 'She didn't really want this baby. When it started, when we were in America, she said that she was too old for little babies. But then she got used to the idea and got quite excited about it, and we bought clothes in New York and things like that. But the last month, it's all changed again. She seems so tired, and . . . frightened, almost.'

'I've never had a baby,' said Miss Cameron, 'so I don't

know how people feel. But I imagine it is rather an emotional time. And you can't help how you feel. It's no good other people telling you not to be depressed.'

'She says she's too old. She's nearly forty.'

'My mother was forty before I was born, and I was her first and only child. And there's nothing wrong with me and there was nothing wrong with my mother.'

Bryony looked up, her attention caught by this revelation. 'Was she really? Did you mind, about her being so old?'

Miss Cameron decided that this was one time when the whole truth went out the window. 'No, not at all. And for your baby it will be different, because you'll be there. I can't think of anything nicer than having a sister fourteen years older than oneself. Just like having the very best sort of aunt.'

'The awful thing is,' said Bryony, 'I wouldn't mind so much if something happened to the baby. But I couldn't bear anything to happen to my mother.'

Miss Cameron leaned forward and gave her a pat on the shoulder. 'It won't. Don't think about it. The doctors will take every care of her.' It seemed time to try to talk about something else. 'Now. It's Christmas Eve. There are carols on television. Would you like to listen to them?'

'No, if you don't awfully mind. I don't want to think about Christmas, and I don't want to watch television.'

'Then what would you like to do?'

'I think I'd just like to talk.'

Miss Cameron's heart sank. 'Talk. What shall we talk about?'

'Perhaps we could talk about you.'

'Me?' Despite herself she had to laugh. 'My goodness, what a boring subject. An old maiden lady, practically in her dotage!'

'How old are you?' asked Bryony with such simplicity that Miss Cameron told her. 'But fifty-eight's not old!

That's only a year or two older than my father and he's young. At least, I always think he is.'

'I'm afraid I'm still not very interesting.'

'I think everybody's interesting. And do you know what my mother said when she first saw you? She said you had a beautiful face and that she would like to draw you. So how's that for a compliment?'

Miss Cameron flushed with pleasure. 'Well, that's very gratifying . . . '

'So tell me about you. Why did you buy this little house? Why did you come *here*?'

And so Miss Cameron, normally so reserved and silent, began painfully to talk. She told Bryony about that first holiday in Kilmoran, before the war, when the world was young and innocent and you could buy an ice cream cone for a penny. She told Bryony about her parents, her childhood, the old, tall house in Edinburgh. She told her about University, and how she had met her friend Dorothy, and all at once this unaccustomed flood of reminiscence was no longer an ordeal, but a kind of relief. It was pleasant to remember the old-fashioned school where she had taught for so many years, and she was able to speak dispassionately about those bleak times before her father finally died.

Bryony listened avidly, with as much interest as if Miss Cameron were telling her of some amazing personal adventure. And when she got to the bit about old Mr Cameron's will, and being left so comfortably off, Bryony could not contain herself.

'Oh, how marvellous. It's just like a fairy story. It's just such a terrible pity there isn't a good-looking, white-haired prince to turn up and claim your hand in marriage.'

Miss Cameron laughed. 'I'm a little old for that kind of thing.'

'What a pity you didn't marry. You'd have been a marvellous sort of mother. Or even if you'd had sisters and brothers and then you could have been the marvellous sort of aunt!' She looked around the little sitting room with satisfaction. 'It's just exactly right for you, isn't it? This house must have been waiting for you, knowing that you were going to come and live here.'

'That's a fatalistic sort of attitude.'

'Yes, but a positive one. I'm terribly fatalistic about everything.'

'You mustn't be too fatalistic. God helps those who help themselves.'

'Yes,' said Bryony. 'Yes, I suppose so.'

They fell silent. A log broke and collapsed into the fire, and as Miss Cameron leaned forward to replace it, the clock on the mantelpiece chimed half-past seven. They were both astonished to realise that it was so late, and Bryony at once remembered her mother.

'I wonder what's happening?'

'Your father will ring the moment he has anything to tell us. And meantime, I think we should wash up these tea things and decide what we're going to have for supper. What would you like?'

'My most favourite would be tinned tomato soup and bacon and eggs.'

'That would be my most favourite, too. Let's go and get it.'

The telephone call did not come through until half-past nine. Mrs Ashley was in labour. There was no saying how long it would be, but Mr Ashley intended staying at the hospital.

'I'll keep Bryony here for the night,' said Miss Cameron firmly. 'She can sleep in my spare bedroom. And I have a telephone by my bed, so don't hesitate to ring me the moment you have any news.'

'I'll do that.'

'Do you want to speak to Bryony?'

'Just to say goodnight.'

Miss Cameron shut herself in the kitchen while father and daughter talked together. When she heard the ring of the receiver being replaced, she did not go out into the hall, but busied herself at the sink, filling hot-water bottles and wiping down the already immaculate draining board. She half-expected tears when Bryony joined her, but Bryony was composed and dry-eyed as ever.

'He says we just have to wait. Do you mind if I stay the night with you? I can go next door and get my toothbrush and things.'

'I want you to stay. You can sleep in my spare room.'

Bryony finally went to bed, with a hot-water bottle and a tumbler of warm milk. Miss Cameron went to say goodnight, but she was too shy to stoop and kiss her. Bryony's flame of hair was spread like red silk on Miss Cameron's best linen pillowcase, and she had brought an aged teddy along with the toothbrush. The teddy had a threadbare nose and only one eye. Half an hour later, when she herself went to bed, she looked in and saw that Bryony was fast asleep.

Miss Cameron lay between the sheets, but sleep did not come easily. Her brain seemed to be wound up with memories, people and places that she had not thought about in years.

I think everybody's interesting, Bryony had said and Miss Cameron's heart lifted in hope for the state of the world. Nothing could be too bad if there were still young people who thought that way.

She said you had a beautiful face. Perhaps, she thought, I don't do enough. I have allowed myself to become too self-contained. It is selfish not to think more about other people. I must do more. I must try to travel. I shall get in touch with Dorothy after the New Year and see if she would like to come with me.

Madeira. They could go to Madeira. There would be blue skies and bougainvillia. And jacaranda trees . . .

She awoke with a terrible start in the middle of the night. It was pitch dark, it was bitterly cold. The telephone was ringing. She put out a hand and turned on the bedside light. She looked at her clock and saw that it was not the middle of the night, but six o'clock in the morning. Christmas morning. She picked up the telephone.

'Yes?'

'Miss Cameron. Ambrose Ashley here . . . ' He sounded exhausted.

'Oh.' She felt quite faint. 'Tell me.'

'A little boy. Born half an hour ago. A lovely little boy.'

'And your wife?'

'She's asleep. She's going to be fine.'

After a little, 'I'll tell Bryony,' said Miss Cameron.

'I'll get back to Kilmoran some time this morning – around midday, I should think. I'll ring the hotel and take you both there for lunch. That is, if you'd like to come?'

'How kind,' said Miss Cameron. 'How very kind.'

'You're the kind one,' said Mr Ashley.

A new baby. A new baby on Christmas morning. She wondered if they would call it Noel. She got up and went to the open window. The morning was black and cold, the tide high, the inky waves lapping at the sea wall. The icy air smelt of the sea. Miss Cameron took a deep breath of it, and felt, all at once, enormously excited and filled with boundless energy. A little boy. She revelled in a great sense of accomplishment, which was ridiculous because in fact she had accomplished nothing.

Dressed, she went downstairs to put a kettle on to boil. She laid a tea tray for Bryony and put two cups and saucers upon it.

I should have a present, she told herself. *It's Christmas and I have nothing to give her*. But she knew that with the tea tray she was taking Bryony the best present she had ever had.

Now, it was nearly seven. She went upstairs and into Bryony's room, set the tray down on the bedside table and turned on the lamp. She went to draw the curtains. In the bed, Bryony stirred. Miss Cameron went to sit by her, to take her hand. The teddy was visible, its ears beneath Bryony's chin. Bryony's eyes opened. She saw Miss Cameron sitting there, and at once they were wide and filled with apprehension.

Miss Cameron smiled. 'Happy Christmas.'

'Has my father rung?'

'You've got a baby brother, and your mother's safe and sound.'

'Oh . . . ' It was too much. Relief opened the flood-gates, and all Bryony's anxieties were released in a torrent of tears. 'Oh . . . ' Her mouth went square as a bawling child's, and Miss Cameron could not bear it. She could not remember when she had last had physical, loving contact with another human being, but now she opened her arms and gathered the weeping girl up into them. Bryony's arms came round her neck and Miss Cameron was held so closely and so tightly that she thought she would choke. She felt the thin shoulders beneath her hands; the wet cheek, streaming with tears, was pressed against her own.

'I thought . . . I thought something awful was going to happen. I thought she was going to die.'

'I know,' said Miss Cameron. 'I know.'

It took a little time for them both to recover. But at last it was over, the tears mopped up, the pillows plumped, the tea poured, and they could talk about the baby.

'I'm certain,' said Bryony, 'that it is terribly *special* to be born on Christmas Day. When shall I see them?'

'I don't know. Your father will tell you.'

'When's he coming?'

'He'll be here in time for lunch. We're all going out to the hotel to eat roast turkey.'

'Oh, good. I'm glad you're coming too. What shall we do till he comes? It's only half-past seven.'

'There's lots to do,' said Miss Cameron. 'We've got to have a great big breakfast, and light a great big Christmas fire. And if you'd like to, we could go to church.'

'Oh, let's. And sing carols. I don't mind thinking about Christmas now. I didn't want to think about it last night.' She said, 'I suppose I couldn't have a simply boiling hot bath, could I?'

'You can do anything you like.' She stood up and picked up the tea tray and carried it to the door. But as she opened the door, Bryony said, 'Miss Cameron,' and she turned back.

'You were so sweet to me last night. Thank you so much. I don't know what I would have done if you hadn't been there.'

'I liked having you,' said Miss Cameron truthfully. 'I liked talking.' She hesitated. An idea had just occurred to her. 'Bryony, after all we've been through together, I don't really think you should go on calling me Miss Cameron. It sounds so very formal, and after all, we're past that now, aren't we?'

Bryony looked a little surprised, but not in the least put out.

'All right. If you say so. But what *shall* I call you?'

'My name,' said Miss Cameron, and found herself smiling, because, really, it was a very pretty name, 'is Isobel.'

Tea With the Professor

They had arrived at the station far too early, but this was the way that James liked it, because he had a horror of missing the train. They had parked the car, bought his ticket, and now walked slowly up the ramp together, Veronica carrying his bag and James with his rugger ball tucked under one arm and his raincoat trailing over the other.

The platform was deserted. Out of the wind it was still warm, and they found a seat in a sheltered corner and sat together in a blaze of gold September sunshine. James kicked at the gravel with the toe of his shoe. Above them the dry and dusty leaves of a palm tree rattled in the breeze. A car passed on the road, and a porter appeared from a little shed with a trolley, which he proceeded to haul the length of the platform. They watched his progress in silence. James looked up at the face of the clock.

'Nigel's late,' he said with satisfaction.

'There's five minutes yet.'

He kicked the gravel again. She observed his profile, cool and detached, the lashes of his lowered eyelids brushing the still-baby curves of his cheek. He was ten years old, her only son, returning to boarding school. They had said goodbye at home, in a passionate hug that made her feel as though she was being torn apart. Now, with this over, it was as though he had already gone. She blessed him for his composure.

A car raced up the hill, changed down, swung into

the station yard. There was a screech of brakes and a rattle of loose stones.

James squirmed round on the seat to peer out through the slats of the wooden railing.

'It's Nigel.'

'I thought they wouldn't be long.'

They sat waiting. A moment later Nigel and his mother came up the ramp, she all breathless and blonde, he chubby and sleek as a mole. Nigel was the same age as James and the boys had started school together, but James had no affection for him. Their only common bond was this journey to and from school, when they shared a carriage and comics and, one imagined, a little stilted conversation. Veronica sometimes felt guilty about James's lack of enthusiasm for Nigel. 'Why don't we ask him over in the holidays? It would be someone for you to play with.'

'I've got Sally.'

'But she's a girl, and she's your sister. And she's older than you are. Wouldn't it be nice to have a boy your own age?'

'Not Nigel.'

'Oh, James, he's not as bad as all that.'

'He opened all the windows in my Advent calendar. He found it in my desk and he opened them all. Even Christmas Eve.'

He would never forget this. Never forgive. Veronica stopped trying, but it was embarrassing when she came face to face with Nigel's mother. Nigel's mother, however, was not in the least embarrassed. *She thinks*, decided Veronica, *that I am much too dull to bother about. She probably thinks that James is dull, too.*

'Heavens, we thought we were going to be late, didn't we, Nigel? Hello, James, how are you? Have you had fabulous holidays? Did you get away? We went to Portugal, but Nigel got a beastly tummy and had to stay in bed for a week. Much better if we'd stayed home, really . . .'

She chattered on, feeling in her bag for a cigarette, lighting it up with her gold lighter. She wore a pale blue jumpsuit with a zip up the front, gold ballet slippers, and a fluffy sweater knotted round her shoulders. Veronica, watching her, wondered how she found the time to put on all that make-up *every* day. The reflection was full of admiration and without rancour, but Veronica wore an old pleated skirt and sneakers and felt that her face was naked.

Nigel's mother was asking after Sally.

'She went back to school last week.'

'She'll be leaving soon, I expect.'

'She's only fourteen.'

'Only fourteen! Goodness, you can hardly believe it.'

'The train's coming,' said James, and they turned to face the train as though it were an enemy approaching. It thundered out of the cutting, slowed down as it reached the curve of the track, then drew in alongside the platform, shutting out the sunlight, filling the little station with noise. Doors opened and people got out. Nigel's mother was off like a shot, seeking a non-smoker, and Veronica and the two boys meekly followed.

'Here we are, and empty too . . . in you get.'

They clambered up the step, found their seats, came back for their coats and their bags.

'Goodbye, my darling,' said Nigel's mother. She embraced her child, kissing him soundly on both cheeks, leaving traces of lipstick which, later on, he would remove with his handkerchief. Over their heads James and his mother watched each other. The guard came down the platform to pack them in and shut the door, for the train was an express and only stopped for a few minutes at this small junction. Penned in, imprisoned, the boys let down the window and hung out, Nigel in front and James easing himself into a corner so that he could still see his mother's face. The guard waved the green flag, the train began to move.

I love you, she thought and hoped that he heard. 'Have

a good journey!' He nodded. 'Send me a postcard as soon as you arrive.' He nodded again. The train gathered speed. Nigel leaned out, waving, taking up all the space in the window. But James had already disappeared. He did not believe in prolonging misery. He had gone to his seat, Veronica knew, would already be settled, unfolding his comic, making the best he could of an intolerable situation.

The two mothers walked together out of the station and over to where the white Jaguar and the old green estate car stood side by side.

'Oh, well,' said Nigel's mother. 'That's that. Now we'll have a bit of peace, I suppose. Roger and I thought we'd go away for a bit. I don't know, the house feels empty without them, doesn't it?' She seemed to realise she had said the wrong thing, for she knew that Veronica's house, except for Toby the dog, was entirely empty. 'You must come over,' she said quickly, for she was a kind-hearted girl, 'for a meal or something. I'll phone.'

'Yes, do that. I'd love it. Goodbye.'

The white Jaguar went ahead, up the steep lane to the road, turning left and away towards the town. Veronica took the estate car more slowly. It stalled at the top, and she had to start the engine again, and then wait while a lorry thundered by. It didn't matter. She was in no hurry. The rest of the day and tomorrow and tomorrow stretched emptily ahead, the inevitable vacuum of aimless hours, which had to be endured before she could bring herself to change gear, to pick up occupations that had nothing to do with her children. To paint the kitchen and plant some roses; to organise a charity coffee morning, start thinking about Christmas.

Christmas. The idea was ridiculous on a day that appeared to be suspended in midsummer. Trees were still full of leaves and, beyond them, the sky blue and cloudless. She turned down the narrow road that led to the village and it was spattered with shade and sunshine which filtered through the tall elms. She came to a crossroads and stopped again. A man drove a herd of cows to be milked. Waiting for them to pass, Veronica glanced into her driving mirror to see if there was another car behind and caught sight of her own reflection. *You look like a girl*, she told herself angrily. An elderly girl. Sun-tanned and with no make-up and your hair as untidy as your daughter's. She remembered Nigel's mother with her darkly coated lashes and the blue on her eyelids. She thought, *At least I'll have time to get my hair done. And my eyebrows tidied up. And perhaps a facial.* A facial was good for the morale. She would have a facial and her morale would soar.

The cows went by. The man driving them waved to her with his stick. Veronica waved back, started up her engine, and drove on, up the hill and around a corner and so into the main street of the village. At the War Memorial she turned down the lane that led to the sea, and the trees fell away and the fields dipped to the creaming coast, the sea green and blue and streaked with purple, flecked with white horses. She came to a tall hedge of fuchsia, changed down, turned sharply and went in through the white gate. The house was grey, square, and thoroughly old-fashioned. She was home.

She went in, knowing how it would be. The hall clock ticked slowly. Toby heard her coming; his claws clicked across the polished floor of the kitchen and he appeared in the doorway, not barking because he always knew when it was family. He came to greet her, searched for James, found no James, returned with dignity to his bed.

It was cool indoors. The house was old and thick-walled, and the furniture was old too, so that it smelt old, but in a pleasant way, like a well-kept antique shop. It was very quiet. When Toby had settled once more, there was only the clock and a tap dripping from the kitchen and the hum of the refrigerator.

She thought, *I could make tea, although it's only half-past three. I could get the washing in and iron it. I could go upstairs to James's room and pick up his clothes.* She saw them, the jeans worn and crumpled, bent to his shape; the grey socks, the disreputable sandals, the Superman T-shirt that was his favourite garment. He had worn them this morning; they had gone to the beach for a final swim, abandoning the dishes, the dusting, the bed-making. Afterwards she had cooked his favourite lunch, chops and baked beans, and eaten it with him, and the clock had ticked away their last moments together.

She dropped her bag, went through the cool hall, out across the sitting room, through the French windows, and down the two stone steps that led to the lawn. There was a sagging deck chair and she sank into it in a sort of exhausted apathy that was beyond time or reason. The sun was in her eyes, and she put up her arm to shut away the glare and at once sounds closed in, demanding attention. The children were being let out of the village school; the church clock, always a little slow, chimed the half hour. A car came down the road, turned into the gate, and ground up the gravel drive to the second front door on the other side of Veronica's house.

She thought, idly, *The Professor's home.*

She had been widowed now for two years. As a married woman she had lived in London, in a roomy flat near the Albert Hall, but after the death of her husband and on the advice of Frank Kirdy, their lawyer, who was also their best friend, she had returned to the village and to the house where she had lived as a child. It seemed a natural and a sensible thing to do. The children loved the country and the beach and the sea; she was surrounded by neighbours and people she had known all her life.

There had, however, been one or two objections.

'But the house, Frank, it's so big. Far too big for me and two children.'

'But it would divide perfectly easily, and you could let the other side.'

'But the garden . . . '

'You could divide the garden, too. Plant a hedge. You'd still have two good-sized lawns.'

'But who would come and live there?'

'We'll look around. There's bound to be someone.'

There was, too. Professor Rydale.

'Who's Professor Rydale?' she asked.

'I was at Oxford with him,' said Frank. 'He's an archaeologist, amongst other things. A professor at Brookbridge University.'

'But if he's at Brookbridge, why does he want to come to Cornwall to live?'

'He's taking a year's sabbatical. He has to write a book. Don't look so agonised, Veronica, he's a bachelor and perfectly self-contained. No doubt some homely female will come in from the village and take care of him, and you won't even know he's there.'

'But what if I don't like him?'

'My dear, people are exasperated by Marcus Rydale, amused by him, and informed by him, but he is impossible to dislike.'

'Well . . . ' Reluctantly, she had agreed. 'All right.'

And so the house was duly divided, and the lawn discreetly sliced in two, and the Professor informed that he could move in when he pleased. After a little, Veronica received an illegible and unstamped postcard which, when deciphered, announced that she was to expect him on Sunday. Sunday, Monday, and Tuesday came and went. On Wednesday, in the middle of lunch, the Professor arrived, driving a sports car that looked as though it had been stuck together with Sellotape. He wore spectacles, a tweed hat, and a sagging tweed suit, but offered neither apologies nor explanations.

Veronica, already amused and exasperated, gave him his keys. The children, fascinated, hung around longing to be asked in to help him unpack, but he faded away as unexpectedly as he arrived and was scarcely seen again. Within two days Mrs Thomas, the postman's wife, was coming and going, keeping house for him, baking him pastries and large sustaining fruit cakes. Before the week was out they had almost forgotten his existence. He settled down, cosy as a squirrel, and in all the months that were to pass, Veronica was only reminded of his presence when his typewriter started tapping at odd hours in the middle of the night, or his little car went roaring out of the gate and up the road to the village, to disappear on strange errands that sometimes lasted two or three days.

But every now and then he appeared to make contact with the children. Sally fell off her bicycle, and by some chance he was driving by and stopped to pick her out of the ditch, straighten the buckled front wheel, and lend her a handkerchief for her bleeding knee.

'He was nice, Mummy, honestly, he was so nice, and he pretended not to see that I was bawling, don't you think that was *tactful?*'

Veronica wanted to thank him, but she did not set eyes on him again for three weeks, and by then she was sure he would have forgotten the incident altogether. But another time James came in for supper bearing a device of chestnut branch and string and a bundle of lethally sharpened twigs.

'What *have* you got there?'

'It's a bow and arrows.'

'It looks deadly. Where did you get it?'

'I met the Professor. He made it for me. You see, you have to keep the string loose when you're not using it, and then when you want to use it, you bend the stick a bit and loop the string on . . . there! See? Isn't it super? It shoots for miles.'

'You mustn't point it at anyone,' said Veronica nervously.

'I wouldn't anyway, even if I knew someone I hated enough,' he said. 'I ought to make a target.' James snapped at the string. It made a satisfactory twang, like playing a harp.

'Well, I hope you said thank you,' said his mother.

'Of course I did. You know, he's terribly nice. Couldn't you ask him in for a drink or supper or something?'

'Oh, James, he'd hate that. He's working, he doesn't want to be disturbed. I think it would embarrass him terribly.'

'Yes, perhaps it would.' He twanged the bow again, and took it upstairs to the safety of his bedroom.

From inside the house, from the Professor's half, came the sound of a window being shut. Then he opened the French windows of his sitting room – which had been the dining room in the days when the house was undivided – and came out into the garden. The next moment, his bespectacled head appeared over the top of the fence, and he said, 'I wonder if you'd like a cup of tea?'

For a mad moment Veronica thought he was talking to someone else. She looked round frantically to see who it could be. But there was no one else. He was talking to her. He was asking her to have a cup of tea, but if he had suggested that they waltz together, then and there, around the lawn, she could not have been more astounded. She stared at him. He wore no hat and she noticed that the breeze made his dark hair stand up in a coxcomb, just as James's did.

He tried again. 'I've just made a fresh pot. I could bring it out here.'

She jerked herself out of her bad manners. 'Oh, I am sorry . . . it was such a surprise. Yes, I'd love one . . . ' She began, awkwardly, to scramble out of the deck chair, but he stopped her.

'No, don't move. You look so peaceful. I'll bring it round.'

She sank back into the chair. The Professor disappeared. Veronica took stock of this startling new situation. She found that she was smiling, at herself, at him, at the absurdity of it all. She pulled her skirt down over her knees and tried to compose herself. She wondered what on earth they were going to talk about.

When he returned, easing himself from his own garden into hers by way of a narrow gap at the bottom of the fence, she saw that he was remarkably organised. She had expected a mug of tea, no more, but he carried a laden tray, and had slung a thick rug, like a Scottish plaid, over one shoulder. He laid the tray down on the grass beside Veronica, spread the rug and sat himself down on it, his long, angular body folding up like a jack-knife. He wore old corduroys that someone had tried to mend at the knee and there was a button missing at the collar of his checked shirt, but he looked in no way pathetic . . . more like a cheerful gypsy. She found herself wondering how he managed to stay so tanned and lean when he appeared to spend so much of his time indoors.

'There,' he said, safely settled. 'Now you must pour.'

The china didn't match, but he had forgotten nothing, and there was even some of one of Mrs Thomas's fruit cakes for them to eat.

She said, 'It looks splendid. I don't usually bother with tea – when I'm on my own, that is.'

'The children have gone.' It was a statement, not a question.

'Yes . . . ' She occupied herself with the tea pot. 'I've just put James on the train.'

'Does he have far to go?'

'No. Only Carmouth. Do you take sugar?'

'Yes, lots. At least four spoonfuls.'

'You'd better put it in yourself.' She handed him his cup and he ladled sugar copiously. She said, 'I never thanked you for making him the bow and arrows.'

'I thought you'd be angry . . . giving him such a dangerous toy.'

'He's very sensible.'

'I know. I wouldn't have done it otherwise.'

'And . . . ' She turned her teacup in her hand. It had roses on it and looked as though it had once belonged to an elderly female relation. 'You rescued Sally the day she fell off her bike, too. I should have made a point of thanking you for that . . . but somehow I never seemed to see you.'

'Sally thanked me herself. And she took to me.'

'I'm glad.'

'It's quiet without them.'

'Oh, dear, do they make so much noise?'

'Only a little, and I like it. It's sort of company when I'm working.'

'They don't disturb or distract you?'

'I said I like it.' Thoughtfully, he cut himself a chunk of cake. He took a mouthful and ate it, and then said, abruptly, 'He seems so small. James, I mean. Such a small chap. Do you have to send him away to school?'

'No, I don't suppose I have to.'

'Wouldn't it be more fun for you both if he stayed?'

She said, 'Yes it would.'

'But he has to go?'

Veronica looked at him then, and wondered why she was not offended by his persistence; why she knew that his questions stemmed from deep interest and not a mere curiosity. His eyes behind the spectacles were very dark and kindly. He was not in the least intimidating.

She said, 'It sounds ridiculous, but it's very simple really. He is my only son. He is also my baby. We've always been together, and very close, all his life. I adore Sally, but in some way she is a person apart from me, that's one of the reasons we get on so well. But James and I are, I don't know, like two branches on the same stem. After my – ' She leaned over to put down her teacup, hiding her face from the Professor with a curtain of hair, for still, even now, she could not trust herself to say it and not to weep. 'After my husband died, there wasn't anyone for James but me.' She straightened up and pushed her hair out of her eyes and faced him again.

She smiled. 'I've always had a horror of smothering mothers and sons that were never able to break away.' He watched her thoughtfully, not answering her smile. She went on, briskly, 'It's a nice school, small and friendly. He's very happy there.'

He was, too. She knew this, but was still bedevilled with doubts. After the agony of this morning, of the last lunch and the journey to the station, and the final parting, she felt that she could not go through it again. She was haunted by James's face, the pale wedge showing over Nigel's shoulder, growing smaller and more blurred as the express sucked him away from her.

'Perhaps,' said the Professor, 'if you lived in a different sort of place, where there was a similar sort of school, and other boys, and things for him to do?'

'It's a father,' said Veronica without thinking. 'Something to do with not having a father.'

'But you're lonely without them? You must be.'

'It's sometimes selfish to be lonely . . . and now, please, can we not talk about it anymore.'

'All right,' said the Professor amiably, as though he had never brought the matter up. 'What shall we talk about?'

'Your book?'

'My book is finished.'

'Finished?'

'Yes. Finished. Typed, corrected, and typed again; not by me, I may add. Not only is it typed and bound up in buff covers and red tape, but it has reached the desk of a publisher and been accepted.'

'But that's wonderful. When did you hear?'

'Today. This very day. I got a telegram over the phone and I went over to the post office to pick up the confirmation.' He reached into his jacket pocket and took it out and flapped it around in the breeze. 'I always feel safer when things are in writing. It proves I didn't imagine anything.'

'Oh, I am pleased. And what happens now?'

'I still have three months of my year's leave to run and then I go back to lecturing at Brookbridge.'

'What are you going to do with the three months?'

'I don't know.' He grinned at her. 'Perhaps go off to Tahiti and become a beachcomber. Perhaps stay here. Would you mind?'

'Why should I mind?'

'I thought perhaps I'd been so rude and unfriendly you wouldn't be able to wait to see the back of me. The thing is that I find being sociable, and organising things and arranging things, takes the most enormous amount of concentration. I mustn't have anything else on my mind. Especially when writing a textbook on archaeology. Can you understand that?'

'Easily. And I never thought you were rude or unfriendly. Anyway, I'm just as bad. James wanted me to ask you in for supper one night and I said you wouldn't want to come. I said you'd be too busy.'

'Perhaps I was.' He appeared to be embarrassed; he frowned, tried to flatten the coxcomb of hair with the palm of his hand. He said, 'James came in to say goodbye to me last night. While you were getting his supper. Did you know?'

It was Veronica's turn to frown. 'James did? No, he never said a word.'

'He told me then that you wouldn't ask me to supper because you thought I wouldn't want to come.'

'He shouldn't have . . .'

'But he did add, in a man-to-man sort of way, that perhaps I might ask *you* to supper.'

'He *what* . . . ?'

'He's concerned about you living on your own. He knows how much you miss him and Sally. And you mustn't be annoyed about it, because I think it's the nicest thing I've ever known a small boy to do.'

'But he had no right!'

'He has every right. He is your son.'

'But . . .'

99

He overrode her objections. 'So of course I said I would. And that's what I'm doing now. And I've even gone so far as to book a table at that new place over at Porthkerris. For eight o'clock. So if you refuse to come, it's going to be very difficult for me, because I'll have to go and cancel it and the head waiter will be furious. You won't say no, will you?'

For a moment she couldn't say anything. But watching him, she remembered what Frank had said about him and all her resentment and annoyance melted away. *People are exasperated by Marcus Rydale, amused by him . . . but he is impossible to dislike.* And she thought, and was taken unaware by the thought, that he was the nicest man she had met in years. She had shared her house with him all these months and never even guessed. But the children guessed. They knew. James had known from the very first.

She began to laugh, defeated by a multitude of pressures. 'No, I won't say no. I couldn't say no, even if I wanted to.'

'But you don't want to, do you,' said the Professor, and once more it was a statement, not a question.

Amita

The notice of Miss Tolliver's death was in this morning's paper. My husband handed it to me across the breakfast table and the name sprang at me from the column of close print like a cry from the past:

TOLLIVER. On the 8th July, in her 90th year, Daisy Tolliver, daughter of the late Sir Henry Tolliver, some time Governor of the Province of Barana, and Lady Tolliver. Private cremation

I had not thought of the Tollivers in years. I am fifty-two now, well into middle age, with a husband on the point of retirement, and children and grandchildren of my own. We live in Surrey, and Cornwall and childhood seem a long way away, another time and another world. But every now and then something happens to bring it all back, like a note struck on a seldom-played piano, and then it is as though the crowded years between had never happened. The old, aimless days are back, bright with perpetual sunshine (did it *never* rain?) and crowded with remembered voices, running footsteps, and marvellously nostalgic smells. Bowls of sweet peas in my mother's drawing room, and the fragrance of pastries baking in the oven of the black-leaded Cornish range.

The Tollivers. When my husband had said goodbye and taken himself off to catch the London train, I went out into the garden with the newspaper and sat in the swing chair by the rose bed and read the lonely little paragraph again – *the late Sir Henry Tolliver, some time*

Governor of the Province of Barana. I remembered him with his red face and great white moustache and his panama hat. And I remembered Angus. And Amita.

To be a child of British India in the early 1930s was a hybrid existence. My father was in the Indian Civil Service, posted to Barana to run the Port and River Department. His terms of duty ran for four years, when he would disappear out of our lives completely, to return for six months' leave that passed like a perpetual holiday.

We were typical of thousands of families in which the burden of rearing the family and running the home in England inevitably fell upon the wife, whose life was constantly bedevilled by the agonising decision of whether she should stay with her children or accompany their father out east. If she did the former, then any sort of married life went by the board. If the latter, then arrangements for the children's welfare had to be made: boarding schools found, and kindly relatives or friends approached and invited to care for the children during the holidays. Whichever she did there were always, inevitably, heart-breaking goodbyes. There was no air service to India then. The days of Imperial Aiways were to come later, and the P&O boats, sailing from London, took three weeks to complete their journey. It was indeed a very complete separation.

My own mother went twice to India. Once before either of us was born, and once again when we were still so small we scarcely noticed her going.

It was on her first trip, as a young and lively bride, that she met Lady Tolliver. The friendship which sprang up between them was an unusual one, for Lady Tolliver was a good generation older than my mother, and the Governor's lady to boot, while my mother was simply the new wife of a young official.

But Lady Tolliver was both unpretentious and friendly. She found my mother refreshing and natural. To their mutual satisfaction and everybody else's surprise, their deck chairs were placed side by side on the boat deck, and there they sat in the pleasant sunshine, with their needlework and their lively conversation to keep them amused as the great liner slid through the Mediterranean, through the Suez Canal, and into the blue Indian Ocean beyond.

In England, the Tollivers lived in Cornwall, and it was because of this that my mother, on her return home from India, heavily pregnant and in need of some sort of a base, rented a little house nearby. It was a very modest house, with a tiny garden, for she could afford nothing more; and there my sister and I were born, and there, in certain austerity but total contentment, we were brought up, and there we stayed until the war came and tore us all apart forever.

It was, looking back, a very uneventful life we led, punctuated by school and holidays; by the letters that we wrote to and received from my father; by Christmas, when packages came, smelling spicy and wrapped in newspaper printed, amazingly, in Indian characters. Every three or four years came the long bright excitement of my father's home leave. And every so often the Tollivers abandoned their Indian palace and their many servants, their garden parties and soirées, and came home too, to see their friends and open their house and live like ordinary mortals.

Daisy was their eldest daughter, unmarried and very musical. She used to play the violin at musical evenings and accompany, on the piano, any person who felt impelled to sing. Then there was Mary, married to a soldier and stationed in Quetta, and then Angus.

Angus was the family's darling, and everybody else's darling as well. Handsome, fair-haired, blue-eyed, he was in his last year at Oxford. He drove about at a great pace in an open Triumph with great polished headlamps, and he played dashing tennis looking like a matinée idol in his white flannels and surf-white shirt.

My sister Jassy, who was two years older than I, was

madly in love with him, but she was only ten at the time, and Angus was never without some pretty girl at his side. But I could see why she was in love with him, because when we did manage to catch him in an uninvolved moment, he was always willing to play French cricket with us, or help to build huge sandcastles on the beach, with deep moats which the flood tide would fill while we splashed and screamed and dug like mad, trying, Canute-like, to shore up the embankments and keep the water out.

Angus finally left Oxford and, inevitably, accompanied his parents back to India. Not, however, as a servant of the state, but working for Ironsides, the huge shipping company which had taken over when the East India Company packed up. This meant that he did not live at Government House with his parents, but had his own establishment in the town, which he shared with a couple of other young men of similar age. A chummery, it was called.

It is hard to remember when the rumours started filtering through. Impossible to remember how Jassy and I caught on to the fact that all was not well. My mother had a letter from my father. She read it at breakfast; her mouth closed in a secret way I knew well. She folded the letter and put it away. For the rest of the meal, she was silent. A feeling of doom sank into my stomach and stayed with me for the rest of the day.

Then Mrs Dobson came for tea with my mother. Mrs Dobson was another Indian grass widow, who stayed in England not for her children's sake, but because she was delicate and could not stand the fierce climate of the East. I was playing in the garden and walked in on them unexpectedly to catch the tail-end of their conversation.

'But how could he have met her?'

'You never know. He always had an eye for a pretty girl.'

'But he could have had *anybody*. How could he be so stupid. Why jeopardise all his chances . . . ?'

My mother caught sight of me. She made a swift

movement with her hand, and Mrs Dobson broke off, turned, and quickly smiled as though pleased to see me. 'Well, if it isn't Laura. Aren't you getting a tall girl?' And I was allowed to have tea with them, and eat all the cucumber sandwiches, as if, by doing this, I would forget anything I might have overheard.

It was Doris, our maid, who finally spilled the beans. Doris's boyfriend was Arthur Penfold, who looked after the Tollivers' garden. On Doris's day off, Arthur would call for her on his motor bicycle, and away they would go to the bright lights of Penzance, Doris with her arms around Arthur's waist, and her skirts blowing back from her long, shapely, artificial-silk legs.

Sometimes in the evenings, if I wanted my hair washed, or felt in need of company, Doris would come upstairs and help me with my bath.

She was kneeling on the bathmat, scrubbing the day's dirt off my knees. The damp air was filled with the smell of Pears' soap. Doris said, 'Angus Tolliver's going to be married.'

I felt a momentary pang of pity for Jassy. She had planned on marrying him herself if he'd only wait long enough for her to grow up.

I said, 'How do you know?'

'Arthur told me.'

'How does he know?'

'His mother had a letter from Agnes.' Agnes was Lady Tolliver's personal maid, a boot-faced woman who travelled resignedly to and from India and suffered agonies of prickly heat, simply because she could not abide the thought of some black woman ironing Lady Tolliver's underclothes. 'There's some turvy going on out there, by all accounts.'

'Why?'

'They don't want Mr Angus to get married.'

'Why not?'

'Because she's an Indian. That's why. Mr Angus is going to marry an Indian.'

'An *Indian!*'

'Well, half Indian.'

That was worse. Anglo-Indian. Chi-chi. I hated the nickname, because I hated the way people used it. But still, I was horror-struck. I had never been to India, but over the years I had absorbed, like a sponge, from my parents and the grown-ups who were their friends, their traditions, their slang, and most of their prejudices. I knew about India. I knew about the hot weather and the rains. I knew about going up-country. I knew about Durbars, and ceremonial elephants, and sunshine sparkling on great, proud parades. I knew the butler was called the bearer, the gardener the mali, the groom the syce. I knew *burra* was big and *chota* was small. If my sister wanted to madden me, she called me Missy Baba.

And I knew about Anglo-Indians. Anglo-Indians were neither one thing nor the other. They worked in offices and ran the railways. They wore topis and spoke in Welsh accents and (unmentionable) they did not use paper when they went to the lavatory.

And Angus Tolliver was going to marry one of them.

I could not speak about it. Angus, the pride of the Tollivers, the only son of the Governor, to marry an Anglo-Indian. Their shame was my shame, because even at eight years old, I knew that if he did this thing, he would cut himself off from everything he had ever known. He would have to step down and out of our lives. He would be lost forever.

I carried my misery around with me for three days, until my mother, unable to stand my gloom for another moment, asked me what was the matter. Painfully, not looking into her face, I told her.

'How did you know?' my mother asked.

'Doris told me. Arthur Penfold told her. His mother had a letter from Agnes.' I made myself look up at my mother and discovered that she was not looking at me. She was trying to arrange some flowers in a bowl, but her usually neat fingers were clumsy. 'Is it true?'

'Yes, it's true.'

My last hope died. I swallowed. 'Is she . . . Anglo-Indian?'

'No. Her mother was Indian and her father French. She's called Amita Chabrol.'

'Will it be very terrible if he marries her?'

'No. It won't be terrible. But it's wrong.'

'Why is it so wrong?' I knew about the chi-chi accent, the topis, the social stigma. But this was *Angus*. 'Why is it wrong?'

My mother shook her head, almost as if she were trying to keep from crying out, or slapping me, or bursting into tears.

'It just *is*. Races shouldn't mix. It's . . . it's not fair to the children.'

'You mean it's not fair to have babies that are half one thing and half the other?'

'No, it's not.'

'But, *why*?'

'Because life is hard for them.'

'Why is life hard for them?'

'Oh, *Laura*. Because it is. Because people look down on them. People are cruel to them.'

'But only horrid people.' I longed for her to give me some reassurance that she would not be cruel to a little Anglo-Indian child. She loved children, and babies in particular. '*You* wouldn't be unkind,' I pleaded.

In the middle of stripping a rose of its leaves, she was still. Her eyes closed tightly as though she were trying to hide something away. I think at that moment her natural instincts were begging her to take my side, but she had lived with the old prejudices for too long, and the rigid cords of convention were too tightly bound for her to be able to break loose. I waited for her to defend herself, but when she opened her eyes again, and continued with her task, she only said, 'It's wrong. That's all I can tell you. And it's specially wrong when Angus's father is the Governor of the province.'

'What can they do?'

They could do nothing. Angus and his bride were married quietly in a small, insignificant church in the least fashionable part of Barana. The Tolliver parents were not present. They went for their honeymoon to a hill station in Kashmir. When they returned, Angus resigned from Ironsides and after some casting about, found himself a modest job in a business owned by a hardworking Tamil. He and Amita moved into a little house in a district far removed from the British residencies. The long exile into the wilderness had begun.

Three years later, in 1938, they came home. By now the Tollivers had retired and taken up permanent residence in their house in Cornwall. They were older, they had lost some of their glitter. Sir Henry passed his days writing his memoirs and weeding the flowerbeds. Lady Tolliver did the shopping with a little basket and played Mah Jong in the afternoons. Daisy Tolliver immersed herself in good works and led the local orchestra with her violin.

Doris and Arthur Penfold got married, and Jassy and I were bridesmaids, dressed in white organdie with blue ribbon sashes. It was at this wedding that Lady Tolliver told us about Angus and Amita.

'He's bringing her back to Europe for a little visit. They're going to stay with her grandparents in Lyons and then come and visit us for a few days.' Her face, now grown so wrinkled, bunched up with pleasure at the very prospect, and I thought how wonderful for her to be able to show her happiness, without fear of offending somebody or letting her husband down. She must be, I decided, thankful to be an ordinary person again, and free of all the social restrictions of her old, grand life.

'I know he'll want to see you and Jassy. He used to be so fond of you both. I'll speak to your mother and see if we can arrange something.'

Jassy was fourteen now. 'Are you excited,' I asked her, 'about seeing Angus Tolliver again?'

'Not particularly,' said Jassy, in her most offhand way. 'And I wish he wasn't bringing *her* with him.'

'You mean Amita?'

'I don't want to meet her. I don't want to have to have anything to do with her.'

'Because she's married to Angus, or because she's half-Indian?'

'Half-Indian,' Jassy sneered. 'She's chi-chi. I don't know how Lady Tolliver can bear to have her in the house.'

I was silenced. I could understand Jassy being jealous, but not spiteful. Much upset, I turned away and left her alone.

It had been arranged that Lady Tolliver and Daisy should bring Angus and Amita for tea with us, and as the appointed day drew near and Jassy's disposition showed no signs of improvement, I found myself dreading it more and more. I imagined Angus, shabby in an ill-cut dhirzi-made suit, with his pathetic wife in tow. Perhaps she would not know how to use the butter knife. Perhaps she would cool her tea by blowing upon it. Perhaps already he was tired of her, and ashamed of her, and regretting his impetuous marriage. And his embarrassment would spread to all of us, like some agonising, paralysing illness.

After lunch, on the day of the tea party, Jassy and I went down to the beach with some friends to swim. The friends had a picnic tea with them, but at three o'clock, the two of us said goodbye and left them, walking home across the golf links, with our damp bathing things clutched to our sides, and our legs and feet encrusted with sand.

It was a day of warmth and wind. There was thyme growing underfoot, and as we walked on it and bruised it, it gave out a sweet and minty smell. We stopped by the church to put on our shoes, then hurried on. Jassy, usually loquacious, was silent. Looking at her, I realised that she probably hadn't meant to be so disagreeable all this time. She was just as nervous and strung up as I was about meeting Angus and Amita, but it affected us in different ways.

At home, our mother was in the kitchen, buttering the freshly made scones. 'Upstairs and change,' she told us. 'Quickly. I've put everything out on your beds.'

She wore, I had time to notice, her turquoise linen, with the hemstitching, and the blue glass beads my father had given her for her birthday. Her best, in fact. For us she had laid out matching cotton dresses and knickers, butcher blue patterned in little white flowers. There were clean white socks and red shoes with straps and buttons. We washed our hands and faces, and Jassy was helpful about my hair, which was thick and curly and, that afternoon, full of sand.

While we were doing this, we heard the car arrive. It came down the road and stopped outside our gate. Downstairs the front door opened and we heard my mother going down the path to greet her visitors.

'Come on,' said Jassy. We started to go downstairs, but at the last moment, she turned back and took the gold locket out of the drawer and fastened the chain around her neck. I wished I had a locket, a talisman, something to boost my courage.

They were in the sitting room. The door to the hall stood open and we could hear soft voices, laughter. Jassy, perhaps emboldened by her locket, led the way and I followed, fearfully, behind. As I came through the door, I heard Angus say, 'Why, Jassy!' and the next thing was that he had put his arms around her in a hug, just as though she were still a little girl. I had time to notice that Jassy went very pink, and then I looked beyond them. Lady Tolliver was already esconced in the best armchair.

Daisy Tolliver sat on a low stool, and, on the window seat, side by side with their backs to the garden, sat my mother and . . . Amita.

The first thing I noticed was that she wore, like a shout of defiance, a flame-red sari. But how else to describe her? A bird of paradise, perhaps, magnificent and incongruous amidst the muted sweet pea shades of an English sitting room on a hot summer afternoon.

She was small, beautifully proportioned, her skin the smooth, dark gold of a brown egg. Her eyes were immense, dark, tip-tilted and marvellously made up. Jewels glowed in her ears, sparkled from wrists and fingers, and her bare feet were thrust into delicate gold thong sandals. All this was pure Indian, but her hair betrayed her European origins, being thick and black and curly. She wore it shoulder length and it framed her face like a child's. She carried a little handbag of gold kid and the room was filled with the musky, subtle undertones of her scent.

I couldn't take my eyes off her. I was kissed by Angus, kissed by Lady Tolliver, and all the time I stared at Amita. By the time I was introduced to her, she was laughing. Perhaps it was her brown skin, but I thought I had never seen teeth so shining white.

She said, 'Am I going to kiss you, too?'

Her voice enchanted me, the pure vowels overlaid with the suggestion of a French intonation.

I said, 'I don't know.'

'Why don't we try?'

So I kissed her. Nothing so magical had ever happened to me before, and as I did so, bewildered and bewitched by her beauty, a thought crossed my mind; gently, like the passing touch of a moth's wing, something to be brushed aside. *What was all the fuss about?*

I cannot remember very much about that afternoon, except for a feeling of unaccustomed glamour, which seemed to blow through my mother's little house like a gust of cool, bright air. Angus had changed, indeed, but

I thought, for the better. He was a man now. The boyish good looks and high spirits had gone; there was a certain wariness, a reserve about him, but as well something stronger. Perhaps a pride, or a sense of achievement. I don't know. He seemed taller, which was strange, because as I grew older, grown-ups had an odd way of becoming smaller. Perhaps I had forgotten how he held himself so erect and straight. Forgotten the width of his shoulders and the clean shape of his capable hands.

Even the conversation over the tea table was marvellously sophisticated. They spoke of Venice and Florence, which they had just visited, and the El Grecos they had seen in Madrid. They had visited Paris, and Angus teased Amita because she had bought so many new clothes, and she only laughed and said to my mother, 'How can a man be expected to understand that everything, the hats and the shoes, and all the shops are irresistible?' Only she made it sound like 'irreseeestible,' and then we all laughed too.

Angus told us that they were leaving India and going to live in Burma because Angus had been made manager of a new office that was opening in Rangoon. They were going to find a house there, and Angus was going to have a little boat and was threatening to teach Amita how to sail. And this provoked more mirth because Amita swore that she only had to look at a boat and she was seasick, and the most energetic thing she had ever done in the whole of her life was to turn the pages of a book.

After tea, we went out into the garden. Lady Tolliver, Daisy, and my mother talked together, and Jassy, who had apparently forgiven Angus and was now restored to her usual good spirits, sat by him and begged him for tales of tiger shoots and houseboats in Kashmir. Amita asked me to show her the garden, so I led her down to

112

the rose bed and tried to remember the names of all the various roses. 'Elizabeth of Glamis, and Ena Harkness, and that little rambler is called Albertine. It smells very like sweet apples.'

She was smiling down at me. She said, 'Do you like flowers?'

'Yes. Almost better than anything.'

She said, 'In Rangoon, I am going to have the most beautiful garden that anybody has ever dreamed about. It will have bougainvillia and temple flowers and jacaranda trees and hollyhocks taller than a man. And there will be green lawns with peacocks and white cranes, and round pools of water, ringed with roses and blue with the reflection of the sky. And when you are grown up, maybe seventeen or so, you must come out and stay with Angus and me, and I will show it all to you. We will have dinner parties for you, and dances, and moonlit picnics down by the shore. And there will be young men around you, falling in love with you, droves of them, like moths around a candle flame.'

I gazed at Amita, dazzled, hypnotised by the visions of myself at seventeen, beautiful and slender as Amita, with a proper bosom and a tiny waist. I saw all those admirers, tall and straight and wearing glittering uniforms. I heard music and smelt the heavy fragrance of the temple flowers and saw moonlight on water . . .

She said, 'Will you come?'

Her voice broke the dream. It had lost its laughter. And now her dark eyes were lustrous with unshed tears. And I knew that it was all a fantasy. She would never have that great, beautiful garden in Rangoon, because the life that she and Angus had chosen for themselves could not encompass such riches. And I would never go and stay with her. She would never ask my mother, and even if she did, I should never be allowed to go. It was all make-believe. She knew it and so did I; but still, I could not bear to see her look so sad, so I smiled up into

113

her face and said, 'Of course I'll come. I'd love to come. More than anything in the world.'

She smiled then, and blinked the tears away. She put a hand on either side of my head and turned my face up to hers. She said, 'One day I will have a little girl of my own. And I would like her to be just as sweet as you are.'

We were all at once very close. I felt, almost, that I had known her all my life and was going to know her forever. And in that instant, I knew, with piercing certainty, that they had all been wrong. My mother and my father, and the Tollivers, and their parents and their parents before them. The preconceived prejudices, the snobbery, the traditions, tumbled like a pack of cards and have stayed that way ever since.

By stripping the truth from a confused morass of childish impressions, Amita changed my whole life. *What was all the fuss about?* I had asked myself, and the answer was *Nothing*. People are people. Some good, some bad, some black, some white, but whatever the colour of our skin, or the difference in creeds and traditions, we all have something to give each other, and we all have something to share, even if it is only life itself.

Before she left, Amita went out to the car and came back with two parcels, one for Jassy and one for me. When the Tollivers had gone, we opened them, and found the dolls. We had never seen dolls like them, so neat and grown-up and beautifully fashioned, even down to the lacquered toenails on the tiny papier-mâché feet and the little glittering earrings. Our other dolls had names like Rosemary and Dimples, but the dolls Amita gave us were never given names. We did not play with them. We looked at them, and kept them in a glass-fronted cupboard in our bedroom along with my grandmother's dolls' tea set and the set of carved wooden animals that had come to us from an aged aunt.

* * *

I could not bear to discuss Amita with anybody. 'Did you like her?' my mother asked one day when Jassy was out for tea with a friend and we were alone.

But I could not tell her how I felt or what I had learned, because now, she and I were on opposite sides of the fence. We were by no means enemies, but we held different opinions, and for the rest of our lives were going to have to learn to live with this.

So I only said 'Yes,' and went on eating my bread and butter.

I never saw Angus and Amita again. The war broke out and they were unable to come home. Amita was pregnant when the Japanese invaded Burma, but she escaped from Rangoon by marching north into Assam, along with some Forestry Department officials, a number of valuable elephants and their mahouts, and a whole horde of British women and children. Angus stayed behind, ostensibly to close up his office and destroy all the important papers. He promised to follow her, but he left it too late, was captured by the Japanese, and died a year later in a prison camp.

As for Amita, the long march, for a girl who had done nothing more energetic than turn the pages of a book, proved too much. A day after the exhausted band of refugees struggled into Assam, Amita went into premature labour. They found a bed for her in a military hospital, but little could be done for her. Her child was stillborn, and a few hours later, Amita died too.

I still have the doll she gave me. The painted hair lies dark on the dusky head, the tip-tilted eyes are ringed with kohl, the little sari glitters with its sequins and its gold thread. One day, when my fat granddaughter is old enough, I shall give her the doll to play with and tell her about Amita.

I could tell her, as well, the truth that Amita, on

that summer afternoon, made so blindingly clear to
me. But I hope, and believe, that by the time she is
old enough to be given the doll, she will have found
it out for herself.

The Blue Bedroom

As the sun slipped down out of the sky and long shadows grew and stretched out over the sandy dunes, the beach slowly emptied. Mothers called to reluctant children, coaxing them out of the warm shallows of a summer flood tide. Sleepy sunburned toddlers were strapped into push-chairs, picnic baskets were repacked, missing sandals and towels finally run to earth. By seven o'clock the beach was almost deserted. Only the lifeguard, sitting in his camp chair by the beach hut; a couple of determined surfers; a woman with a rambunctious dog.

And Emily and Portia.

Emily was fourteen and Portia a year older. Emily lived in the village – had been born here and spent all her life in the rambling old house that lay just beyond the church. But Portia came from London. Ever since Emily could remember, Portia's parents had rented the Luscombes' house for the month of August, while the Luscombes took themselves off to stay with their daughter who lived in some remote corner of Scotland that had a name like a sneeze.

As small children, Emily and Portia had played together every summer. In the normal course of events they would probably have taken little notice of each other, for they had, in fact, little in common. But Portia's brothers and sisters were all older than she, and Emily was an only child. Thus, thrown together with the encouragement of their parents, they had formed a companionship that was quite satisfactory in its own practical fashion. They exchange confidences.

117

It was Portia who had suggested this afternoon's excursion to the beach. She had telephoned Emily after lunch.

' . . . I'm all on my own. Giles and his friends have gone to watch stock car racing . . . ' Giles was her brother, an undergraduate at Cambridge and terrifyingly witty and erudite. ' . . . and I don't want to go. It's too hot and smelly.' Emily hesitated, and Portia caught the hesitation. 'You haven't got anything else you want to do, have you?'

Emily, grasping the receiver of the telephone, listened to the silence of the house, drowsing in the heat of the early afternoon. Mrs Wattis, having cleared the lunch, had departed for Fourbourne, where she was to spend the night with her sister. Emily's father was in Bristol. He had gone this morning on a business trip and would not return for another two days. Stephanie was upstairs in her bedroom, resting.

'No. Nothing, really,' said Emily. 'I'd like to come.'

'Bring a biscuit or a sandwich or something. I've got a bottle of lemonade. I'll meet you at the church.'

Emily had not seen Portia for a year, and as soon as she set eyes on her, her heart sank. It had happened again. At school, all her friends seemed to be growing up and outstripping Emily, moving on to higher forms, more advanced examinations, added privileges, while Emily stumbled along behind, clinging to the security of childhood, the known, the familiar. Longing to advance with the others, but lacking the courage to take the first, deliberate step.

And now Portia.

Portia was growing up. She had a proper figure. In a mere twelve months, she had turned from a child to a young woman. Her skimpy shorts and T-shirt revealed a proper waist, slender hips, long, brown legs. She had grown her dark curls down to her shoulders, she had had her ears pierced and wore shining gold earrings. They glinted when she tossed back her hair, tangled in the glossy dark locks. She had pink varnish on her toenails and she had shaved her legs.

Walking down over the golf links towards the sea, they passed a couple of young men, golfers, making their way to the next tee. Last year the young men would not even have glanced at Portia and Emily, but now she saw their eyes on Portia, and she observed Portia's reaction. The pantomime of not being aware of admiring stares. The sudden self-consciousness of her walk, the toss of her head as a gust of wind blew her hair across her eyes. The young men did not look at Emily and Emily did not expect them to. For who would want to look at a stringy fourteen-year-old, with no shape and no curves, hair the colour of straw, and horrible spectacles?

'You've still got specs,' Portia remarked. 'Why don't you get contact lenses?'

'Perhaps I will, but I can't till I'm older.'

'A girl at school's got them, but she said they were agony to begin with.'

Emily felt sick. She couldn't bear to think about putting contact lenses into her eyes any more than she could bear to have her fingernails cut (Mother had taught her how to use a little emery board) or to eat sandwiches that the sand had got into.

She said, not wanting to talk about contact lenses, 'Did you do O Levels this summer?'

Portia made a bored face. 'Yes, but I haven't had the results yet. I think I'm all right, but now my parents say I have to do A Levels. That's another two years at school and I simply don't think I can bear it. I'm trying to get them to say I can leave next summer and go to an A Level crammer or something. School's so stifling.' Emily made no comment on this. 'How about you? O Levels, I mean.'

Emily looked away from Portia because sometimes her eyes filled with tears, and this felt as though it was going to be one of them.

'I'm taking them next year.' Across the bay, a car was crawling down the road towards the distant beach. Sunlight flashed signals from its windows. She watched it minutely, concentrating, and after a little the tears receded, unshed. She said, 'I was meant to take them. But Miss Myles, she's my headmistress, said it would be better to wait another year.'

The interview had been a nightmare. Miss Myles had been so kind, so sympathetic, and all Emily had been able to do was sit and stare at her, numb with misery, scarcely able to listen to what she was saying, scarcely able to hear the sensible words. *Nobody would expect you to pass, Emily, not just at this time. And after all, what rush is there? Why not give yourself another twelve months? Time is a great healer. In twelve months you won't have forgotten, because you'll never forget your mother, but I think you'll find that things will be better.*

They came to the railway bridge, the wooden footbridge that separated the golf links from the dunes. Halfway across they stopped, as they had always stopped, to lean over the wooden barrier and gaze down at the curving rails, glittering today in the brazen sunshine.

Portia said, 'My mother told me that your father had married again.'

'Yes.'

'Is she nice?'

'Yes.' The silence that followed this single word seemed an indictment against Stephanie, so she added, 'She's very young. She's only twenty-nine.'

'I know. My mother told me. She told me about the baby coming, too.'

'Do you mind?'

'No,' lied Emily.

'It must be funny, having a baby coming. Now, I mean. At our age.'

'It's all right.'

They had bought a new cot for the new baby, but

Emily's father had brought Emily's old pram down from the attic, and Stephanie had cleaned and oiled and polished it, and made a little patchwork quilt for it, and now it waited, in a corner of the wash-house, for the new occupant.

'I mean,' pursued Portia, 'you've never had brothers and sisters. It'll be strange for you.'

'It'll be all right.' The wooden parapet of the bridge felt warm to her hand, splintery and smelling of creosote. 'It'll be all right.' She threw a splinter of wood down onto the railway lines. 'Come on. I'm hot and I want to swim,' and they went on over the bridge, their footsteps sounding hollow on the planks, and started out across the sandy footpath that led to the dunes.

They swam and sunbathed, lying face down on the sand with their heads turned towards each other. Portia chattered endlessly, about next holidays when she might be going skiing; about the boy she had met who had promised to take her roller-discoing; about the suede jacket her father had said that he would give her for her birthday. She did not talk about Stephanie and the baby again, and for this Emily was silently grateful.

And now, at the end of the day, at the start of the evening, it was time to make tracks for home. The tide was at the turn, a rim of dark sand lay wetly just beyond the reach of the breakers. The sea was a welter of dazzling light, the sky still cloudless and a deepening blue.

Portia looked at her watch. She said, 'It's nearly seven. I've got to go.' She began to brush damp sand from her bikini. 'We've got a supper party. Giles is bringing his friends home and I promised my mother I'd give her a hand.' Emily imagined the house, filled with young people all knowing each other very well, eating enormous quantities of food, drinking beer, playing the latest discs on their stereo. The image was both enviable and frightening. She began to pull her T-shirt over her bathing suit. She said, 'I ought to go too.'

Portia said, with unaccustomed politeness, 'Are you having a party?'

'No, but my father's away, and Stephanie's on her own.'

'So it'll just be you and the wicked stepmother.'

Emily said, quickly, 'She's not wicked.'

'Just a manner of speech,' said Portia, and started to gather up towels and sun oil, stuffing them into a canvas bag that had ST TROPEZ printed in huge red letters upon its side.

They parted at the church.

'It's been fun,' said Portia. 'We'll do it again,' and she gave a casual wave, and sauntered off. The saunter speeded up, turned into a run. Portia was hurrying home, to wash her hair and get ready for the evening's fun.

She had not invited Emily to the party and Emily had not expected to be asked. She did not want to go to any party. She didn't much want, either, to return home and face an evening spent in the company of Stephanie.

Stephanie and Emily's father had been married now for nearly a year, but this was the first time that she and Emily had been left on their own. Without her father to act as buffer and keep the conversation going, Emily was in an agony of apprehension. What would they talk about?

She began to walk in the direction of home. Across the green, under the deep shade of the oaks, down the rutted lane, with a glimpse of sea at the end of it. In through the open white gates, the house revealing itself beyond the curve of the drive.

Reluctant, filled with a strange foreboding, Emily stopped, and stood looking at it. Home. But it had not been home since her mother died. Worse, since her father married Stephanie, it had become another person's home.

What had changed? Small and subtle things. The

rooms were tidier. Knitting and bits of sewing, books and old magazines no longer lay about the place. Cushions were plumped up, rugs lay flat and straight.

The flowers indoors had changed. Emily's mother had loved flowers, but had no great refinements as to their disposal. Great bunches were crammed into jugs, just the way they had been picked. But Stephanie was a magician with flowers. Formal arrangements stood on pedestals in huge cream-coloured urns. Spikes of delphinium and gladiola, massed with roses and sweet peas and strangely shaped leaves that no person but Stephanie would even think of picking.

All of this was inevitable, and quite bearable. But what was almost unbearable and had really turned Emily's world upside down had been the total transformation of her mother's bedroom. Nothing else in the house had been altered, or redecorated or repainted, but the big double room that faced out over the garden and the blue waters of the creek had been stripped of furniture, gutted, rebuilt, and made totally new and unfamiliar.

In all fairness to her father, he had told Emily that this was going to be done.

He had written to her at school. 'A bedroom is a personal thing,' his letter had said. 'It wouldn't be fair to Stephanie to ask her to use your mother's bedroom, any more than it would be fair to your mother if Stephanie were simply to take over all her most treasured possessions. So we are going to change it all, and when you come back for the holidays, it will be unrecognisable. Don't be upset about this. Try to understand. It is the only thing we are changing. The rest of the house remains the way you have always known it.'

She thought of the room. In the old days, before her mother died, it had been shabby and comfortable, with nothing actually matching anything else but everything living happily together, like the random sowing of flowers in a border. The curtains and the rug were faded.

123

The huge brass bed, which had belonged to Emily's grandmother, wore a bedspread of crocheted white lace, and there were a great number of photographs about the place and old-fashioned water colours upon the walls.

But that had all gone. Now everything was eggshell blue, with a fitted pale blue carpet, and beautiful satin curtains lined with the palest yellow. The old brass bed had gone, and in its place was a luxurious king-size divan, frilled in the same material as the curtains, and draped in a white muslin canopy that was suspended from a gilded coronet, high on the wall. There were a lot of white furry rugs, and the bathroom was lined in mirror glass and glittering with enticing bottles and jars. And everything smelt of lilies-of-the-valley. It was Stephanie's own scent. But Emily's mother had always smelt of Eau-de-Cologne and face powder.

Standing there in the evening sunlight, with her hair wet from swimming and sand encrusting her bare brown legs, Emily suddenly ached for things to be the way they had been. To be able to run in through the front door, calling for her mother, and to have her mother's voice answer from upstairs. To go to her, curling up on the big hospitable bed, and to watch while her mother, at her dressing table, brushed her short, wayward hair, or dusted her nose with a swansdown puff that had been dipped into the crystal bowl of fragrant face powder.

She could never feel close to Stephanie. It wasn't that she didn't like her. Stephanie was beautiful and youthful and loving and had tried her hardest to find some niche in Emily's heart. Bu they were both, basically, shy. Both wary of intruding on the other's privacy. Perhaps it might have been easier for both of them if the baby had not happened. In a month the baby would be here, sleeping in the new cot in Emily's old nursery. An entity to be reckoned with, bringing with it more claims on Emily's father's affections.

Emily did not want the baby. She did not much like babies. Once she had seen a television film of some person bathing a new born baby and had been horrified. It looked like trying to bathe a tadpole.

She longed to be able to go back in time. To be twelve years old again and have none of these disturbing things happen to her. She was always longing to go back in time, which was why she had done badly in her lessons, had failed so miserably at games, had been kept back a year in the same form. Next term she must keep company with a gang of younger girls with whom she had nothing in common. Her confidence had been hopelessly eroded, like the face of a cliff too long pounded by the sea and scoured by the winds, so that at times she felt she would never be able to make a decision, or achieve something, successfully, ever again.

But brooding did no good. The evening stretched ahead and had to be faced. She went on up the drive, and when she had pegged her bathing things out on the line, let herself into the house through the back door. The kitchen was spotlessly neat and orderly. The round, wooden-framed clock over the dresser ticked away at the minutes, making a sound like a pair of snipping shears. Emily dumped the remains of her picnic onto the table and went through the door and into the hall. Evening sunshine lay in a long yellow beam through the open front door. Emily stood in its warmth and listened. There was no sound. She looked into the sitting room, but it was empty.

'Stephanie.'

She had probably gone out for a walk. She liked to walk in the evenings when it was cooler. Emily started upstairs. On the landing, she saw that the door to the big, pale blue bedroom stood open. She hesitated. From within a voice spoke her name.

'Emily. Emily, is that you?'

'Yes.' She crossed the landing and went in through the open door.

'Emily.'

Stephanie lay on the beautiful bed. She was still dressed, in her loose cotton maternity smock, but she had kicked off her sandals and her feet were bare. Her red-gold hair spread its tangle over the white pillowcase, and her face, innocent of make-up and freckled as a child's, was very pale and shone with sweat.

She stretched out a hand. 'I'm so glad you're here.'

'I was on the beach with Portia. I thought you were out for a walk.' Emily approached the bed, but she did not take Stephanie's outstretched hand. Stephanie's eyes closed. She turned her head away from Emily, and her breathing was suddenly long and laboured.

'Is something wrong?'

But she knew that there was. And she knew what it was. Even before Stephanie relaxed at last and opened her eyes again. She and Emily gazed at one another. Stephanie said, 'the baby's started.'

'But it's not due for a month.'

'Well, I think it's coming now. I know it is. I've been feeling odd all day, and I tried to go out for a bit of fresh air after tea, and I had this pain. So I came home to lie down. I thought it might just go away. But it hasn't, it's got worse.'

Emily swallowed. She tried to remember everything she had ever known about having babies, which was not much. She said, 'How often are the pains coming?'

Stephanie reached out for her gold wristwatch which lay on the bedside table. 'That was only five minutes.'

Five minutes. Emily could feel her heart pounding. She looked down at the swollen, ludicrous mound that was Stephanie's abdomen, taut with incipient life beneath the sprigged cotton of her voluminous dress. Without thinking, she laid her hand, gently, upon it.

She said, 'I thought first babies took ages to arrive.'

'I don't think there's any hard and fast rule.'

'Have you rung the hospital? Have you rung the doctor?'

'I haven't done anything. I was frightened to move in case something happened.'

'I'll ring,' said Emily. 'I'll ring now.' She tried to remember what had happened when Mrs Wattis's Daphne had had her baby. 'They'll send an ambulance.' Mrs Wattis's Daphne had cut things a bit too fine and very nearly had her child on the way to hospital.

'Gerald was going to take me,' said Stephanie. Gerald was Emily's father. 'I don't want to have it without him here . . . ' Her voice broke, and there were tears in her eyes.

'You may have to,' said Emily. Stephanie started to weep in earnest, and then suddenly stopped. 'Oh . . . there's another one!' She grabbed for Emily's hand, and for a minute or so there was nothing in existence except the frenzied clasp of her fingers, the slow, determined breathing, the escaping gasps of pain. It seemed to go on for eternity, but at last, gradually, it passed. It was over. Exhausted, Stephanie lay there. Her grasp on Emily's hand loosened. Emily took her hand away. She went across the room and into Stephanie's bathroom. She found a clean washcloth, wrung it out in cold water, and took it back to the bedside. She wiped Stephanie's face, then made the cloth into a pad and laid it on her forehead.

She said, 'I have to leave you for a moment. I'll go downstairs and telephone. But I'll be listening, and you only have to yell . . . '

There was a phone in the study, on her father's desk. She hated using the telephone, so she sat in his big chair for confidence, and because it was the nearest she could get to him. The number of the hospital was written in her father's desk directory. She dialled it carefully and waited. When a man's voice answered the call, she asked, making her voice as calm as she could, for the Maternity Ward. There was another delay, that seemed to last forever. Emily felt sick with anxiety and impatience.

'Maternity Ward.'

Relief made her incoherent. 'Oh ... this ... I mean ... ' She swallowed and started again, more slowly. 'This is Emily Bradley. My stepmother's meant to be having a baby in a month's time, but she's having it now. I mean, she's having pains.'

'Oh, yes,' said the voice, cool and blessedly business-like. Emily imagined somebody starched and neat, drawing a notepad towards her, unscrewing her pen, all set to take down lists of statistics. 'What is your stepmother's name?'

'Stephanie Bradley. Mrs Gerald Bradley. She's booked in at the hospital in a month, but I think she's going to have the baby today. Now.'

'Has she timed her pains?'

'Yes. They're every five minutes.'

'You'd better bring her in.'

'I can't. I haven't got a car, and I can't drive, and my father's away from home and there's nobody but me.'

The blatant urgency of the situation finally got through.

'In that case,' said the voice, wasting no more time, 'we'll send an ambulance.'

'I think,' said Emily, remembering Mrs Wattis's Daphne, 'you'd better send a nurse as well.'

'What is the address?'

'The Wheal House, Carnton. We're past the church and down the lane.'

'And who is Mrs Bradley's doctor?'

'Dr Meredith. But I'll ring him, if you'll get the ambulance here and a bed ready at the hospital.'

'There'll be an ambulance with you in about fifteen minutes.'

'Thank you. Thank you very much.'

She put down the receiver. Sat for a moment, biting her lip. Thought about calling the doctor, and then remembered Stephanie and went back upstairs, two at a time, urgency and responsibility and importance lending wings to her feet.

Stephanie lay with her eyes still shut. She did not appear to have moved. Emily said her name, and she opened her eyes. Emily smiled, trying to reassure her. 'All right?'

'I've had another pain. That's four minutes now. Oh, Emily, I'm so frightened.'

'You mustn't be frightened. I've phoned the hospital and they're sending an ambulance and a nurse . . . they'll be here in about a quarter of an hour.'

'I feel so hot. I feel such a mess.'

'I could help you out of your dress. Put on a clean nightie. That would make you feel more comfortable.'

'Oh, could you? There's one in the drawer.'

She opened the drawer and found the white lawn nightdress, scented and lacy. Gently, she eased Stephanie out of the crumpled maternity dress, helped her off with her bra and pants. Naked, the huge bulge of her abdomen was revealed. Emily had never seen such a sight before, but rather to her own surprise, she did not find it horrifying. Instead, it seemed a sort of miracle; a safe, dark nest containing a living child, which already was making its presence felt and announcing to the world that it was time to make its appearance. Suddenly it was not alarming anymore but rather exciting. She slipped the nightdress over Stephanie's head, and helped her put her arms into the lacy sleeves. She fetched a hairbrush from the dressing table and a length of velvet ribbon, and Stephanie took the brush and smoothed back her tangled hair, then tied it with the ribbon and lay back once more to await the next onslaught of pain. It was not long in coming. When it was over, Emily, feeling as exhausted as Stephanie looked, checked once more on the watch. Four minutes again.

Four minutes. Emily did a few panic-stricken calculations. It looked as though there was every chance that the baby would not wait for that drive to the hospital.

In which case, it would be born right here, in this house, in the blue bedroom, in the immaculate bed. Having a baby was a messy business. Emily knew that much from books she had read, to say nothing of having once watched a pet tabby cat produce a litter of striped kittens. Precautions must be taken, and Emily knew what they were. She went to the linen cupboard and found a rubber sheet, newly purchased for the new baby, and a pile of thick white bathtowels.

'You're brilliant,' said Stephanie, as Emily, with some difficulty, remade the bed with her stepmother still in it. 'You've thought of everything.'

'Well, your waters might break.'

Stephanie, despite everything, dissolved into weak laughter. 'How do you know so much?'

'I don't know. I just do. Mummy told me all about having babies when she told me about the facts of life. She was peeling Brussels sprouts at the time, and I can remember standing by the sink and watching her, and thinking that there must be an easier way to have children.' She added, 'But of course there isn't.'

'No, there isn't.'

'My mother only had me, but I know other people say that once it's all over, you forget about the pain, you just think how marvellous it was. Having the baby, I mean. And then when you have another you remember the same old pain, and you think, "I must have been out of my mind to do it a second time," only then, of course, it's too late. Now if you're all right, I'll go and ring the doctor.'

Mrs Meredith answered the call, and said that the doctor was out on his rounds, but she would leave a message at the surgery, as he frequently rang in to see if there were any extra calls to be made.

'It's terribly urgent,' said Emily, and explained what was happening, and Mrs Meredith said in that case, she would try to find him herself. 'You've rung the hospital, Emily?'

'Yes, and they're sending an ambulance and a nurse. It shoud be here in a little while.'

'Is Mrs Wattis with you?'

'No. She's gone to Fourbourne.'

'And your father?'

'He's in Bristol. He doesn't know what's happening. There's just Stephanie and me.'

There was a little pause. 'I'll find the doctor,' said Mrs Meredith, and rang off.

'Now,' said Emily, 'we just have to get hold of Daddy.'

'No,' said Stephanie. 'Let's wait, until it's all safely over. Otherwise he'll be panic-stricken, and there's nothing he can do. We'll wait until the baby's arrived, and then we'll tell him.'

They smiled at each other, a conspiracy of two women who both loved, and wished to protect, the same man. The next instant Stephanie's eyes widened, her mouth opened in a gasp of agony. 'Oh, Emily . . . '

'It's all right . . . ' Emily took her hand. 'It's all right. I'm here. I won't go away. I'm here. I'll stay with you . . . '

Five minutes later, the village was astounded by the blare of sirens. The ambulance, everything ringing, came thundering down the rutted lane, turned in at the gate, and shot up the drive. Emily scarcely had time to get downstairs before they were into the house, two burly men with a stretcher and a nurse with a bag. Emily met them in the hall. 'I don't think there's time to take her to the hospital . . . '

'We'll see,' said the nurse. 'Where is she?'

'Upstairs. The first door on the left. There are towels and a rubber sheet on the bed.'

'Good girl,' said the nurse briskly, and disappeared up the stairs with the ambulance men behind her. Almost at once another car appeared, hard on the heels of the ambulance, stopped with a screech of brakes on gravel, and discharged, like a bullet, the doctor.

Dr Meredith was an old friend of Emily's. He said, 'What's happening?'

She told him. 'It's a month early. I think it must be the heat.' He allowed himself a small, private smile. 'Is that bad, or is it going to be all right?'

'We'll see.' He headed for the stairs.

'What shall I do now?' Emily asked him.

He stopped and turned to look back at her. There was an expression on his face that Emily had never seen before. He said, 'It seems to me that you've done just about everything already. Your mother would be proud of you. Why don't you take yourself off. Go out in the garden and sit in the sun. I'll let you know everything, just as soon as there's anything to tell.'

Your mother would be proud of you. She went through the sitting room, the open French windows, and onto the terrace. She sat on the top step of the little flight of steps that led down to the lawn. All at once, she felt very tired. She put her elbows on her knees and rested her chin in her hands. *Your mother would be proud of you.* She thought about her mother. It was funny, but it didn't make her miserable any longer The aching need for a person no longer there had gone. She pondered on this. Perhaps you only needed people if other people didn't need you.

She was still sitting there, mulling all this over, when, half an hour later, Dr Meredith came to find her. She heard his step on the flags as he came out through the French windows and twisted around to face him. He had taken off his jacket and his shirt sleeves were rolled up. He came, slowly, to sit beside her. He said, 'You've got a little sister. Six and a half pounds and quite perfect.'

'And Stephanie?'

'A bit weary, but blooming. A copybook mother.'

Emily felt a smile creeping up into her face, and at the same time a lump grew in her throat and her eyes started to fill with tears. Dr Meredith, with no words, handed over a large white cotton handkerchief, and Emily took off her spectacles and wiped her eyes and blew her nose.

'Does Daddy know?'

'Yes. I've just been speaking to him on the phone. He's coming home right away. He'll be here by midnight. The ambulance has gone back to the hospital, but nurse is going to stay the night.'

'When can I see the baby?'

'You can see her now if you want to. Just for a moment.'

Emily stood up. 'I want to,' she said.

They went back into the house. Upstairs, the nurse, bustling and competent, gave Emily a cotton mask to tie over her face. 'Just in case,' she said. 'She's an early baby and we don't want to take any risks.'

Emily, not minding, obediently tied it on. She went with Dr Meredith into the blue bedroom. And there, in the beautiful bed, propped up with pillows, lay Stephanie. And in her arms, cocooned in a shawl, its little head downed with hair the same colour as Stephanie's, lay the new baby. A person. A sister.

She stooped and laid her face against Stephanie's. She couldn't kiss her, because of the mask, but Stephanie kissed Emily. All constraint between them had melted away. They were no longer shy of each other, and Emily knew that they would never be shy again. She looked down into the baby's face. She said, wonderingly, 'She's beautiful.'

'We had her together,' Stephanie told her, sleepily. 'I feel she's yours as much as mine.'

'A rare little nurse you'd make, Emily,' the nurse chipped in. 'I couldn't have coped with things better myself.'

Stephanie said, 'We're a family now.'

'Is that what you wanted?' asked Emily.

'It's all I've ever wanted.'

*   *   *

133

A family. Everything had changed, everything was different, but that didn't mean that it couldn't be good. When she had seen the doctor off, and watched his car disappear around the curve of the drive, Emily did not immediately return indoors. It was growing dark now, the garden dusky and sweet-scented after the long, hot day. The first of the stars shone from a sapphire-coloured sky. A beautiful evening. Just the right sort of evening for a person to start living. Just the right sort of evening for a person to start growing up.

She was very tired. She took off her spectacles and rubbed her eyes. She looked at the spectacles thoughtfully. Perhaps contact lenses wouldn't be so bad. If Stephanie could bear having a baby, then surely Emily could learn to wear contact lenses.

She would try. Just as soon as she was old enough, she would try.

Gilbert

Awaking; aware, without opening his eyes, of sunlight and a band of warmth lying across the bed, Bill Rawlins was pervaded with a sense of marvellous contentment and well-being. A number of pleasant thoughts crossed his mind. That it was a Sunday so he didn't have to go to work. That it was going to be a fine day. That the warm, soft body of his wife lay close to him, her head pillowed in the curve of his arm. That he was, in all probability, one of the most fortunate men in the world.

The bed was huge and downy. An old aunt of Bill's had given it to them as a wedding present when he had married Clodagh two months ago. It had been her marriage bed, his aunt had informed him with certain relish, and to make the gift more acceptable, had thrown in a beautiful new mattress and six pairs of heirloom linen sheets.

It was about the only thing in the house, apart from his desk and his clothes, that actually belonged to Bill. Marrying a widow had posed certain complications, but where they were to live was not one of them, because there could have been no question of Clodagh and her two small girls moving into Bill's two-roomed bachelor flat, and there seemed little point going to all the hassle and expense of buying themselves a new house when hers was already so perfect. His flat had been in the middle of the town, within walking distance of the office, but this house lay a mile or so out into the country, and had as well the advantage of a large and rambling garden. Besides, Clodagh pointed out, it was the

135

children's home. Here were their secret hideouts, the swing in the sycamore tree, the playroom in the attic.

Bill needed no persuasion. It was the right and obvious thing to do.

'You're going to live in Clodagh's house?' his friends exclaimed, looking astonished.

'Why not?'

'A bit tricky, surely. After all, that's where she lived with her first husband.'

'Very happily, too,' Bill pointed out. 'And I hope she'll be just as happy with me.'

Clodagh's husband, and the father of her two little girls, had been killed in a tragic car smash three years ago. Bill, although he had worked and lived in the district for some years, did not meet her until two years later, when he was asked, as a suitable man to make up numbers, to a dinner party, and there found himself sitting next to a tall and slender girl, whose thick blonde hair was wound up into a knot at the back of her elegant head.

Her finely boned face he instantly found beautiful, and yet, at the same time, sad. Her eyes were grave, her mouth hesitant. It was this very sadness that caught at his tough and experienced heart. Her fragile neck, exposed by the old-fashioned hairstyle, seemed to him vulnerable as a child's, and when at last he made her laugh, and her smile came into its own, he fell, like any young man, head over heels in love.

'You're going to *marry* her?' asked those same astonished friends. 'One thing, marrying a widow. Another, marrying a ready-made family.'

'That's a bonus.'

'Glad you think so, old boy. Ever had anything to do with children?'

'No,' he admitted, 'but it's never too late to start.'

Clodagh was thirty-three; Bill was thirty-seven. A confirmed bachelor. That's what he was known as. A handsome, cheerful sort of fellow, good for a game of golf, and a useful player at the local tennis club, but definitely a confirmed bachelor. How would he manage?

He managed by treating the two small girls like grown-ups. They were called Emily and Anna. Emily was eight and Anna was six. Despite his determination not to be intimidated by them, he found their straight stares unnerving. They were both fair, with long hair and blue eyes of startling brightness. These two pairs of eyes watched him incessantly; moved around the room as he moved, showed neither affection nor dislike.

They were very polite. From time to time during his courtship of their mother, he gave them small presents. Tubes of sweets, puzzles, or games to play. Anna, the less complicated child, was pleased by these, opened them at once, and showed her delight in smiles and the occasional hug of appreciation. But Emily was a different kettle of fish. Politely, she would thank him, then disappear with the parcel unwrapped, to deal with her loot in private, and presumably decide, on her own, to give or withhold approval.

Once, he was able to mend Anna's Action Man – she did not play with dolls – and after that there was a certain rapport between them, but any affection that Emily had to show was bestowed only on her pets. She had three. A hideous tom cat, which hunted ferociously and had no conscience about stealing any food he could get his brazen claws into; a smelly old spaniel who could not go for a walk without returning home filthy; and a goldfish. The cat was called Breeky, the dog was called Henry, and the goldfish was called Gilbert. Breeky, Henry, and Gilbert were three of the many good reasons why Bill moved into Clodagh's house. One could not imagine these three demanding creatures being domiciled anywhere else.

Emily and Anna came to the wedding in pink and white dresses with pink satin sashes. Everybody said that they looked angelic, but all through the ceremony,

Bill was uncomfortably aware of their cool blue eyes boring holes in the back of his neck. When it was over, they dutifully flung a bit of confetti and ate some wedding cake, and then departed to stay with Clodagh's mother, while Clodagh and Bill went off on their honeymoon.

He took her to Marbella, and the sun-drenched days slipped by, each a little better than the one before, enriched by laughter and shared experiences and starlit nights when, with the windows open wide to the warm velvety darkness, they made love to the sound of the sea whispering on the beach below the hotel.

By the end, though, Clodagh was missing her children. She said a sad goodbye to Marbella, but Bill knew that she was looking forward to getting back. When they drove up the short approach to her house, Emily and Anna were there, waiting for them, with a homemade banner held aloft, proclaiming, in wobbly capitals, that they were WELCOME HOME.

Welcome home. Now, it was his home. Now, he was not only husband, but father as well. Now, when he drove to the office, he had two small girls in the back of his car, to be unloaded out onto the pavement in front of their school. Now, at weekends he did not play golf, but cut grass and planted out lettuces and mended things. A house without a handyman can slide into disrepair, and this house had had no man in it for nearly three years. There seemed no end to the squeaking hinges, defunct toasters, and balky lawnmowers. Out of doors gates sagged, fences collapsed, and sheds demanded creosote.

As well, there were Emily's animals, which seemed to thrive on emergency and drama. The cat disappeared for three days and was given up for dead, only to reappear with a torn ear and a hideous wound in his side. No sooner had he been wheeled off to the vet than the old dog ate something unspeakable and was sick for four days, lying in his basket and gazing at Bill with red-rimmed, reproachful eyes, as though the whole thing were his fault. Only Gilbert the goldfish remained boringly healthy, swimming around his tank in aimless circles, but even he needed constant care and attention, his tank cleaned, and special food purchased from the pet shop.

Bill coped with all this as best he could, remaining deliberately patient and cheerful. When tantrums blew up and there were quarrels and fights, usually ending with cries of 'It's not fair!' and an earth-shaking slam of a door, he kept out of the way, leaving the necessary arbitration to Clodagh, terrified of getting involved and saying or doing the wrong thing.

'What was all that about?' he would ask, when Clodagh returned to him, looking exasperated, amused, exhausted, but never cross, and she would try to explain, and then stop explaining, because after about one minute of her explanation he would probably have put his arms around her and started kissing her, and it is almost impossible to explain and be kissed at the same time. He found himself amazed that despite all these domestic ups and downs, the magic they had discovered in Marbella was not lost to them. Things still seemed to get better with each passing day, and he loved his wife to the very extent of his being.

And now it was Sunday morning. Warm sun, warm bed, warm wife. He turned his head and buried his face in her neck, smelled her silky, fragrant hair. As he did this, a warning chord struck. He was being watched. He turned his head back and opened his eyes.

Emily and Anna, in their nightdresses, and with their long straight hair tousled from sleep, sat on the brass rail at the end of the bed, observing him. Eight and six. Was that too young to start sex education at school? He hoped so.

He said, 'Hello there.'

Anna said, 'We're hungry. We want breakfast.'

'What time is it?'

139

She spread her hands. '*I* don't know.'

He reached out and found his watch. 'Eight o'clock,' he told them.

'We've been awake for ages, and we're starving.'

'Your mother's still asleep. I'll cook you breakfast.'

They did not move. He eased his arm from beneath Clodagh's shoulders and sat up. Their faces showed disapproval of his naked state.

He said, 'You go and get your clothes on, and clean your teeth, and by the time you're ready, I'll have breakfast on the table.'

They went, their bare feet pattering on the polished floor. When they were safely out of sight, he climbed out of bed, pulled on a towelling robe, closed the door of the bedroom silently behind him, and went downstairs. In the kitchen, Henry snored in his basket. Bill stirred him awake with a toe, and the old dog yawned, had a good scratch, and finally deigned to climb out of his bed. Bill led him to the back door and opened it onto the garden, and Henry made his way out of doors. As he did this, Breeky appeared from nowhere, looking more like a battered old tiger than ever, and shot past Bill's bare legs into the kitchen. In his mouth was a large, dead mouse, which he laid in the middle of the floor and then settled down to devour.

It was too early in the day for such cannibalism. At risk to life and limb, Bill removed the mouse and dropped it into the trash can under the sink. Breeky was furious and set up such a caterwauling that Bill was forced to calm him with a saucer of milk. Breeky drank this as messily as he could, splashing milk all over the linoleum, and then, when the saucer was emptied, leapt up onto the window seat, closed his eyes to yellow slits, and started to wash himself.

After he had wiped up the milk, Bill put on a kettle, found the frying pan, the bacon and eggs. He put the bread in the toaster and laid the scrubbed pine table. When this was done, the two little girls had still not appeared, so he went back upstairs to dress. As he pulled on an old cotton shirt, he heard them going down to the kitchen, chattering in their high-pitched voices. They sounded happy, but a moment later there floated up to him a wail of despair that chilled his heart.

With his shirt still unbuttoned, he shot out onto the landing. 'What is it?'

Another wail. Imagining every sort of horror, he bolted downstairs and into the kitchen. There Emily and Anna stood with their backs to him, staring into the goldfish tank. Anna's eyes brimmed with tears, but Emily seemed too stricken to weep.

'What's happened?'

'It's *Gilbert!*'

He crossed the floor, and over their heads, peered into the tank. At its bottom, on his side, with one round lifeless eye staring upwards, lay the goldfish.

'He's dead,' said Emily.

'How do you know?'

'Because he is.'

He certainly looked dead. 'Perhaps he's having a sleep?' Bill suggested, without much hope.

'No. He's dead. He's *dead*.'

With that, the two of them burst into tragic tears. With an arm for each, Bill tried to comfort them. Anna pushed her face into his stomach and wound her arms around his thigh, but Emily stood rigid, sobbing uncontrollably, her skinny arms crossed over her bony chest, as though she were trying to hold herself together.

It was terrible. His first instinct was to free himself and go to the foot of the stairs and yell for help. Clodagh would know what to do . . .

And then he thought, No. Here was a chance to show his mettle. Here was a chance to break down the barriers; to cope on his own, and earn their respect.

He calmed them down at last. Found a clean tea towel to use as a handkerchief, led them to the window seat, and sat them down, one on either side of him.

'Now,' he said. 'Listen.'

'He's dead. Gilbert's dead.'

'Yes, I know he's dead. But when people, or pets, that we're fond of, die, what we do is to bury them decently, give them a beautiful funeral. So why don't the pair of you go out into the garden and find a really peaceful spot, where you can dig a nice hole. And I'll see if I can rustle up an old cigar box or something to use as a coffin for Gilbert. And you can make wreaths to put on the top of his grave, and perhaps a little cross.'

The two pairs of blue eyes, watchful as ever, slowly showed some interest. Tears were still wet on their cheeks, but drama and high tragedy had great appeal, and were too attractive to resist.

'When Mrs Donkins in the village died, her daughter wore a black veil on her hat,' Emily remembered.

'Perhaps your mother can find a black veil for your hat.'

'There's one in the dressing-up box.'

'There you are. You can wear that!'

'What am I going to wear?' Anna wanted to know.

'I'm sure Mummy will find something for you.'

'I want to make the cross.'

'No. I do.'

'But . . .'

He interrupted quickly. 'The first thing to do is decide on a good place. Why don't you both nip off and do that, while I cook you some breakfast. And then after breakfast . . .'

But they did not listen for more. On the instant, they were up and away, not able to wait. At the back door, Emily stopped.

'We'll need a spade,' she said, in her most businesslike manner.

'You'll find a trowel in the toolshed.'

They sped across the garden, brimming with enthusiasm, all sorrow forgotten in the excitement of a real, grown-up funeral, with black veils on their hats. With mixed feelings, he watched them go. The little scene had left him drained, and ravenously hungry. Grinning wryly to himself, he went back to the stove and began frying up the bacon.

As he did this, there came the sound of soft footsteps on the stair, and the next moment his wife appeared through the door. She wore her nightdress and a loose cotton dressing gown. Her hair was all over her shoulders, her feet bare, her eyes still cloudy with sleep.

'What was all that about?' she asked, through a yawn.

'Hello, my darling. Did we wake you?'

'Was somebody crying?'

'Yes. Emily and Anna. Gilbert is dead.'

'Gilbert? Oh, no. I don't believe it.'

He went to kiss her. 'I'm afraid it's true.'

'Oh, poor Emily.' She drew away from his embrace. 'He's really dead?'

'See for yourself.'

Clodagh went to the fish tank and peered inside. 'But *why?*'

'I don't know. I don't know much about goldfish. Perhaps he ate something that disagreed with him.'

'But he wouldn't just die, like that.'

'You obviously know more about goldfish than I do.'

'When I was Anna's age, I had goldfish of my own. They were called Sambo and Goldy.'

'Original names.'

They fell silent while she observed the lifeless Gilbert. Then she said, thoughtfully, 'I remember Goldy once behaving just like that. And my father gave him a tot of whisky, and he started swimming around again. Besides, when fish are dead, they float to the top of the water.'

Bill ignored this last observation. 'A tot of *whisky?*'

'Have you got any?'

'Yes. I have one precious bottle which I keep for my closest friends. I suppose Gilbert qualifies, and if you want you can certainly try a reviver, but it seems rather a waste to pour the stuff over a dead fish. Like casting pearls before swine.'

Clodagh did not reply to this. Instead, she rolled up her sleeve, put her hand into the tank, and touched Gilbert's tail with a gentle finger. Nothing happened. It was hopeless. Bill went back to the pan of sizzling bacon. Perhaps he was being a bit mean about the whisky. He said, 'If you want, you can . . . '

'He's waggled his tail!'

'He has?'

'He's all right. He's swimming . . . oh look, darling.'

And, indeed, Gilbert was. Had righted himself, shaken out his little golden fins, and was once more on his regular circuit, right as rain.

'Clodagh, you're a miracle worker. Look at him.' In passing, Gilbert's fishy eye met Bill's. He knew a moment's annoyance. 'Stupid bloody fish, giving me a fright like that,' he said to it, and then he grinned in real relief. 'Emily will be overjoyed.'

'Where is she?'

He remembered the funeral. He said, 'She's in the garden with Anna.' For some reason he did not tell Clodagh about the plans that had been made. He did not tell her what they were doing.

Their mother smiled. 'Well, now that that little problem's been resolved, I'm going up to have a bath. I'll leave you to break the happy news,' and she blew him a kiss and took herself off upstairs.

Minutes later, as the bacon sizzled and the coffee perked, the two little girls reappeared, exploding through the open back door in a whirlwind of excitement.

'We've found a lovely place, Bill, under the rose bush in Mummy's border, and we've dug a huge hole . . . '

'And I've made a daisy chain . . . '

'And I've made a sort of cross out of two bits of wood, but I'll need string or a nail or something to hold them together . . . '

'And we're going to sing a *hymn*.'

'Yes. We're going to sing "All Things Bright and Beautiful." '

'And we thought . . . '

'Let *me* tell him . . . '

'We *thought* . . . '

'Now, just listen.' He had to raise his voice in order to make himself heard over the din. They fell silent. 'Just listen for a moment. And look.' He led them over to the fish tank. 'Look.'

They looked. They saw Gilbert, swimming around in his usual pointless fashion, his fragile, translucent tail flicking, his round eyes looking no more lively than when he had been presumed dead.

There was, for a moment, total silence.

'See? He wasn't dead at all. Just having a kip. Mummy gave him a tickle, and that stirred his stumps.' Still silence. 'Isn't that great?' Even to himself, he sounded quite sickeningly hearty.

Neither little girl said a word. Bill waited, and then, finally, Emily spoke.

She said, 'Let's kill him.'

He found himself torn between horrified shock and uncontrollable mirth, and for a second it was touch and go as to whether he actually struck the child or dissolved into laughter. By a superhuman effort he did neither of these things, but there was a long and pregnant pause before he finally said, with monumental calmness, 'Oh, I don't think we want to do that.'

'Why not?'

'Because . . . it's wrong to kill any living creature.'

'Why is it?'

'Because life is given to us by God. It's sacred.' Even as he said this, he felt slightly uncomfortable. Although he had been married to Clodagh in a church, he had not thought about God, in this everyday sort of way, for a number of years, and now knew a pang of guilt, as though he were taking the name of an old friend in vain.

'It's wrong to kill anything, even if it is only a goldfish. Besides, you love Gilbert. He belongs to you. You can't kill the thing you love.'

Emily's bottom lip protruded. 'I want to have a funeral. You promised.'

'But not Gilbert. We'll bury someone else.'

'*What?* Who?'

Anna knew her sister well. 'Not my Action Man,' she stipulated firmly.

'No, of course not Action Man.' He cast about for ideas, and was visited with a brainwave. 'A mouse. A poor, dead mouse. Look . . . ' Like a conjurer, he opened the trash can with his toe on the lever, and produced, with a certain flourish, Breeky's hunting trophy, holding its small stiff body up by the tail. 'Breeky brought it in this morning and I took it away from him. Surely you wouldn't want a poor old mouse to end up in the dustbin? Surely he deserves a bit of ceremony?'

They stared at his offering. After a bit, Emily said, 'Can we put him into the cigar box like you said?'

'Of course.'

'And sing hymns, and everything?'

'Of course. All Creatures Great and Small. Nothing could be much smaller than this.' He found a paper towel, laid it on the dresser, and placed the body of the mouse carefully upon it. Then he washed his hands, and drying them, turned to face the two little girls.

'What do you say?'

'Can we do it right away?'

'Let's eat breakfast first. I'm starving.'

Anna went at once to the table, to pull out a chair and settle herself, but Emily lingered for another reassuring check on Gilbert. Her nose was pressed against the glass wall of the tank, her finger traced a pattern, following his convolutions. Bill waited patiently. Presently she turned her head to look at him. Their eyes met in a long, steady stare.

She said, 'I'm glad he wasn't dead.'

'Me too.' he smiled, and she smiled back, and all at once looked so like her mother that, without thinking, he opened his arms to her, and she came to him, and they hugged, without words, without needing words. He stooped and kissed the top of her head, and she did not try to wriggle away or detach herself from this, their first tentative embrace.

'You know something, Emily,' he told her. 'You're a good girl.'

'You're good, too,' she said, and his heart was filled with gratitude, because somehow, by the grace of God, he had neither said nor done the wrong thing. He had got it right. It was a beginning. Not much, but a beginning.

Then Emily enlarged on this. 'Really, really good.'

Really, really good. Perhaps in that case, it was more than a beginning, and he was just about halfway there. Filled with gratification, he gave her a final hug and let her go, and at last, in happy anticipation of the mouse's funeral, they all sat down to breakfast.

The Before-Christmas Present

Two weeks before Christmas, on a black and bitterly cold morning, Ellen Parry, as she had been doing every morning for the past twenty-two years, drove her husband, James, the short distance to the station, kissed him goodbye, watched his black-coated, bowler-hatted figure disapear through the barrier, and then cautiously, because of the ice on the road, drove home again.

As she trundled down the slowly waking village street and out into the gentle country that lay beyond, her thoughts, disjointed and undisciplined at this early hour of the day, flew around the back of her mind like birds in a cage. There was always, at this time of the year, an enormous amount to be done. After she had washed up the breakfast dishes she would compose a shopping list for the weekend, perhaps make mince pies, send a few last-minute Christmas cards, buy a few last-minute presents, turn out Vicky's bedroom.

No. She changed her mind. She would not turn out Vicky's bedroom and make the bed until she knew for certain that Vicky would be with them for Christmas. Vicky was nineteen. In the autumn, she had managed to find herself a job in London, and a small flat, which she shared with two other girls. The break, however, was not total, because at weekends she usually came home, bringing sometimes a friend, and always a bag of dirty laundry for her mother's washing machine. The last time she had been back, Ellen had started making Christmas plans, but Vicky had looked discomfited and had finally plucked up the courage to tell Ellen that, perhaps, this year, she wouldn't be there. There was some talk about joining a young party who were taking a villa in Switzerland for the skiing.

Ellen, taken completely unawares by this bombshell, had managed to hide her dismay, but privately she reeled from the prospect of a Christmas spent without her only child, and yet knew that the worst thing any parent can do is to become possessive, to refuse to let go, to expect, in fact, anything at all.

It was all very difficult. Perhaps, when she got home, the post would have arrived, and there would be a letter from Vicky. She saw the envelope lying on the door mat, Vicky's huge writing.

Darling Ma. Kill the fatted calf and deck the halls with holly, Switzerland is off, so I'll be home to spend the festive season with you and Dad.

So certain was she that the letter would be there, so impatient to read it, Ellen allowed the car to pick up a little speed. The pale light of a midwinter morning now revealed the frozen ditches and black, frosty hedgerows. Small lights shone from cottage windows, and the local hill was capped with a drift of snow. She thought of Christmas carols and the smell of spruce, brought indoors, and was suddenly touched with excitement, the old magic of childhood.

Five minutes later, she parked the car in the garage and went into her house through the back door. The kitchen felt blissfully warm after the icy outdoors; the remains of breakfast lay on the table, but she ignored this and went through to the front hall to look for mail. The postman had called, and a pile of envelopes lay on the door mat. She stooped and picked them up, so certain of a letter from Vicky that when she found none, she thought she must be mistaken, and leafed through the pile for a second time. But there was nothing from her daughter.

For a moment she was overwhelmed with disappointment, and then, with an effort, pulled herself together. Perhaps the afternoon post . . . It is better to travel hopefully than to arrive. She took the pile of envelopes back into the kitchen, shrugged off her sheepskin coat, and sat down to open the mail.

Mostly cards. She opened them, one by one, stood them up in a semicircle. Robins and angels and Christmas trees and reindeer. The last was huge and extravagant, a Breugel reproduction of a skating party. With much love from Cynthia. Cynthia, as well, had written a letter. Ellen poured herself a mug of coffee and sat down to read it.

A long time ago Ellen and Cynthia had been best friends at school. But after they had grown up, their ways had diverged and their lives taken totally different directions. Ellen married James, and after a spell in a small London flat had moved, with their new baby daughter, to this very house where they had lived ever since. Once a year, she and James went on holiday . . . usually to places where James could play golf. That was all. The rest of the time she did the sort of things that women, all over the world, spend their time doing. That is, shop, cook, sew, weed the garden, wash clothes and iron them. Entertain, and be entertained by a few close friends; dabble in a little social work and make cakes for the Women's Institute fair. It was all quite undemanding, and, she knew, a little dull.

Cynthia, on the other hand, had married a brilliant physician, produced three children, started her own antique business, and made a lot of money. Her holidays were unimaginably exciting, driving across the United States, or walking the mountains of Nepal, or going to visit the Great Wall of China.

While Ellen and James's friends were doctors or lawyers or business colleagues, Cynthia's house in Campden Hill was a gathering point for the most fascinating people. Famous faces from television peppered her parties, writers discussed existentialism, artists argued abstractionism, politicians indulged in weighty debate. Once, staying overnight with Cynthia after a day's shopping, Ellen had found herself at dinner between a Cabinet minister and a young man with pink hair and a single earring, and trying to make conversation to either of these individuals had been a testing experience.

Afterwards, Ellen had blamed herself. 'I've got nothing to talk about,' she told James. 'Except making marmalade and getting my washing white, like those awful women on television advertisements.'

'You could talk about books. You get through more books than any person I know.'

'You can't talk about *books*. Reading is simply experiencing other people's experiences. I should be *doing* something, making experiences of my own.'

'How about the time we lost the cat? Doesn't that count as an experience?'

'Oh, *James*.'

It was then that the idea was born. She'd never done anything about it, but it was at that moment that it had been born. When Vicky left home, perhaps she could . . . ? She mentioned it in a casual way to James a few evenings later, but he had been reading the paper and scarcely listened, and when she brought it up again a few days after that, he had, in a quite kindly way, doused it with unenthusiasm, as though he were emptying a bucket of water over a fire.

She sighed, abandoned ambition, and read Cynthia's letter.

Darling Ellen. Just had to put a note into the card to say hello, and give you some news. Don't think you ever met the Sanderfords, Cosmo and Ruth, when you were here.

Ellen had not met the Sanderfords, but that did not mean that she did not know exactly who they were. Who had not heard of the Sanderfords? He a brilliant film director, and she a novelist, creator of wry, funny novels of family life. Who had not watched them in discussion panels on television? Who had not read her articles on the bringing up of their four children? Who had not marvelled at his films, with their oblique and original approach, their sensitivity and visual beauty? The Sanderfords, whatever they did, were news. Just to consider them was enough to make an ordinary, humdrum mortal feel completely inadequate. The Sanderfords. With a sinking heart, Ellen read on:

> They divorced a year ago, very amicably, and can still be observed from time to time, lunching together. But she has bought a house near you, and I'm sure would love a visit. Her address is Monk's Thatch, Trauncey, and the telephone is Trauncey 232. Give her a ring and say I told you to call. Have a marvellous Christmas, with very much love, Cynthia.

Trauncey was only a mile away, practically next door. And Monk's Thatch was an old gamekeeper's cottage, which had had a For Sale sign up for months. Now, presumably, the For Sale sign had gone, because Ruth Sanderford had bought it and was living there, on her own, and Ellen was expected to get in touch.

The prospect was daunting. If only the newcomer had been an ordinary person, a woman alone, needing company and the solace of a comfortable friend, then it would have been a different matter. But Ruth Sanderford was not an ordinary person. She was famous, clever, probably relishing her newfound solitude after a glittering life of artistic achievement, coupled with the sheer grind of bringing up four children. She would be bored by Ellen, resentful that Cynthia had ever even suggested that Ellen should get in touch with her.

The thought of the cold reception her tentative advances might precipitate caused Ellen's imagination to turn and flee in horror. Sometime, she would go. Not before Christmas. Perhaps at New Year. Anyway, now, she was too busy. There was so much to do. Mince pies to make, lists to be written . . .

Firmly, putting Ruth Sanderford out of her head, she went upstairs and made her bed. Across the landing, the door of Vicky's bedroom stood shut. Ellen opened it and looked inside, saw the dust on the dressing table, the bed, piled with folded blankets, the closed windows. Without Vicky's possessions, it had a strangely impersonal air, a room belonging to anybody, or nobody. Standing there in the open doorway, Ellen suddenly knew, beyond doubt, that Vicky would be going to Switzerland. That Christmas must somehow be endured without her.

What would they do, she and James? What would they talk about, sitting at either end of the dining-room table with a turkey too big to eat? Perhaps she should cancel the turkey and order lamb chops. Perhaps they should go away, to one of those hotels that cater to lonely, elderly people.

She closed the door swiftly, shutting away not just Vicky's deserted room, but the frightening images of old age and loneliness that must come to us all. At the far end of the landing, a narrow staircase led up to the loft. Without any reason in mind, Ellen went up these stairs and through the door that led into the huge attic with its slope-ceilinged roof. It was empty save for a few suitcases and the bulbs she had planted for the spring now shrouded in thick blankets of newspaper. Dormer windows and a spacious skylight let in the first pale rays of the low sun, and there was a pleasant smell of wood and camphor.

In a corner stood a box containing the Christmas tree decorations. But would they have a tree this year? It was always Vicky's job to dress the tree, and there seemed little point, if she wasn't going to be here. There seemed, in fact, little point in anything.

Say I told you to call.

Ruth Sanderford was back again. Living at Monk's

Thatch, a short walk away across the frosty fields. All right, so she was famous, but Ellen had read all her books and loved them, identifiying with the harassed mothers, the angry, misunderstood children, the frustrated wives.

But I am not frustrated.

The attic was part and parcel of the idea that she had had; the scheme that James had dismissed out of hand; the plan that she had allowed to die because there was no person to give her a little encouragement.

James and Vicky. Her husband and her child. All at once Ellen was fed up with the pair of them. Fed up with worrying about Christmas, fed up with the house. She longed for escape. She would go, now, this minute and call on Ruth Sanderford. Before this brave new courage seeped away, she went downstairs, bundled herself into her coat, found a jar of homemade marmalade and another of mincemeat and put them into a basket. As though she were setting out on some intrepid and dangerous journey, she stepped out into the icy morning and slammed the door shut behind her.

It had turned into a beautiful day. A pale, cloudless sky, sparkling frost on the bare trees, the furrows of plough iron hard. Rooks cawed from topmost branches, and the air was icy and sweet as wine. Her spirits rose; she swung the basket, savouring her rising energy. The footpath lay along the edge of the fields, over wooden stiles. Soon, beyond the hedgerows, Trauncey came into view. A little church with a pointed spire, a cluster of cottages. Over the last stile, and she was in the road. Smoke rose serenely from chimneys, grey plumes in the still air. An old man, driving a pony and trap, clip-clopped by. They said good morning. Ellen went on, up the winding street.

At Monk's Thatch, the For Sale sign was gone. Ellen opened the gate and went up the brick path. The house was long and low, very old, half-timbered with a thatched roof that hung over the small windows like beetling eyebrows. The door was painted blue, with a brass knocker, and, with some trepidation, she gave this a rap, but then, as she stood there waiting, became aware of the sound of sawing.

Nobody answered the door, so after a little, she followed this sound, and in a yard at the side of the house came upon a figure hard at work. A woman, and instantly recognisable from her appearances on Ellen's television screen.

Raising her voice, she said, 'Hello.'

Thus interrupted, Ruth Sanderford stopped sawing and looked up. For an astonished instant, she stayed as she was, bent over the sawhorse, then straightened up, leaving the saw, which stayed where it was, stuck halfway through an old tree branch. Dusting her hands on the seat of her trousers, she came forward.

'Hello.'

She was a person of great distinction. Tall, slim, strong as a man. Grey hair was drawn back into a knot at the back of her head, and her face was tanned, dark-eyed, cleanly featured. She wore, with her stained trousers, a navy guernsey and a spotted handkerchief knotted around her neck. 'Who are you?'

She did not sound rude, but as though she really wanted to know.

'I . . . I'm Ellen Parry. A friend of Cynthia's. She told me to come and see you.'

Ruth Sanderford smiled. It wa a beautiful smile, warm and friendly. Ellen instantly stopped feeling nervous. 'Of course. She told me about you.'

'I only came to say hello. I won't disturb you if you're busy.'

'You're not disturbing me. I've just about finished.' She went back to the sawhorse, stooped, and gathered up into her capable arms a bundle of newly sawn logs. 'I don't need to do this – I've got a store of firewood up to the ceiling – but I've been writing for two days, and I find a bit of physical work good therapy. Besides, it's such a magic morning, it's almost a crime to stay indoors. Come on in, I'll give you a cup of coffee.'

She led the way back down the path, freed a hand to turn the latch of the door, and pushed it open with her foot. She was so tall that she had to duck her head in order not to hit it on the lintel, but Ellen, who was a good deal smaller, did not have to duck, and, filled with a sort of amazed relief that the initial introduction was safely over, followed Ruth Sanderford into the house, closing the door behind them.

They had descended two steps straight into a living room, which was so long and spacious that it must surely take up most of the ground floor of the little house. At one end was an open fireplace, at the other a great cherry-wood table. On this stood an open typewriter, boxes of paper, reference books, a mug of sharpened pencils, and a Victorian ewer filled with dried flowers and grasses.

Ellen said, 'what a lovely room.'

Her hostess piled the logs into an already brimming basket and turned to face Ellen.

'Sorry about the mess. Like I said, I've been working.'

'I don't think it's a mess.' Shabby perhaps, and a bit untidy, but so welcoming, with its book-lined walls and worn old sofas, drawn up either side of the fireplace. As well, there were a great many photographs standing about, and odd pieces of beautiful china. 'It's just the way a room should look. Lived in and warm.' She put her basket on the table. 'I brought you something. Marmalade and mincemeat. Not very exciting.'

'Oh, how kind.' She laughed. 'A before-Christmas present. And I've run out of marmalade. Let's take it into the kitchen and I'll put the kettle on.'

Ellen shed her sheepskin coat and followed Ruth through a latched door at the back of the room, into a small and humble kitchen which might once have been a wash-house. Ruth filled the kettle and put it to boil on the gas cooker. She rummaged in a cupboard for coffee and took two mugs from a shelf. She then produced a tin tray with *Carlsberg Lager* written on it, but had something of a hunt before she found the sugar. Despite the fact that she had brought up four children, she was obviously not the domestic type.

'How long have you been living here?' Ellen asked.

'Oh, a couple of months now. It's heaven. So peaceful.'

'You're writing a new novel?'

Ruth grinned wryly. 'That's about it.'

'At the risk of sounding banal, I've read all your books and revelled in them. And watched you on television.'

'Oh, dear.'

'You were good.'

'I was asked to do a programme the other day, but somehow, without Cosmo, there didn't seem much point. We were very much a team. On television, I mean. But actually, now we're divorced, I think we're both much happier. And our children are, too. The last time I lunched with him, he told me he was thinking of marrying again. A girl who's been working with him for the past two years. She's so nice. She'll make him a marvellous wife.'

It was a little disconcerting to be so instantly on the receiving end of another woman's confidences, but she spoke so naturally and warmly that it made what was happening seem perfectly normal, even desirable.

Ruth went on, spooning instant coffee into the mugs, 'Do you know, this is the first time in my life I've ever lived on my own? I was one of a big family, married at eighteen and started a baby right away. After that, there was never a dull moment. People seem to multiply in the most extraordinary way. I had friends, and Cosmo had friends, and then the children started bringing their friends home, and the friends had friends, and so it went on. I never knew how many people I was expected to produce food for. As I'm not a particularly expert cook,

it was usually bowls of spaghetti.' The kettle boiled and
she filled the mugs, and picked up the tray. 'Come along,
let's go back to the fire.'

They sat, each in a corner of a sagging sofa, and faced
one another across the warmth of the blazing fire. Ruth
took a mouthful of coffee and then set down the mug
on the low table that stood between them. She said,
'One of the good things about living alone is that I can
cook when I want, and what I want. Work till two in the
morning if it suits me, and sleep till ten.' She smiled. 'Is
Cynthia a friend of long standing?'

'Yes, we were at school together.'

'Where do you live?'

'In the next village.'

'Do you have a family?'

'A husband and a daughter, Vicky. That's all.'

'Do you know, I'm going to be a grandmother soon.
The very idea I find astonishing. It doesn't seem a moment since my eldest child was born. Life rushes by,
doesn't it? There's never time to do anything.'

It seemed to Ellen that Ruth had done just about
everything, but she didn't say this. She said instead, not
meaning to sound wistful, 'Do your children come and
see you?'

'Oh, yes. They wouldn't let me buy this house until
they'd approved of it first.'

'Do they come and stay?'

'One of my sons came and helped me move in, but
he's gone off to South America, so I don't suppose I'll
see him again for months.'

'What about Christmas?'

'Oh, I'll be alone for Christmas. They've all grown up
now, lead their own lives. They'll maybe land themselves on their father if they're short of a bed. I don't
know. I never know. I never did know.' She laughed,
not at her children, but at herself, for being vague and
foolish.

Ellen said, 'I don't think Vicky's coming home for

Christmas. I think she's going to Switzerland to ski.'

If she expected sympathy and commiseration, she did not get it. 'Oh, what fun. Christmas in Switzerland is perfect. We took the children once when they were little and Jonas broke his leg. What do you do with yourself when you're not being a wife and mother?'

The blunt question was unexpected and a little disconcerting. 'I . . . I really don't do anything . . . ' Ellen admitted.

'I'm sure you do. You look immensely capable.'

This was encouraging. 'Well . . . I garden. And I cook. And I'm on a committee or two. And I sew.'

'Goodness, you're clever to sew. I can't even thread a needle. You only have to look at my chair-covers to see that. They all need to be patched . . . no, they don't, they're beyond patching. I suppose I should buy more chintz and have new covers made. Do you make your own clothes?'

'No, not clothes. But curtains and things.' For a moment she hesitated, and then said, in a rush, 'If you wanted, I could patch your covers. I'd like to do it for you.'

'What about making new ones? Could you do that?'

'Yes.'

'With piping, and everything?'

'Yes.'

'Then will you? Professionally, I mean. As a job. After Christmas, when things have quieted down and you aren't so busy?'

'But . . . '

'Oh, say you will. I don't mind what you charge me. And the next time I go to London I can go to Liberty's and buy yards of the most beautiful Morris chintz.' Ellen could only gaze at her. Ruth looked a little deflated. 'Oh, dear. Now I've offended you.' She tried again, coaxing. 'You could always give the money to the Church, and write it off as good works.'

'It isn't that!'

'Then why are you looking dumbfounded?'

'Because I am. Because this is what I've been *thinking* I should do. Professionally, I mean. Making loose covers and curtains and things like that. Upholstery. Last year I went to evening classes and learned how. And now, with Vicky being in London, and James away all day . . . You see, I've got a lovely attic in my house, very light and warm. And I've got a sewing machine. All I'd have to buy would be a big table . . .'

'I saw one last week in a sale room. An old laundry table . . .

'But the only thing is, that James – my husband – he doesn't seem to think it was a very good idea.'

'Oh, husbands are notoriously bad at thinking anything is a good idea.'

'He said I'd never manage the business side of it. The income tax and the bills and the VAT. And he's right,' Ellen finished sadly, 'because he knows I can't even add two and two.'

'Get an accountant.'

'An *accountant*?'

'Don't say "*An accountant*" like that, as though it were something shameful. You look as though I was telling you to acquire a lover. Of course, an accountant, to do your sums for you. No more buts. You're onto a marvellous idea.'

'Supposing I didn't get any work?'

'You'll get more work than you can cope with.'

'That's even worse.'

'Not at all. You'll enrol some nice village ladies to help you. Give employment. Better and better. Before you know where you are, you'll be running a real little business.'

A real little business. Doing something creative, that she enjoyed and was good at. Employing people. Perhaps, like Cynthia, making money. She thought about it. After a bit, she said, 'I don't know if I've got the nerve.'

161

'Of course you've got the nerve. And you've already got your first order. Mine.'

'It's James. I . . . don't *suppose* he'd mind?'

'Mind? He'll be thrilled to bits. And as for your daughter, it would be the best thing you could do for her. It's not easy for children to leave the nest, especially only children. If you're busy and happy, she need be devilled by no stirrings of guilt. It'll make all the difference to her, and your relationship with her. Come on! You've probably never had the chance to do something on your own, and now here it is. Grab it, Ellen, with both hands.'

Watching her, listening, Ellen suddenly began to laugh. Ruth wrinkled her brow. 'Why do you laugh?'

'I realise now just why you were such a success on television.'

'I tell you why, because I've gone into what my children call my tub-thumping act. Cosmo always called me a rampant feminist, and perhaps I am. Perhaps I always was. I only know that the most important person in the world is oneself. *You* are the person you have to live with. *You* are your own company, your own pride. Self-reliance has nothing to do with selfishness . . . it's simply a well that doesn't run dry until the day you die and you don't need it any more.'

Ellen, oddly touched, could think of nothing to say to this. Ruth turned her head, looked into the firelight. Ellen saw the lines about her eyes, the generous curve of her mouth, the smooth grey hair. Not young, but beautiful; experienced, bruised, perhaps – probably sometimes exhausted – but never defeated. In middle age she had started a new life, in good heart, and without malice, on her own. Surely, with James behind her, it shouldn't be too difficult to follow her example?

She said, 'How soon do you want your loose covers made?'

It was time, at last, to go home. Ellen stood up, pulled on her sheepskin coat, and picked up the empty basket.

Ruth opened the door and they went out together into the frosty garden.

Ellen said, 'You've got a mulberry tree. That'll give you shade when the summer comes.'

'I can't imagine summer.'

'If . . . if you are alone at Christmas, would you like to come and spend the day with James and me? I've made him sound stuffy but he's really very nice.'

'How very kind. I'd love it.'

'That's settled then. Thank you for the coffee.'

'Thank you for my before-Christmas present.'

'You've given me a before-Christmas present, too.'

'I have?'

'Encouragement.'

Ruth smiled. 'That,' she said, 'is what friends are for.'

Ellen walked slowly home, swinging the empty basket, her head buzzing with plans. As she opened the door and went into the kitchen, the telephone started to ring, and she picked up the receiver in her still-gloved hand.

'Hello.'

'Mummy. It's Vicky. I am sorry I haven't been in touch, but I just rang to let you know that I *am* going to Switzerland. I do hope you don't mind, but it's such a lovely chance, and I've never been skiing and I thought perhaps I could come home for New Year. Do you mind dreadfully? Do you think I'm being dreadfully selfish?'

'Of *course* I don't.' And it was true. She didn't think Vicky was being selfish. She was doing what she should be doing, making her own decisions, having fun, meeting new friends. 'It's a wonderful opportunity and you must grab it with both hands.' (*Grab it, Ellen, with both hands.*)

'You are angelic. And you and Dad won't be lonely on your own?'

'I've already asked someone to spend Christmas with us.'

163

'Oh, good. I imagined you both being gloomy and eating a chop and not having a Christmas tree.'

'Then you imagined wrong. I'll post your presents this afternoon.'

'And I'll post you mine. You are a darling to be so understanding.'

'Send us postcards.'

'I will. I promise. I will. And Mummy . . . '

'Yes, my darling?'

'Merry Christmas.'

Ellen replaced the receiver. Then, still wearing her coat, she went upstairs, past Vicky's bedroom, and on up to the attic. There it was, the scent of wood and camphor. There they were, the spacious windows and the wide skylight. There, her table would stand; here, the ironing board, here her sewing machine. Here she would cut, tack, and stitch. In her mind's eye stood images of bolts of linen and chintz, braiding for curtains, rolls of velvet. She would make a name for herself – Ellen Parry. A life for herself. A real little business.

She might have stood there all day, lost in plans, hugging herself with satisfaction, had not she suddenly caught sight of the box containing the Christmas tree decorations.

Christmas.

Less than two weeks away, and still so much to do. The mince pies, the cards, the presents to be posted, the tree to be ordered. She hadn't, she remembered without guilt, even washed up the breakfast things. Jerked back from the future to the even more exciting present, she crossed the empty floor and picked the box up in her arms, and then, bearing the precious load with considerable care, she made her way downstairs.

The White Birds

From the garden, where she was engaged in cutting the last of the roses before the frost set in, Eve Douglas heard the telephone ringing inside the house. She did not instantly rush indoors, because it was a Monday, and Mrs Abney was there, pushing the vacuum cleaner around like a mad thing and filling the house with the smell of furniture polish. Mrs Abney loved to answer the telephone, and, sure enough, a moment later the sitting-room window was flung open to reveal Mrs Abney, waving a yellow duster to attract Eve's attention.

'Mrs Douglas! Telephone.'

'Coming.'

Carrying the prickly bunch in one hand and her secateurs in the other, Eve made her way up the leaf-strewn grass, shucked off her muddy boots, and went indoors.

'I think it's your son-in-law, from Scotland.'

Eve's heart gave a faint lurch. She put the flowers and the secateurs down on the hall chest and went into the sitting room. The furniture was all over the place, the curtains draped over chairs to facilitate floor-polishing. The telephone stood on her desk. She picked up the receiver.

'David?'

'Eve.'

'Yes?'

'Eve . . . look . . . it's Jane.'

'What's happened?'

'Nothing's happened. It's just that we thought last night that the baby was coming . . . and then the pains

165

sort of stopped. But this morning the doctor came, and her blood pressure was a bit high, so he's taken her into hospital . . . '

He stopped. After a little Eve said, 'But the baby isn't due for another month.'

'I know. That's it.'

'Do you want me to come?'

'Could you?'

'Yes.' Her mind flew ahead, checking the contents of the deep freeze, cancelling small appointments, trying to work out how she could abandon Walter. 'Yes, of course. I'll catch the five-thirty train. I should be with you at about a quarter to eight.'

'I'll meet you at the station. You're an angel.'

'Is Jamie all right?'

'He's all right. Nessie Cooper's keeping an eye on him; she'll look after him till you get here.'

'I'll see you, then.'

'I'm sorry to spring this on you.'

'That's all right. Give Jane my love. And, David . . . ' She knew it was a ludicrous thing to say, even as she said it. ' . . . try not to worry.'

Slowly, carefully, she replaced the receiver. She looked up at Mrs Abney, who stood in the open doorway. Mrs Abney's cheerful expression had gone, to be replaced by one of anxious concern which Eve knew was mirrored by her own. There was no need for spoken word or explanation. They were old friends. Mrs Abney had worked for Eve for more than twenty years. Mrs Abney had watched Jane grow up, had come to Jane's wedding wearing a turquoise two-piece and a matching turban hat. When Jamie was born, Mrs Abney had knitted him a blue blanket for his pram. She was, in every sort of way, one of the family.

She said, 'Nothing's gone wrong?'

'It's just that they think the baby's on the way. It's a month early.'

166

'You'll have to go.'

'Yes,' said Eve faintly.

She had been going to go anyway, had everything planned for next month. Walter's sister was going to come up from the south to keep him company and do the cooking, but there could be no question of her coming now, at such short notice.

Mrs Abney said, 'Don't you worry about Mr Douglas. I'll keep an eye on him.'

'But, Mrs Abney, you've got enough to do – your own family . . . '

'If I can't make it in the mornings, I'll nip up in the afternoons.'

'He can make his own *breakfast* . . . ' But somehow that only worsened the situation, as though poor Walter was capable of nothing more than boiling an egg. But it wasn't that, and Mrs Abney knew it. Walter had the farm to run; he was out working from six o'clock in the morning until sunset or later. He needed, got, and consumed meals of enormous proportions because he was a big man and a hard-working one. He took, in fact, a good deal of looking after.

'I – I don't know how long I'll be away.'

'All that matters,' said Mrs Abney, 'is that Jane's all right and the baby too. That's your place . . . that's where you've got to be.'

'Oh, Mrs Abney, what would I do without you?'

'Lots of things, I expect,' said Mrs Abney, who was a true Northumbrian and didn't believe in showing emotion. 'And now, why don't I make us a nice hot cup of tea?'

The tea was a good idea. While she drunk it, Eve made lists. When she had finished drinking it, she got out the car, drove the short distance to the local town, went into the supermarket and there stocked up on all the sort of food that Walter could, if necessary, cope with for himself. Tins of soup, quiches, frozen pies, frozen vegetables. She stocked up on bread, butter, pounds of cheese. Eggs and milk came from the farm, but the butcher wrapped chops and steaks and sausages, found scraps and bones for the dogs, agreed to send a van out to the farm should the need arise.

'Going away?' he asked, slicing a marrow bone in two with his cleaver.

'Yes. Just up to Scotland to stay with my daughter.' The shop was full and she did not say why she was going.

'That'll be a nice change.'

'Yes,' said Eve faintly. 'Yes, it will be very nice.'

She got home and found Walter, who had come in early, sitting at the kitchen table and eating his way through the stew, boiled potatoes, and cauliflower cheese which Mrs Abney had left for him in the bottom oven of the Aga stove. He wore his old working clothes and looked like a ploughman. Once, and it seemed a long time ago, he had been in the Army; Eve had married him as a tall and dashing captain, and they had had a traditional wedding with herself in flowing white and an archway of swords awaiting them as they emerged from the church doorway. There had followed postings in Germany and Hong Kong and Warminster, always living in married quarters, never having a home of their own. And then Jane arrived, and soon after that Walter's father, who had spent his life farming in Northumberland, announced that he had no intention of dying in harness, and what was Walter going to do about it?

Eve and Walter made the great decision together. Walter said goodbye to the Army, spent two years at an Agricultural College, and then took over the farm. It was a decision neither of them regretted, but the hard physical work had left its mark on Walter. He was now fifty-five, his thick hair quite grey, his brown face seamed with lines, his hands permanently engrained with engine oil.

He looked up as she appeared, borne down with laden baskets. 'Hello, darling.'

She sat down at the other end of the table without even taking off her coat. 'Did you see Mrs Abney?'

'No, she'd gone before I came in.'

'I have to go to Scotland.'

Across the table their eyes met. 'Jane?' said Walter. 'Yes.'

The sudden shock of anxiety seemed, visibly, to drain him, to diminish him in some horrible way. Every instinct was to comfort him. She said quickly, 'You mustn't worry. It's just that the baby's going to arrive a little early.'

'Is she all right?'

Matter-of-factly, Eve explained what David had told her. 'These things happen. And she's in hospital. I'm sure she's getting the best of attention.'

Walter said what Eve had been trying not to tell herself ever since David's telephone call. 'She was so ill when Jamie was born.'

'Oh, Walter, *don't* . . . '

'In the old days she'd have been told never to have another child.'

'It's different now. Things are so different. The doctors are so clever – ' she went on, vaguely, trying to reassure not only her husband, but herself. 'You know . . . scans and things . . . ' He looked unconvinced. 'Besides, she wanted another child.'

'We wanted another child, too, but we only had Jane.'

'Yes, I know.' She got up and went to kiss him, putting her arms around his neck, burying her face in his hair. She said, 'You smell of silage.' And then, 'Mrs Abney wil take care of you.'

He said, 'I should be coming with you.'

'Darling, you can't. David knows that, he's a farmer himself. Jane knows it. Don't think about it.'

'I hate you having to go alone.'

'I shan't be alone. I'm never alone as long as I know

that you're around somewhere, even if it's a hundred miles away.' She drew away from him, and smiled down at his upturned face.

'Would she be so special,' Walter asked, 'if she hadn't been an only child?'

'Just as special. No person could ever be as special as Jane.'

When Walter had taken himself off, Eve busied herself, putting the shopping away, making a list for Mrs Abney, stacking up the deep freeze, washing the dishes. She went upstairs to pack a suitcase, but when all this was accomplished, it was still only half-past two. She went downstairs and pulled on her coat and her boots and whistled up the dogs, then set off across the fields to wards the cold North Sea and the little sickle of beach which they had always thought of as their own.

It was October now, still and cool. The first frosts had turned the trees to amber and gold, the sky was overcast, and the sea grey as steel. The tide was out, the sand lay smooth and clean as a newly laundered sheet. The dogs bounded ahead, leaving trails of paw-marks in the pristine sand. Eve followed, the wind blowing her hair across her face, humming in her ears.

She thought of Jane. Not now, lying in some anonymous hospital bed waiting for God knew what was going to happen. But Jane as a little girl, Jane growing up, Jane grown up. Jane with her tangle of brown hair and her blue eyes and her laughter. The small, industrious Jane, sewing dolls' clothes on her mother's old machine, mucking out her little pony, making rock buns in the kitchen on wet winter afternoons. She remembered Jane as a leggy teenager, the house filled with her friends, the telephone endlessly ringing. Jane had done all the maddening, harum-scarum things that all teenagers do, and yet had never herself become maddening. She had never been plain, never sulky, and her natural friendliness and vitality ensured that there had never been a time when she had not had some adoring male in attendance.

'You'll be getting married next,' Mrs Abney used to tease her, but Jane had ideas of her own.

'I'm not getting married until I'm at least thirty. I'm not getting married until I'm too old to do anything else.'

But when she was twenty-one, she had gone to spend a weekend in Scotland, and had met David Murchison and fallen instantly in love, and the next thing Eve was in the thick of wedding plans, trying to work out how the marquee was going to fit onto the front lawn and searching the shops of Newcastle for a suitable wedding dress.

'Marrying a farmer!' Mrs Abney marvelled. 'You'd have thought, being brought up on a farm, you'd have had enough of that sort of life.'

'Not me,' said Jane. 'I'm jumping out of one dung-heap into another!'

She had never been ill in her life, but she was very ill when Jamie was born four years ago, and the baby had been kept in intensive care for two months before he was allowed home. Eve had gone to Scotland at that time, to take care of the little household, and Jane had taken so long to recover and get back her strength that privately Eve prayed that she would never have another child. But Jane thought differently.

'I don't want Jamie to be an only child. It isn't that I didn't adore being one, but it must be more fun to be one of a family. Besides, David wants another.'

'But, darling . . . '

'Oh, it'll be all right. Don't fuss, Mumma. I'm as strong as a horse, it's just that my insides don't seem to be very cooperative. It only goes on for a few months, anyway, and then you've got something marvellous for the rest of your life.'

The rest of your life. The rest of Jane's life. All at once Eve was gripped in a freezing panic. Two lines of a poem she had once read rose from her subconscious and rang through her head like a roll of drumbeats:

Unstoppable blossom
above my rotting daughter . . .

She shivered, chilled to the bone, overwhelmed by every sort of cold. She was now out in the middle of the beach, where an outcrop of rock, invisible at flood tide, was revealed, abandoned like a wrecked hulk by the sea. It was crusted with limpets, fringed with green weed, and on it sat a pair of herring gulls, beady-eyed, screaming defiance at the wind.

She stood and watched them. White birds. For some reason white birds had always been an important, even symbolic, part of her life. She had loved the gulls of childhood, sailing against the blue skies of seaside summer holidays, and their cry never failed to evoke those endless, aimless sunlit days.

And then there were the wild geese which, in winter, flew over David and Jane's farm in Scotland. Morning and evening the great formations crossed the skies, skimming down to settle on the reedy mudflats by the shores of the great tidal estuary that bordered David's land.

And fantail pigeons. She and Walter had spent their honeymoon in a small hotel in Provence. Their bedroom window had faced out over a cobbled courtyard with a dovecote in the centre of it, and the fantails had woken them each morning with their cooing and fluttering and sudden idyllic bursts of flight. On the last day of their honeymoon, they had gone shopping, and Walter had bought her a pair of white porcelain fantails, and they lived still at either end of her sitting-room mantelpiece. They were two of her most precious possessions.

White birds. She remembered being a child during the war, with an older brother reported missing. Fear and anxiety, like a sort of canker, had filled the house,

172

destroying security. Until that morning when she had
looked from her bedroom window and seen the gull
poised on the roof of the house opposite. It was winter,
and the early sun, a scarlet fireball, had just crept up
into the sky, and as the gull suddenly launched itself
into flight, she saw the underside of its wings stained
with rosy pink. The delighted shock of such marvellous
and surprising beauty filled her with comfort. She knew
then that her brother was alive, and when, a week later,
her parents heard officially that he was safe and well
although a prisoner-of-war, they could not understand
why Eve took the news so calmly. But she never told
them about the gull.

And these gulls . . . ? But these were giving nothing
away, no reassurances for Eve. They turned their heads,
searching the empty sands, spied some distant gobbet
of edible rubbish, screamed, stood tiptoe, spread their
massive snowy wings and were away, wheeling and
floating on the arms of the wind.

She sighed, looked at her watch. It was time to return.
She whistled for the dogs, and started the long walk
home.

It was nearly dark when the train drew into the station,
but she saw her tall son-in-law waiting for her on the
platform, standing beneath one of the lights, huddled
into his old working jacket, with the collar turned up
against the wind. Eve got herself out of the warm interior
of the train and felt that wind, which on this particular
station always seemed to blow with piercing chill, even
in the middle of summer.

He came towards her. 'Eve.' They kissed. His cheek
felt icy beneath her lips, and she thought he looked
terrible, thinner than ever, and with no colour to his
face. He stooped and picked up her suitcase. 'Is this all
you've got?'

'That's all.'

Not speaking, they walked together down the platform, up the steps, out into the yard where his car waited. He opened the boot and slung her case in, then went around to unlock her door. It was not until they were away from the station and on the road that led out into the country that she steeled herself to ask, 'How is Jane?'

'I don't know. Nobody will say for certain one way or the other. Her blood pressure soared, that's what really started it all.'

'Can I see her?'

'I asked, but not this evening, Sister said. Maybe tomorrow morning.'

There was nothing much else to be said. 'And how's Jamie?'

'He's fine. I told you, Nessie Cooper's been marvellously kind, she's been looking after him, along with her own brood.' Nessie was married to Tom Cooper, who was David's foreman. 'He's excited at the thought of you coming to look after him.'

'Dear little boy.' In the darkness of the car, she made herself smile. Her face felt as though it had not smiled for years, but it was important, for Jamie's sake, to arrive looking cheerful and calm, whatever horrors were going on in the inside of her head.

When they arrived at last, Jamie and Mrs Cooper were watching television together in the sitting room. Jamie was in his dressing gown and drinking a mug of cocoa, but when he heard his father's voice, he set this down and came to meet them in the hall, partly because he was fond of Eve and looking forward to seeing her again, and partly because he had a very good idea that she might have brought him a present.

'Hello, Jamie.' She stooped and they kissed. He smelled of soap.

'Granny, I had lunch today with Charlie Cooper and he's six and he's got a pair of football boots.'

'Heavens above! With proper studs?'

'Yes, just like real, and he's got a football and he lets me play with him, and I can nearly do a drop kick.'

'More than I can,' Eve told him.

She pulled off her hat and began to unbutton her coat, and as she did this, Mrs Cooper emerged through the open sitting-room door and took her own coat off the hall chair.

'Nice to see you again, Mrs Douglas.'

She was a neat, slim woman, and looked far too young to be the mother of four – or was it five? – children. Eve had lost count.

'And you too, Mrs Cooper. You've been so kind. Who's looking after your lot?'

'Tom. But the baby's teething, so I must get back.'

'I can't thank you enough for all you've done.'

'Oh, it's nothing. I . . . I just hope everything goes all right.'

'I'm sure it will.'

'It doesn't seem fair, does it? I have babies, no trouble. One after the other, easy as a cat, Tom always says. And there's Mrs Murchison . . . well, I don't know. It doesn't seem fair.' She pulled on her coat and did up the buttons. 'I'll come along tomorrow to give you a hand, if you like, if you don't mind me bringing the baby. He can sit in his pram in the kitchen.'

'I'd love you to come.'

'Makes it easier, waiting,' said Mrs Cooper. 'Helps if you've got a body to talk to.'

When she had gone, Eve and Jamie went up to her bedroom and she opened her suitcase, and found his present, which was a model John Deere tractor and which he insisted politely was exactly what he had been wanting, and how had she known? With the tractor safely in his possession, he was happy to go to bed. He kissed her goodnight, and went with his father to have his teeth cleaned and be tucked into bed. Eve unpacked and washed her hands, changed her shoes and did her hair; then she went downstairs, and she and David had a drink together. She went into the kitchen and assembled a little supper for them both, which they ate off a tray by the fire. After supper, David got into the car and went back to the hospital, and Eve washed up. When this was done, she telephoned Walter, and they talked for a little, but somehow there didn't seem to be very much to say. She waited up until David returned, but still he had no news.

'They said they'd ring if anything started,' he told her. 'I want to be with her. I was with her when Jamie was born.'

'I know.' Eve smiled. 'She always said she'd never have had Jamie without you. And I told her that she'd probably have managed. Now, you look exhausted. Go to bed and try to get some sleep.'

His face was haggard with strain. 'If . . . ' The words seemed to be torn from him. 'If anything happens to Jane . . . '

'It won't,' she said quickly. She laid a hand on his arm. 'You mustn't even think about it.'

'What can I think?'

'You must just have faith. And if there's a call in the middle of the night, you will come and tell me, won't you?'

'Of course.'

'Goodnight then, my dear.'

She had told David to sleep, but she could not sleep herself. She lay, in the downy bed, in the darkness, watching the patch of paler darkness that was the night sky beyond the drawn curtains and the open window, and listening to the hours chime by on the grandfather clock that stood at the foot of the stairs. The telephone did not ring. Dawn was breaking before at last she dozed off, and then, almost instantly, was awake again. It was half-past seven. She got up and pulled on her dressing gown and went to find Jamie, who too, was awake, sitting up in bed and playing with his tractor.

'Good morning.'

He said, 'Do you think I can play with Charlie Cooper today? I want to show him the John Deere.'

'Won't he be at school this morning?'

'This afternoon, then?'

'Perhaps.'

'What shall we do this morning?'

'What would you like to do?'

'We could go down to the foreshore and look at the geese. Do you know, Granny, do you know this, there are men who come and shoot them? Daddy hates it, but he says he can't do anything to stop them, because the foreshore belongs to everybody.'

'Wildfowlers.'

'Yes, that's right.'

'I must say it seems hard on the poor geese to fly all the way from Canada and then get shot.'

'Daddy says they *do* make an awful mess of the fields.'

'They have to feed. And talking of feeding, what do you want for breakfast?'

'Boiled eggs?'

'Up you get, then.'

In the kitchen, they found a note from David on the kitchen table:

7 a.m. Have fed the cattle, am just going up to the hospital again. No call during the night. I'll ring you if anything happens.

'What does he say?' asked Jamie.

'Just telling us he's gone to see your mother.'

'Has the baby come yet?'

'Not yet.'

'It's in her tummy. It's got to come out.'

'I don't expect it will be very long now.'

As they finished their breakfast, Mrs Cooper arrived with her large rosy-cheeked baby in a perambulator, which she manoeuvred into a corner of the kitchen.

She gave the baby a rusk to chew. 'Any news, Mrs Douglas?'

'No, not yet. But David's at the hospital now. He'll ring us if there's any.'

She went upstairs and made her bed, and then Jamie's, and then, after a tiny hesitation, went into Jane and David's room in order to make that bed as well.

It was impossible not to feel that she was trespassing. There was the smell of lily-of-the-valley, which was the only perfume Jane ever used. She saw the dressing table, with all Jane's small, personal possessions: her grandmother's silver hairbrushes, the snaps of David and Jamie, the strings of pretty, junky beads that she had hung from the mirror. Clothes lay about: the dungarees that she had been wearing before she was taken off in the ambulance; a pair of shoes, a scarlet sweater. She saw the childish collection of china animals, ranged along the mantelpiece, the big photograph of herself and Walter.

She turned to the bed, and saw that David had spent the night on Jane's side, with his head buried in the huge, white, lace-frilled pillow. For some reason this was the last straw. *I want her back*, she said furiously, to nobody in particular. *I want her back. I want her home, safely, with her family. I can't bear this anymore. I want to know now that she's going to be all right.*

The telephone rang.

She sat on the edge of the bed and reached out and picked up the receiver.

'Yes?'

'Eve, it's David.'

'What's happening?'

'Nothing yet, but there seems to be a bit of a panic on and they don't want to wait any longer. She's being wheeled along to the labour room now. I'm going with her. I'll call you when there's any news.'

'Yes.' *There seems to be a bit of a panic on.* 'I . . . I thought

178

I'd take Jamie out for a walk. But we won't be long, and Mrs Cooper is here.'

'Good idea. Get him out of the house. Give him my love.'

'Take care, David.'

The foreshore lay beyond an old apple orchard, and then a field of stubble. They came to the hawthorn hedge and the stile, and then grass sloped down to the rushes and the water's edge. The tide was out, the great mudflats spread to the further shore. She saw the shallow hills and the huge sky; patches of palest blue, hung with slow-moving grey clouds.

Jamie, climbing over the stile, said, 'There are the wildfowlers.'

Eve looked and saw them, down by the edge of the water. There were two men, and they had built a hide of the brushwood that had been washed up by the high tides. They stood in this, silhouetted against the shining mudflats, their guns at the ready. A pair of brown and white springer spaniels sat nearby, waiting. It was very quiet, very still. From far out in the middle of the estuary, Eve could hear the chatter and gobble of the wild geese.

She helped Jamie off the stile, and hand in hand they made their way down the slope. Where this levelled off they came to a group of plaster birds which the wildfowlers had arranged to resemble a flock of feeding geese.

'They're toy ones,' said Jamie.

'They're decoys. The wildfowlers hope that any geese that fly over will see them and think it's safe to come down and feed.'

'I think that's horrid. I think that's cheating. If any come, Granny, if any come, let's wave our arms and chase them away.'

'I don't think we'll be very popular if we do.'

'Let's tell the wildfowlers to go away.'

'We can't do that. They're not breaking any law.'

'They're shooting our geese.'

'The wild geese belong to everybody.'

The wildfowlers had seen them. The dogs had their ears pricked and were wheeking. One of the men swore at his dog. Nonplussed, not knowing now quite which way to go, Eve and Jamie stood by the ring of decoys, hesitating, and as they did this, a movement in the sky caught Eve's eye and she looked up, and saw, coming from the direction of the sea, a line of birds.

'Look, Jamie.'

The wildfowlers had seen them, too. There was a stir of activity as they turned to face the incoming flight.

'Don't let them come!' Jamie sounded panic-stricken. He pulled his hand free from Eve's, and began to run, stumbling on his short, gum-booted legs, waving his arms, trying to divert the distant birds and turn them away from the guns. 'Go away, go away, don't come!'

Eve felt that she should try to stop him, but there seemed little point. Nothing on earth could halt that relentless flight. And, as well, there was something unusual about these birds. The wild geese flew from north to south on regular flight lines, but this flock approached from the east, from the sea, and with every second they grew larger. For an instant Eve's natural measure of distance was both dazzled and baffled, and then it all clicked into true focus, and she saw that the birds were not geese at all, but twelve white swans.

'They're swans, Jamie. They're swans.'

He heard her and stopped dead, standing silently, his head bent back to watch them fly over. They came, and the air was filled with the drumming and beating of their immense wings. She saw the long white necks stretched forward, the legs tucked up and streaming behind. And then they were over and gone, flying upriver, and the sound of their wings died into the silence, and finally they disappeared, swallowed into the greyness of the morning, the distance of the hills.

* * *

'Granny.' Jamie caught her sleeve and shook it. 'Granny, you're not listening.' She looked down at him. It felt like looking down at a child she had never seen before. 'Granny, the wildfowlers didn't shoot them.'

Twelve white swans. 'They're not allowed to shoot swans. Swans belong to the Queen.'

'I'm glad. I thought they were *beauti*-full.'

'Yes. Yes, they were.'

'Where do you think they're going?'

'I don't know. Up the river. Up to the hills. Perhaps there's a hidden loch where they feed and nest.' But she spoke absently, because she was not thinking about the swans. She was thinking about Jane, and all at once it was intensely urgent that they lose no time at all in getting home.

'Come along, Jamie.' She took his hand, and began to scramble back up the grassy slope towards the stile, dragging him behind her. 'Let's go back.'

'But we haven't had our walk yet.'

'We've walked far enough. Let's hurry. Hurry. Let's see how quick we can be.'

They climbed the stile and ran across the stubble, Jamie's short legs doing their valiant best to keep up with his grandmother's. They went through the orchard, not stopping to look for windfalls or to climb the wizened old trees. Not stopping for anything.

Now, they reached the track that led to the farmhouse and Jamie was exhausted, he could run no further and stopped dead in protest at such extraordinary behaviour. But Eve could not bear to linger, and she swung him up into her arms and hurried on, not minding his weight, scarcely noticing it.

They came to the house at last, and went in through the back door, not even stopping to take off their muddy boots. Through the back porch, into the warm kitchen, where the baby still sat placidly in its perambulator and Mrs Cooper peeled potatoes at the kitchen sink. She turned as they appeared, and as she did this, the telephone began to ring. Eve set Jamie down on his feet and darted to answer it. It had only time to ring once more before she had picked up the receiver.

'Yes.'

'Eve, it's David. It's all over. Everything's all right. We've got another little boy. He had a pretty rough ride, but he's strong and healthy and Jane's fine. A bit tired, but they've got her back into bed, and you can come and see her this afternoon.'

'Oh, *David* . . . '

'Can I speak to Jamie?'

'Of course.'

She handed the little boy the receiver. 'It's Daddy. You've got a brother.' She turned to Mrs Cooper, who was still standing with a knife in one hand and a potato in the other. 'She's all right, Mrs Cooper. She's all right.' She wanted to hug Mrs Cooper, to press kisses on her rosy cheeks. 'It's a little boy, and nothing went wrong. She's all right . . . and . . . '

It wasn't any good. She couldn't say any more. And she could no longer see Mrs Cooper because her eyes had filled with tears. She never cried, and she did not want Jamie to see her crying, so she turned and left Mrs Cooper standing there, and simply went out of the kitchen, out the way they had come in, out into the garden and the cold, fresh morning air.

It was safely over. Relief made her feel so weightless it was as though she could have taken a single leap and floated up, ten or twenty feet into the air. She was crying, but she was laughing too, which was ridiculous, so she felt in her pocket and found a handkerchief, and wiped her eyes and blew her nose.

Twelve white swans. She was glad that Jamie had been with her, otherwise, for the rest of her life, she might have suspected that that astonishing sight had been simply a figment of her own overwrought imagination. Twelve white swans. She had watched them come and watched them go. Gone forever. She knew that she would never witness such a miraculous sight again.

She looked up into the empty sky. It had clouded over, and soon it would probably start to rain. As the thought occurred to her, Eve felt the first cold wet drops upon her face. Twelve white swans. She buried her hands deep in the pockets of her coat, and turned and went indoors to telephone her husband.

The Tree

At five o'clock on a sultry, sizzling London afternoon in July, Jill Armitage, pushing the baby buggy that contained her small son Robbie, emerged through the gates of the park and started to walk the mile of pavements that led to home.

It was a small park and not a very spectacular one. The grass was trodden, the paths fouled by other people's dogs, the flower beds filled with things like lobelia and hot red geraniums and strange plants with beetroot-coloured leaves, but at least there was a children's corner, and a shady tree or two, and some swings and a see-saw.

She had packed a basket with some toys and a token picnic for the two of them, and this was now slung on the handles of the buggy. All that could be seen of her child was the top of his cotton sun hat and his red canvas sneakers. He wore a skimpy pair of shorts and his arms and shoulders were the colour of apricots. She hoped that he had not caught the sun. His thumb was in his mouth, he hummed to himself, *meh, meh, meh,* a sound he made when he was sleepy.

They came to the main road and stood, waiting to cross. Traffic, two lanes deep, poured in front of them. Sunlight flashed on windscreens, drivers were in shirt sleeves, the air was heavy with the smell of exhaust and petrol fumes.

The lights changed, brakes screeched, and traffic halted. Jill pushed the buggy across the road. On the far side was the greengrocer's shop, and Jill thought about

185

supper that evening, and went in to buy a lettuce and a pound of tomatoes. The man who served her was an old friend – living in this run-down corner of London was a little like living in a village – and he called Robbie 'My love' and gave him, free, a peach for his supper.

Jill thanked the greengrocer and trudged on. Before long she turned into her own street, where the Georgian houses had once been quite grand, and the pavements were wide and flagged with stone. Since getting married and coming to live in the neighbourhood, she had learned to take for granted the decrepitude of everything, the dingy paint, the broken railings, the sinister basements with their grubby drawn curtains and damp stone steps sprouting ferns. But over the last two years, hopeful signs of improvement had begun to show in the street. Here, a house changed hands intact, scaffolding went up, great Council skips stood at the road's edge and were filled with all sorts of interesting rubbish. There, a basement flat sported a new coat of white paint, and a honeysuckle was planted in a tub, and in no time at all had reached the railings, twisting and twining with branches laden with blossom. Gradually, windows were being replaced, lintels repaired, front doors painted shiny black or cornflower blue, brass handles and letter boxes polished to a shine. A new and expensive breed of car stood at the pavement's edge and a whole new and expensive breed of mothers walked their offspring to the corner shop, or brought them home from parties, carrying balloons and wearing false noses and paper hats.

Ian said that the district was going up in the world, but really, it was just that people could no longer afford to buy property in Fulham or Kensington, and had started to try their luck further afield.

Ian and Jill had bought their house when they were married, three years ago, but still they had the dead weight of a mortgage hanging around their necks, and since Robbie was born and Jill had stopped working, their financial problems were even more acute. And now, to make matters worse, there was another baby on the way. They had wanted another baby; they had planned for another baby, but perhaps not quite so soon.

'Never mind,' Ian had said when he got over the shock. 'We'll have it all over and done with in one fell swoop, and just think what fun the children will be for each other, only two years apart.'

'I just feel we can't afford it.'

'It doesn't cost anything to have a baby.'

'No, but it costs a lot to bring them up. And buy them shoes. Do you know what it costs to buy Robbie a pair of sandals?'

Ian said that he didn't know and he didn't want to. They would manage somehow. He was an eternal optimist and the best thing about his optimism was that it was catching. He gave his wife a kiss and went out to the off-licence around the corner and bought a bottle of wine which they drank that evening, with their supper of sausage and mash.

'At least we've got a roof over our heads,' he told her, 'even if most of it belongs to the Building Society.'

And so they had, but even their best friends had to admit that it was an odd house. For the street, at its end, turned in a sharp curve, and Number 23, where Jill and Ian lived, was tall and thin, wedge-shaped in order to accommodate the angle of the bend. It was its very oddness that had attracted them in the first place, as well as its price; for it had been allowed to reach a sad state of dilapidation and needed much done to it. Its very oddness was part of its charm, but charm didn't help much when they had run out of the time, energy, and means to attend to the outside painting, or apply a coat of Snowcem to its narrow frontage.

Only the basement, paradoxically, sparkled. This was where Delphine, their lodger, lived. Delphine's rent helped to pay the mortgage. She was a painter who had turned, with some success, to commercial art, and she used the basement as a London pied-à-terre, commuting between this and a cottage in Wiltshire, where a decrepit barn had been converted into a studio, and an overgrown garden sloped down on the reedy banks of a small river. Every so often, Jill and Ian and Robbie were invited to this enchanting place for a weekend, and these visits were always the greatest treat – a feast of ill-assorted guests, enormous meals, quantities of wine, and endless discussions on esoteric subjects usually quite beyond Jill's comprehension. They made, as Ian was wont to point out when they returned to humdrum old London, a nice change.

Delphine, enormously fat in her flowing caftan, was sitting now outside her own front door, basking in the shaft of sunlight which, at this time of the day, penetrated her domain. Jill lifted Robbie out of the buggy, and Robbie stuck his head through the railings and stared down at Delphine, who put down her newspaper and stared back at him from behind round, black sunglasses.

'Hello, there,' she said. 'Where have you been?'

'To the park,' Jill told her.

'In this heat?'

'There's nowhere else to go.'

'You should do something about the garden.'

Delphine had been saying this, at intervals, over the last two years, until Ian told her that if she said it once more, he, personally, would strangle her. 'Cut down that horrible tree.'

'Don't start on that,' Jill pleaded. 'It's all too difficult.'

'Well, at least you could get rid of the cats. I could hardly sleep last night for the yowling.'

'What can we do?'

'Anything. Get a gun and shoot them.'

'Ian hasn't got a gun. And even if he had, the police would think we were murdering someone if we started blasting off at the cats.'

'What a loyal little wife you are. Well, if you won't

shoot the cats, how about coming down to the cottage this weekend? I'll drive the lot of you in my car.'

'Oh, Delphine.' It was the best thing that had happened all day. 'Do you really mean it?'

'Of course.' Jill thought of the cool country garden, the smell of elderflowers; of letting Robbie paddle his feet in the shallow pebbly waters of the river.

'I can't think of anything more heavenly . . . but I'll have to see what Ian says. He might be playing cricket.'

'Come down after dinner and I'll give you both a glass of wine. We'll discuss it then.'

By six o'clock, Robbie was bathed, fed – on the juicy peach – and asleep in his cot. Jill took a shower, put on the coolest garment she owned, which was a cotton dressing gown, and went down to the kitchen to do something about supper.

The kitchen and the dining room, divided only by the narrow staircase, took up the entire ground floor of the house, but still were not large. The front door led straight into this, so that there never seemed to be anywhere to hang coats or park a pram. At the dining-room end, the window faced out onto the street; but the kitchen had enormous French windows of glass, which seemed to indicate that once there had been a balcony beyond, with perhaps a flight of steps leading down into the garden. The balcony and the steps had long since disintegrated – been demolished, perhaps – disappeared, and the French windows opened onto nothing but a twenty-foot drop to the yard beneath. Before Robbie was born they used to let the windows stand open in warm weather, but after his arrival, Ian, for safety, nailed them shut, and so they had stayed.

The scrubbed pine table stood against these windows. Jill sat at it and sliced tomatoes for the salad in a preoccupied sort of way, gazing down at the horrible garden. Encased as it was by high, crumbling brick walls, it was a little like looking down into the bottom of a well. Near the house there was the brick yard, and then a patch of straggling grass, and then desolation, trodden earth, old paper bags that kept blowing in, and the tree.

Jill had been born and brought up in the country and found it hard to believe that she could actually dislike a garden. So much so that even if there had been any form of access, she would not hang her washing out, let alone allow her child to play there.

And as for the tree – she positively hated the tree. It was a sycamore, but light-years away from the friendly sycamores she remembered from her childhood, good for climbing, shady in summer, scattering winged seed-pods in the autumn. This one should never have grown at all; should never have been planted, should never have reached such a height, such density, such sombre, depressing size. It shut out the sky, and its gloom discouraged all life except the cats, who prowled, howling, along the tops of the walls and used the sparse earth as their lavatories. In the autumn, when the leaves fell from the tree and Ian braved the cats' messes to go out and build a bonfire, the resultant smoke was black and stinking, as though the leaves had absorbed, during the summer months, everything in the air that was dirty, repellent, or poisonous.

Their marriage was a happy one, and most of the time Jill wanted nothing to be different. But the tree brought out the worst in her, made her long to be rich, so that she could damn the expense and get rid of it.

Sometimes she said this, aloud, to Ian. 'I wish I had an enormous private income of my own. Or that I had a marvellously wealthy relation. Then I could get the tree cut down. Why hasn't one of us got a fairy godmother? Haven't you got one hidden away?'

'You know I only have Edwin Makepeace, and he's about as much good as a wet weekend in November.'

Edwin Makepeace was a family joke, and how Ian's parents had ever been impelled to make him godfather to their son was an enigma that Jill had never got around to solving. He was some sort of a distant cousin, and had always had a reputation for being humourless, demanding, and paranoically mean with his money. The passing years had done nothing to remedy any of these traits. He had been married, for a number of years, to a dull lady called Gladys. They had had no children, simply lived together in a small house in Woking renowned for its gloom, but at least Gladys had looked after him, and when she died and he was left alone, the problem of Edwin became a constant niggle on the edge of the family's conscience.

Poor old chap, they would say, and hope that somebody else would ask him for Christmas. The somebody else who did so was usually Ian's mother, who was a truly kind-hearted lady, and it took some determination on her part not to allow Edwin's depressing presence to totally dampen the family festivities. The fact that he gave her nothing more than a box of hankies, which she never used, did nothing to endear him to the rest of the party. It wasn't, as they pointed out, that Edwin didn't have any money. It was just that he didn't like parting with it.

'Perhaps we could cut down the tree ourselves.'

'Darling, it's much too big. We'd either kill ourselves or knock the whole house down.'

'We could get a professional. A tree surgeon.'

'And what would we do with the bones when the surgeon had done his job?'

'A bonfire?'

'A bonfire. That size? The whole terrace would go up in smoke.'

'We could *ask* somebody. We could get an estimate.'

'My love, I can give you an estimate. It would cost a bomb. And we haven't got a bomb.'

'A garden. It would be like having another room. Space for Robbie to play. And I could put the new baby out in a pram.'

191

'How? Lower it from the kitchen window on a rope?'

They had had this conversation, with varying degrees of acrimony, too many times.

I'm not going to mention it again, Jill promised herself, but . . . She stopped slicing the tomato, sat with the knife in one hand and her chin resting on the other hand, and gazed out through the grimy window that couldn't be cleaned because there was no way of getting at it.

The tree. Her imagination removed it; but then what did one do with what remained? What would ever grow in that bitter scrap of earth? How could they keep the cats away? She was still mulling over these insuperable problems when there came the sound of her husband's latchkey in the lock. She jumped, as though she had been caught doing something indecent, and quickly started slicing the tomato again. The door banged shut and she looked up over her shoulder to smile at him.

'Hello, darling.'

He dumped his briefcase, came to kiss her. He said, 'God, what a furnace of a day. I'm filthy, and I smell. I'm going to have a shower, and then I shall come and be charming to you . . . '

'There's a can of lager in the fridge.'

'Riches indeed.' he kissed her again. 'You, on the other hand, smell delicious. Of freesias.' He began to pull his tie loose.

'It's the soap.'

He made for the stairs, undressing himself as he went. 'Let's hope it does the same for me.'

Five minutes later he was down again, bare-footed, wearing an old pair of faded jeans and a short-sleeved shirt he had bought for his honeymoon.

'Robbie's asleep,' he told her. 'I just looked in.' He opened the fridge, took out the can of lager and poured it into two glasses, then brought them over to the table and collapsed into a chair beside her. 'What did you do today?'

She told him about going to the park, about the free peach, about Delphine's invitation for the weekend. 'She said she'd drive us down in her car.'

'She is an angel. What a marvellous thought.'

'She's asked us down for a glass of wine after dinner. She said we could talk about it.'

'A little party, in fact.'

'Oh, well, it makes a nice change.'

They looked at each other, smiling. He put out a hand and laid it on her flat and slender stomach. He said, 'For a pregnant lady, you look very toothsome.' He ate a piece of tomato. 'Is this dinner, or are we defrosting the fridge?'

'It's dinner. With some cold ham and potato salad.'

'I'm starving. Let's eat it and then go and beat Delphine up. You did say she was going to open a bottle of wine?'

'That's what she said.'

He yawned. 'Better if it was two.'

The next day was Thursday and as hot as ever, but somehow now it didn't matter, because there was the weekend to look forward to.

'We're going to Wiltshire,' Jill told Robbie, flinging a load of clothes into the washing machine. 'You'll be able to paddle in the river and pick flowers. Do you remember Wiltshire? Do you remember Delphine's cottage? Do you remember the tractor in the field?'

Robbie said 'Tractor.' He didn't have many words, but this was one of them. He smiled as he said it.

'That's right. We're going to the country.' She began to pack, because although the trip was a day away, it made the weekend seem nearer. She ironed her best sundress, she even ironed Ian's oldest T-shirt. 'We're going to stay with Delphine.' She was extravagant and bought a cold chicken for supper and a little punnet of strawberries. There would be strawberries growing in Delphine's wild garden. She thought of going out to pick them, the sun hot on her back, the rosy fruits fragrant beneath their sheltering leaves.

The day drew to a close. She bathed Robbie and read to him and put him in his cot. As she left him, his eyes already drooping, she heard Ian's key in the latch and ran downstairs to welcome him.

'Darling.'

He put down his briefcase and shut the door. His expression was bleak. She kissed him quickly and said, 'What's wrong?'

'I'm afraid something rotten has come up. Would you mind most dreadfully if we didn't go to Delphine's?'

'Not go?' Disappointment made her feel weak and emptied as though all her happiness were being drained out of her. She could not keep the dismay out of her face. 'But – oh, Ian, why not?'

'My mother rang me at the office.' He pulled off his jacket and slung it over the end of the banister. He began to loosen his tie. 'It's Edwin.'

'Edwin?' Jill's legs shook. She sat on the stairs. 'He's not *dead?*'

'No, he's not, but apparently, he's not been too well lately. He's been told by the doctor to take things easy. But now his best friend has what Edwin calls "passed on", and the funeral's on Saturday and Edwin insists on coming to London to be there. My mother tried to talk him out of it, but he won't budge. He's booked himself in for the night at some grotty, cheap hotel and Ma's convinced he's going to have a heart attack and die too. But the nub of the matter is that he's got it into his head that he'd like to come and have dinner with us. I told her that it was just because he'd rather have a free meal than one he has to pay for, but she swears it's not that at all. He kept saying he never sees anything of you and me, he's never seen our house, he wants to get to know Robbie . . . you know the sort of thing . . .'

When Ian was upset, he always talked too much. After

a little Jill said, 'Do we *have* to? I wanted so much to go to the country.'

'I know. But if I explain to Delphine, I know she'll understand, give us a rain check.'

'It's just that . . . ' She was near to tears. 'It's just that nothing nice or exciting ever happens to us nowadays. And when it does, we can't do it because of somebody like Edwin. Why should it be us? Why can't somebody else look after him?'

'I suppose it's because he doesn't have that number of friends?'

Jill looked up at him, and saw her own disappointment and indecision mirrored in his face.

She said, knowing what the outcome would inevitably be, 'Do you want him to come?'

Ian shrugged, miserably. 'He's my godfather.'

'It would be bad enough if he was a jolly old man, but he's so gloomy.'

'He's old. And lonely.'

'He's dull.'

'He's sad. His best friend's just died.'

'Did you tell your mother we were meant to be going to Wiltshire?'

'Yes. And she said that we had to talk it over. I said I'd ring Edwin this evening.'

'We can't tell him *not* to come.'

'That's what I thought you'd say.' They gazed at each other, knowing that the decision was made; behind them. No country weekend. No strawberries to be picked. No garden for Robbie. Just Edwin.

She said, 'I wish it wasn't so hard to do good deeds. I wish they just happened, without one having to do anything about them.'

'They wouldn't be good deeds if they happened that way. But you know something? I do love you. More, all the time, if possible.' He stooped and kissed her. 'Well . . . ' He turned and opened the door again. 'I'd better go down and tell Delphine.'

'There's cold chicken for supper.'

'In that case I'll see if I can rustle up enough loose change for a bottle of wine. We both need cheering up.'

Once the dreadful disappointment had been conquered, Jill decided to follow her own mother's philosophy – if a thing is worth doing, it's worth doing well. So what, if it was only dreary old Edwin Makepeace, fresh from a funeral; it was still a dinner party. She made a cassoulet of chicken and herbs, scrubbed new potatoes, concocted a sauce for the broccoli. For dessert there was fresh fruit salad, and then a creamy wedge of Brie.

She polished the gate-leg table in the dining room, laid it with the best mats, arranged flowers (bought late yesterday from the stall in the market), plumped up the patchwork cushions in the first-floor sitting room.

Ian had gone to fetch Edwin. He had said, his voice sounding shaky over the telephone, that he would take a taxi, but Ian knew that it would cost him ten pounds or more and had insisted on making the journey himself. Jill bathed Robbie and dressed him in his new pyjamas, and then changed herself into the freshly ironed sun-dress that had been intended for Wiltshire. (She put out of her mind the image of Delphine, setting off in her car with no one for company but her easel and her weekend bags. The sun would go on shining; the heatwave would continue. They would be invited again, for another weekend.)

Now, all was ready. Jill and Robbie knelt on the sofa that stood in the living-room bay window, and watched for Edwin's arrival. When the car drew up, she gathered Robbie into her arms and went downstairs to open the door. Edwin was coming up the steps from the street, with Ian behind him. Jill had not seen him since last Christmas and thought that he had aged considerably. She did not remember that he had had to walk with a cane. He wore a black tie and a relentless dark suit. He carried no small gift, no flowers, no bottle of wine. He looked like an undertaker.

'Edwin.'

'Well, my dear, here we are. This is very good of you.'

He came into the house, and she gave him a kiss. His old skin felt rough and dry and he smelt, vaguely, of disinfectant, like an old-fashioned doctor. He was a very thin man; his eyes, which had once been a cold blue, were now faded and rheumy. There was high colour on his cheekbones, but otherwise he looked bloodless, monochrome. His stiff collar seemed a good size too large, and his neck was stringy as a turkey's.

'I was so sorry to hear about your friend.' She felt that it was important to get this said at once.

'Oh, well, it comes to all of us, yerknow. Three score years and ten, that's our alloted span, and Edgar was seventy-three. I'm seventy-one. Now, where shall I put my stick?'

There wasn't anywhere, so she took it from him and hung it on the end of the banister.

He looked about him. He had probably never before seen an open-plan house.

'Well, look at this. And this' – he leaned forward, his beak of a nose pointing straight into Robbie's face – 'is your son.'

Jill wondered if Robbie would let her down and burst into tears of fright. He did not, however, simply stared back into Edwin's face with unblinking eyes.

'I . . . I kept him up. I thought you'd like to meet each other. But he's rather sleepy.' Ian now came through the door and shut it behind him. 'Would you like to come upstairs?'

She led the way, and he followed her, a step at a time, and she heard his laboured breathing. In the sitting room she set the little boy down, and pulled up a chair for Edwin. 'Why don't you sit here?'

He sat, cautiously. Ian offered him a glass of sherry,

and Jill left them, and took Robbie upstairs to put him into his cot.

He said, just before he put his thumb into his mouth, 'Nose,' and she was filled with love for him for making her want to laugh.

'I know,' she whispered. 'He *has* got a big nose, hasn't he?'

He smiled back, his eyes drooped. She put up the side of the cot and went downstairs. Edwin was still on about his old friend. 'We were in the Army together during the war. Army Pay Corps. After the war, he went back to Insurance, but we always kept in touch. Went on holiday once together, Gladys and Edgar and myself. He never married. Went to Budleigh Salterton.' He eyed Ian over his sherry glass. 'Ever been to Budleigh Salterton?'

Ian said that no, he had never been to Budleigh Salterton.

'Pretty place. Good golf course. Of course, Edgar was never much of a man for golf. Tennis when we were younger, and then he took up bowls. Ever played bowls, Ian?'

Ian said that no, he had never played bowls.

'No,' said Edwin. 'You wouldn't have. Cricket's yer game, isn't it?'

'When I can get the chance.'

'Yer probably pretty busy.'

'Yes, pretty busy.'

'Play at weekends, I expect.'

'Sometimes.'

'I watched the Test Match on my television set.' He took another cautious sip at his Tio Pepe, his lips puckered. 'Didn't think much of the Pakistanis.'

Jill, discreetly, got to her feet and went downstairs to the kitchen. When she called to them that dinner was ready, Edwin was still talking about cricket, recalling some match in 1956 that he had particularly enjoyed. The drone of this long story was stilled by her interruption.

Presently the two men came down the stairs. Jill was at the table, lighting the candles.

'Never been in a house like this,' observed Edwin, sitting down and unfolding his napkin. 'How much did yer pay for it?'

Ian, after a tiny hesitation, told him.

'When did yer buy it?'

'When we were married. Three years ago.'

'Yer didn't do too badly.'

'It was in rotten shape. It's still not great shakes, but we'll get it straight in time.'

Jill found Edwin's disconcerting stare directed at herself. 'Yer mother-in-law tells me yer having another baby.'

'Oh. Well . . . yes, I am.'

'Not meant to be a secret, is it?'

'No. No, of course not.' She picked up the cassoulet in oven-gloved hands and pushed it at him. 'It's chicken.'

'Always fond of chicken. We used to have chicken in India during the war . . . ' He was off again. 'Funny thing, how good the Indians were at cooking chicken. Suppose they had a lot of practice. Yer weren't allowed to eat the cows. Sacred, you see . . . '

Ian opened the wine, and after that things got a little easier. Edwin refused the fruit salad, but ate most of he Brie. And all the time he talked, seeming to need no sort of response, merely a nod of the head or an attentive smile. He talked about India, about a friend he had made in Bombay; about a tennis match he had once played in Camberley; about Gladys's aunt, who had taken up loom-weaving and had won a prize at the County Show.

The long, hot evening wore on. The sun slid out of the hazed city sky, and left it stained with pink. Edwin was now complaining of his daily help's inability to fry eggs properly, and all at once Ian excused himself, got to his feet, and took himself off to the kitchen to make coffee.

Edwin, interrupted in his free flow, watched him go. 'That yer kitchen?' he asked.

'Yes.'

'Let's have a look at it.' And before she could stop him, he had hauled himself to his feet and was headed after Ian. She followed him, but he would not be diverted upstairs.

'Not much room, have you?'

'It's all right,' said Ian. Edwin went to the French windows and peered out through the grimy glass.

'What's this?'

'It's . . . ' Jill joined him, gazing in an agonised fashion at the familiar horror below. 'It's the garden. Only we don't use it because it's rather nasty. The cats come and make messes. And anyway, we can't get to it. As you can see,' she finished tamely.

'What about the basement?'

'The basement's let. To a friend. Called Delphine.'

'Doesn't she mind living cheek-by-jowl with a tip like that?'

'She's – she's not here very often. She's usually in the country.'

'Hmm.' There was a long, disconcerting silence. Edwin looked at the tree, his eyes travelling from its grubby roots to the topmost branches. His nose was like a pointer and all the sinews in his neck stood out like ropes.

'Why don't yer cut the tree down?'

Jill sent an agonised glance in Ian's direction. Behind Edwin's back, he threw his eyes to heaven, but he said, reasonably enough, 'It would be rather difficult. As you can see, it's very large.'

'Horrible, having a tree like that in yer garden.'

'Yes,' agreed Jill. 'It's not very convenient.'

'Why don't yer do something about it?'

Ian said quickly, 'Coffee's ready. Let's go upstairs.'

Edwin turned on him. 'I said, why don't yer do something about it?'

'I will,' said Ian. 'One day.'

'No good waiting for one day. One day yer'll be as old as me and the tree will still be there.'

'Coffee?' said Ian.

'And the cats are unhealthy. Unhealthy when children are about the place.'

'I don't let Robbie out in the garden,' Jill told him. 'I couldn't even if I wanted to, because there is no way we can get to it. I think there used to be a balcony and steps down to the garden, but they'd gone before we bought the house, and somehow . . . well, we've never got around to doing anything about replacing them.' She was determined that she would not make it sound as though she and Ian were penniless and pathetic. 'I mean, there's been so much else to do.'

Edwin said 'Hmm' again. He stood, his hands in his pockets, gazing through the window, and after a bit Jill wondered if he was drifting off into some sort of a coma. But then he became brisk, took his hands out of his pockets, turned to Ian and said, testily, 'I thought you were making us coffee, Ian. How long do we have to wait for it?'

He stayed for another hour, and his endless flow of deadly anecdote never ceased. At last the clock from a neighbouring church began to chime eleven o'clock, and Edwin set down his coffee cup, glanced at his own watch, and announced that it was time for Ian to drive him back to his hotel. They all went downstairs. Ian found his car keys and opened the door. Jill gave Edwin his stick.

'Been a pleasant evening. Liked seeing yer house.'

She kissed him again. He went out and down the steps and crossed the pavement. Ian, trying not to look too eager, stood with the door of the car open. The old man cautiously got in, stowed his legs and his stick. Ian shut the door and went around to the driving seat. Jill, smiling still, waved them off. When the car disappeared around the corner at the end of the street, and not before, she let the smile drop, and went inside, exhausted, to start in on the washing up.

In bed that night, 'He wasn't too bad,' said Jill.

'I suppose not. But he takes everything so for granted, as though we all owed him something. He could at least have brought you a single red rose, or a bar of chocolate.'

'He's just not that sort of a person.'

'And his stories! Poor old Edwin, I think he was born a bore. He's so terribly good at it. He probably Bored for his school, and went on to Bore for England. Probably captained the team.'

'At least we didn't have to think of things to say.'

'It was a delicious dinner, and you were sweet to him.' He yawned enormously and heaved himself over, longing for sleep. 'Anyway, we did it. That's the last of it.'

But in that Ian was wrong. That was not the last of it, although two weeks passed by before anything happened. A Friday again, and as usual Jill was in the kitchen, getting supper ready, when Ian returned home from the office.

'Hello, darling.'

He shut the door, dumped his briefcase, came to kiss her. He pulled out a chair and sat down, and they faced each other across the table. He said, 'The most extraordinary thing has happened.'

Jill was instantly apprehensive. 'Nice extraordinary or horrid extraordinary?'

He grinned, put his hand in his pocket, and pulled out a letter. He tossed it across to her. 'Read that.'

Mystified, Jill picked it up and unfolded it. It was a long letter and typewritten. It was from Edwin.

My dear Ian
    This is to thank you for the pleasant evening with you both, and the excellent dinner, and to say how much I

appreciated your motoring me to and fro. I must say that it goes against the grain, being forced to pay exorbitant taxi fares. I much enjoyed meeting your child and seeing your house. You have, however, an obvious problem with your garden, and I have given the matter some thought.

Your first priority is obviously to get rid of the tree. On no account must you tackle it yourself. There are a number of professional firms in London who are qualified to deal with such work, and I have taken the liberty of instructing three of them to call on you, at your convenience, and give you estimates. Once the tree has gone, you will have more idea of the possibilities of your plot, but in the meantime I would suggest the following:

The letter continued, by now reading like a builder's specification. Existing walls made good, repointed, and painted white. A trellis fence, for privacy, erected along the top of these walls. The ground cleared and levelled, and laid with flags – a drain to be discreetly incorporated in one corner for easy cleaning. Outside the kitchen window a wooden deck – preferably teak – to be erected, supported by steel joists, and with an open wooden staircase giving access to the garden below.

I think [Edwin continued] this more or less covers the structural necessities. You may want to construct a raised flower bed along one of the walls, or make a small rockery around the stump of the removed tree, but this is obviously up to yourselves.

Which leave us with the problem of the cats. Again, I have made some enquiries and discovered that there is an excellent repellant which is safe to use where there are children about. A squirt or two of this should do the trick, and once the soil and grass have been covered by flags, I see no reason why the cats should return for any function, natural or otherwise.

This is obviously going to cost quite a lot of money. I realise that, with inflation and the rising cost of living, it is not always easy for a young couple, however hard they work, to make ends meet. And I should like to help. I have, in fact, made provision for you in my Will, but it occurs to me that it would be much more in keeping to hand the money over to you now. Then you will be able to deal with your garden, and I shall have the pleasure of seeing it completed, hopefully before I, too, follow my good friend Edgar, and pass on.

Finally, your mother indicated to me that you had given up a pleasurable weekend in order to cheer me up on the evening of Edgar's funeral. Your kindness equals her own, and I am fortunate to be in a financial position when I am able, at last, to repay my debts.

With best wishes,

Yours

Edwin

Edwin. She could hardly see his spiky signature because her eyes were full of tears. She imagined him, sitting in his dark little house in Woking, absorbed in their problems, working them all out; taking time to look up suitable firms, probably making endless telephone calls, doing little sums, forgetting no tiny detail, taking trouble . . .

'Well?' said Ian, gently.

The tears had started to slide down her cheeks. She put up a hand and tried to wipe them away.

'I never thought. I never thought he'd do anything like *this*. Oh, Ian, and we've been so horrible about him.'

'You were never horrible. You wouldn't know how to be horrible about anybody.'

'I . . . I never imagined he had any money at all.'

'I don't think any of us did. Not that sort of money.'

'How can we ever thank him?'

'By doing what he says. By doing just exactly what he's told us to do, and then asking him around to the garden-warming. We'll throw a little party.' He grinned. 'It'll make a nice change.'

She looked out of the window, through the grimy glass. A paper bag had found its way into the garden from some neighbouring dustbin, and the nastiest of the tom cats, the one with the torn ear, was sitting on top of the wall, eyeing her.

She met his cold green stare with equanimity. She said, 'I'll be able to hang out my washing. I shall get some tubs, and plant bulbs for the spring, and pink ivy-leafed geranium in the summer. And Robbie can play there and we'll have a sandpit. And if the deck is big enough, I can even put the baby out there, in the pram. Oh, Ian, isn't it going to be *wonderful*? I won't ever have to go to the park again. Just think.'

'You know what I think?' said Ian. 'I think it would be a good idea to go and give old Edwin a ring.'

So they went together to the telephone and dialled Edwin's number, and stood very close, with their arms around each other, waiting for the old gentleman to answer their call.

The House on the Hill

The village was miniature. Oliver had never, in all the ten years of his life, seen such a tiny place. Six grey granite houses, a pub, an ancient church, a vicarage, and a little shop. Outside this was parked a rackety-looking truck, and somewhere a dog was barking, but apart from that, there did not seem to be anybody about.

Carrying the basket and Sarah's shopping list, he opened the door of the shop, over which was written JAMES THOMAS, PURVEYOR, TOBACCONIST, and went in, down two steps, and the two men who stood on either side of the counter turned their heads to look at him.

He shut the door behind him. 'Won't keep you a moment,' said the shopkeeper, presumably James Thomas, a small, bald gentleman in a brown cardigan. Quite an ordinary sort of person. The other man, who had purchased and was now paying for an enormous amount of groceries, was, however, not ordinary in the very least, but so tall that, standing, he had to stoop slightly in order not to brain himself on the overhead beams. He wore a leather jacket and patched jeans and huge workman's boots, and his hair was red and so was his beard. Oliver, knowing that it was rude to stare, stared, and the man stared back from a pair of bright, pale blue eyes, unblinking and flinty. It was unnerving. Oliver tried a feeble smile, but this roused no response, and the bearded man said nothing. After a moment, he turned to the counter, feeling in his back pocket for a wad of notes. Mr Thomas rang up his account and handed it over.

'Seven pounds fifty, Ben.'

His customer paid the money, then piled one laden grocery carton onto the other, lifted the pair of them with ease, and turned towards the door. Oliver went to open it for him. As he went through the door, the bearded man glanced down. 'Thanks.' His voice was deep as a gong. *Ben*. You could imagine him growling orders from the poop deck of some pirate ship, or allying a murderous band of wreckers. Oliver watched as he loaded his cartons over the tail-gate of the truck, then climbed into the driving seat and started up the engine. With a roar of exhaust and a spatter of chippings, the scarred vehicle took off. Oliver closed the door and turned back into the shop.

'What can I do for you, young man?'

Oliver handed him the list. 'It's for Mrs Rudd.'

Mr Thomas looked at him, smiling. 'You must be Sarah's young brother. She told me you were coming to stay. When did you arrive?'

'Last night. I came on the train. I had my appendix out, so I've come to stay with Sarah for two weeks till I go back to school.'

'Live in London, don't you?'

'Yes. Putney.'

'You'll soon get strong down here. First time you've been, isn't it? How'd you like the valley?'

'It's beautiful. I walked down from the farmhouse.'

'See any badgers?'

'Badgers?' He did not know if Mr Thomas was teasing him or not. 'No.'

'Walk down the valley at half-light and you'll see badgers. And you go down the cliffs and you can watch the seals. How's Sarah keeping?'

'She's all right.' At least, he supposed that she was all right. She was due to have her first baby in a couple of weeks, and it had been something of a shock to find his slender, pretty sister swollen to whalelike proportions. Not that she didn't still look pretty, just enormous.

'You'll be helping Will on the farm.'

'I was up early to watch him milking.'

'We'll make a farmer of you yet. Now, let's see . . . pound of flour, jar of instant coffee, three pounds of granulated sugar . . . ' He packed the basket. 'Not too heavy for you?'

'No, I'll manage.' He paid, from Sarah's purse, and was given a bar of milk chocolate as a present. 'Thank you very much.'

'Keep you going that walk up the hill to the farm. Take care, now.'

Carrying the basket, Oliver left the village, crossed the main road, and started up the narrow lane that wound up the valley back to Will Rudd's farm. It was a pleasant walk, because a small stream kept the road company, sometimes changing sides, so that every now and then there was a little stone bridge, good for leaning over and looking for fish and frogs. It was open, moorland country, patched with tawny bracken and gorse. The stout gorse stems were the fuel for Sarah's fire – those, and scraps of driftwood which she collected on her walks by the sea. The driftwood spat and smelt of tar, but the furze burned cleanly, to a white-hot ash.

Halfway up the valley, he reached the single lonely tree. An ancient oak, which had somehow dug its roots into the bank of the stream, defied the winds of centuries and grown, malformed and twisted, to venerable maturity. Bare-branched, its fallen leaves lay thick on the ground, and, coming down the hill, Oliver had kicked at these with the toes of his rubber boots. But now, coming upon them, he stopped dead in horrified revulsion, for in the middle of the leaves lay the carcass of a rabbit, newly killed, with fur torn and horrible red guts spilling from the wound in its belly.

A fox, perhaps, disturbed in the middle of his snack. Perhaps, at this very minute, he was waiting, watching from the depths of the bracken with cold and hungry eyes. Oliver glanced about, warily, but nothing moved, only the wind, stirring the leaves. He felt fearful. Something impelled him to look up, and there, high in the pale November sky, he saw a hawk hovering, waiting to pounce. Beautiful and deadly. The country was cruel. Death, birth, survival were all about him. He watched the hawk for a little, and then, giving the dead rabbit a wide berth, hurried on up the hill.

It was comforting to get back to the farmhouse, to shuck off his boots and go through the door into the warm kitchen. The table was laid for lunch, and Will sat there reading the paper, but he laid this aside when Oliver appeared.

'We thought you'd got lost.'

'I saw a dead rabbit.'

'Plenty of those around.'

'And a hawk hovering.'

'Little kestrel. I saw it too.'

Sarah, at the stove, ladled soup into bowls. As well, there was a dish of fluffy mashed potatoes and a loaf of wheaty brown bread. Oliver took a slice and buttered it, and Sarah sat opposite him, a bit away from the table because of her size.

'You found the shop all right?'

'Yes, and there was a man there, hugely tall, with red hair and a red beard. He was called Ben.'

'That's Ben Fox. He rents a little house from Will, up on the hill. You can see his chimney from your bedroom window.'

It sounded spooky. 'What does he do?'

'He's a wood carver. He's got a workshop up there, does quite well. Lives on his own, save for a dog and a few chickens. There's no track to his cottage, so he keeps his truck down on the road, carries everything he needs up on his back. Sometimes, if it's heavy stuff, like a new cultivator, Will lends him the tractor, and in return he gives us a hand at lambing time, or hay making.'

Oliver, eating his soup, thought about this. It all

sounded quite friendly and harmless, but did nothing to explain the coldness of those blue eyes, the unfriendliness of the man.

'If you like,' Will said, 'I'll take you up to meet him. One of my cows has got a passion for that bit of the hill, gets out and takes her calf up there at the drop of a hat. She's up there now. Took off this morning. This afternoon I'll have to fetch her back.'

'You'll need to build up that wall,' Sarah pointed out.

'We'll take a couple of posts and some fencing wire and see if we can make a good job of it.' He grinned at Oliver. 'Like to do that, would you?'

Oliver did not answer at once. In truth, he was apprehensive of meeting Ben Fox again, and yet fascinated by the man. Besides, he could come to no harm if Will was there. He made up his mind. 'Yes, I'd like it.' And Sarah smiled, and poured another ladleful of soup into his bowl.

Half an hour later they set off, with Will's sheepdog at their heels. Oliver carried a roll of fencing wire, and Will a couple of sturdy fenceposts across his shoulder. A heavy hammer weighed down the pocket of his dungarees.

They made their way across the first pastures, climbing up towards the moor. At the top of the last field they came upon the gap in the wall, where the errant cow had knocked aside several stones in her determined efforts to get through. Here Will set down the posts and the hammer and the wire, then climbed the wall and led the way into the tangle of bracken and bramble that lay beyond. A tiny path, a warren, led through the undergrowth, scarcely visible through the thorny gorse bushes, but they came at last to the foot of the great cairns, steep as cliffs, which crowned the hill. Between two of these massive boulders, a narrow gulley led them up to the summit, where the mossy turf was studded with outcrops of lichened granite and the cool, salty air,

211

blown straight off the sea, filled Oliver's grateful lungs. He saw the ocean to the north, the moor to the south; and the little house. They had come upon it almost by surprise. Single-storeyed, crouched against the elements, it snuggled into a natural hollow of the terrain. Smoke rose from a single chimney and there was a small garden, sheltered by a drystone wall. By the wall, placidly munching, stood Will's cow and her calf.

'You stupid animal,' Will told her. They left her, browsing, and went around to the front of the house, where stood a spacious wooden shed with a corrugated iron roof. The door of this was open and from inside came the whine of a chain saw, and then a ferocious barking, and the next moment a great black and white dog bounded out at them, making a fearful racket, but not, Oliver was glad to realise, with the intention of doing anything worse.

Will stooped to greet the animal. The sound of the chain saw abruptly ceased. Presently Ben Fox himself appeared in the open doorway.

'Will.' That deep growl of a voice. 'Come for the cow, have you?'

'Hope she's done no damage.'

'Not that I know of.'

'I'll fence the gap.'

'She's better down in the pasture, might come to harm up here.' His eyes moved down to Oliver, who stood, with his face tipped up, staring.

'This is Sarah's brother, Oliver,' Will told him.

'Met you this morning, didn't I?'

'Yes. In the shop.'

'I didn't realise who you were.' He turned back to Will. 'Like a cup of tea?'

'If you're making one.'

'Come on inside, then.'

They followed him through a gate in the wall, which was opened and then firmly latched shut behind them. The garden was neat and marvellously productive, filled with vegetables and little apple trees. Ben Fox toed off his boots and went indoors, ducking his great red head beneath the lintel, and Will and Oliver did likewise, stepping down into a room so unexpected that Oliver could only gaze in disbelief. For every wall was covered with bookshelves, and every shelf was crammed with books. As well as this, the furniture was surprising. A great big sofa, an elegant brocade chair, an expensive hi-fi with stacks of long-playing records. The plain wooden floor was scattered with rugs which Oliver thought beautiful and decided probably precious. A fire burned in the cave of a fireplace, and on the granite slab of the mantleshelf stood an astonishing clock, gold and turquoise enamel, with its slowly turning mechanism visible through glass.

Everything, although cluttered, was nevertheless neat and ship-shape, and there was something of this neatness about Ben Fox, too, as he filled the kettle and plugged it in and reached for mugs and a jug of milk and a sugar bowl. The tea made, the three of them sat at the scrubbed table, and the men talked together, not including Oliver in their discussion. He sat, quiet as a mouse, taking surreptitious glances at his host's face, in between sips of scalding tea. Looking at him, he was certain of mystery, baffled by those empty eyes.

When it came time to go, having contributed nothing to the conversation, he said, 'Thank you.' The ensuing silence was disconcerting. He added, 'For the tea.'

There was no smile. 'You're welcome,' said Ben Fox. That was all. It was time to go. They rounded up the cow and the calf and headed for home. Ben Fox watched them go. At the top of the hill, just before they descended into the gulley, Oliver turned to wave goodbye, but the bearded man had disappeared, and so had his dog, and as Oliver cautiously followed Will down the precipitous track, he heard the sound of the chain saw start up again.

*   *   *

As Will mended the gap in the wall, 'Who is he?' Oliver asked.

'Ben Fox.'

'But don't you know anything about him?'

'No, and I don't want to, either, unless he chooses to tell me. A man has a right to privacy. Why should I pry?'

'How long has he lived here?'

'Couple of years.'

It seemed amazing that a man could be your close neighbour for two years, and still you knew nothing about him.

'Perhaps he's a criminal. On the run from the law. He could be. He looks like a pirate.'

'Never judge a man by his appearance,' said Will, shortly for him. 'All I know is, he's a craftsman, and he's hardworking and seems to be making a living for himself. Pays his rent regularly. What more would I want to know about him? Now you hold the hammer and take this end of the wire . . . '

Later, he tried pumping Sarah, but she was no more informative than Will had been.

'Does he ever come and see you?' he wanted to know.

'No. We asked him for Christmas, but he said he was better on his own.'

'Does he have friends?'

'Not close friends. But sometimes, you'll see him in the pub on a Saturday night, and people seem to like him all right . . . he's just very reserved.'

'Perhaps he's got a secret.'

Sarah laughed. 'Don't we all?'

Perhaps he's a murderer. The thought flashed across the back of his mind, but was too terrible to say aloud. 'His house is full of books and precious things.'

'I think he's a cultured man.'

'Perhaps they're *loot*.'

'I doubt it.'

She maddened him. 'But, Sarah, don't you want to *know?'*

'Oh, Oliver.' She rumpled his hair. 'Leave poor Ben Fox be.'

That night, as they sat by the fire, the wind began to get up. Gently at first, whining and whistling, and then with a greater force, roaring up the valley, striking the thick walls of the old house in great thumps and clouts. Windows rattled and curtains stirred. When he went to bed, Oliver lay for some time and listened, awestruck, to its fury. Every so often there would be a lull, and then he could hear the murmurous roar of the sea breaking against the cliffs beyond the village.

He imagined the monstrous rollers, surging in; thought of the dead rabbit and the hovering hawk and all the terrors of this primaeval countryside. He thought of the little house, high and exposed on the top of the hill, and Ben Fox inside it, with his dog and his books and his unsmiling eyes and his secret. *Perhaps he's a murderer.* He shivered and rolled over in bed, pulling the blankets over his ears, but nothing could keep out the sound of the wind.

The next morning the storm had not abated. The farm-yard lay littered with blown debris and one or two smashed slates that had been torn from the steading roof, but the damage was not instantly visible because the wind had brought rain on its wings, a thick driving mist that blurred and blotted out all visibility. It was like being marooned in a cloud.

'Dirty morning,' said Will at breakfast. He was dressed in his good suit and a collar and tie because he was going to market. Oliver went to the door to watch him leave, driving the truck so that Sarah could have the use of the car. As the truck bumped over the cattle grid of the first gateway, it disappeared, swallowed into the murk. Oliver shut the door and went back into the kitchen.

'What do you want to do with yourself?' Sarah asked him, 'I've got some drawing paper and new felt pens for you. Bought them in case of a rainy day.'

But he didn't feel much like drawing. 'What are *you* going to do?'

'A bit of baking.'

'Rock buns?' He was very fond of Sarah's rock buns.

'I've run out of dried fruit.'

'I could go to the shop and get some.'

She smiled down at him. 'Wouldn't you mind, walking all that way in this fog?'

'No, I'll be all right.'

'Well, if that's what you want to do. But put on your oilskin and your boots.'

With her purse in his pocket, and his oilskin buttoned up to his neck, he set off, feeling adventurous – like an explorer – and exhilarated by the force of the wind. It was aginst him, so that he had sometimes to lean against it, and it drenched him in mist so that in no time his hair was plastered to his head and there was an ominous trickle of water down the back of his neck. The ground beneath his feet was heavy with mud and littered with torn bracken, and when he reached the first bridge and paused to lean over, he saw the swollen brown waters of the stream, pouring in a torrent down towards the sea.

It was very exhausting. To cheer himself on, he thought of the return journey when he would at least have the wind at his back. Perhaps Mr Thomas would give him another bar of chocolate to munch on the way home.

But as it happened, he never got to the village or the shop. Because when he came to the bend of the lane where the oak tree stood, he could go no further. The old tree, after centuries, had succumbed at last to the wind; had been torn up by the roots, and lay in a confusion of massive trunk and shattered limbs across the road, its topmost branches tangled inextricably with the broken wires of the telephone line.

It was an awesome sight. But what frightened him more was the knowledge that this disaster could only just have happened, for Will had got through in his truck. *It could have fallen on me.* He had a vision of himself, trapped beneath that monstrous trunk, dead as the rabbit, for no living being could survive such a horrible fate. His mouth was dry. He swallowed the lump in his throat, shivered with a sudden chill, and then turned and ran all the way home.

'Sarah!'

But she was not in the kitchen.

'Sarah!' He had pulled off his boots, was fumbling with the toggles of his streaming oilskin.

'I'm in the bedroom.'

He raced upstairs in stockinged feet. 'Sarah, the oak tree's fallen across the road. I couldn't get to the village. And . . . ' He stopped. Something was wrong. Sarah, still fully dressed, lay across the bed, her hand over her eyes, her face very pale. 'Sarah?' Slowly, she took her hand away, her eyes met his; she managed a smile. 'Sarah, what is it?'

'I . . . was making the bed. And I . . . Oliver, I think I've started the baby.'

'Started . . . ? But you're not meant to have it for another two weeks.'

'Yes, I know.'

'Are you *sure*?'

After a little she said, 'Yes, I'm sure. Perhaps we should ring the hospital.'

'We can't. The tree's broken the telephone line.'

The road blocked. The telephone dead. And Will far away in Truro. They looked at each other in a silence fraught with apprehension and dismay.

He knew he must do something. 'I'll get to the village. I'll climb through the tree, or go round by the moor.'

'No.' She was herself again, blessedly in charge. She sat up, swinging her legs over the side of the bed. 'That would take too long.'

'Is the baby coming *soon?*'

She managed a grin. 'Not immediately. I'll be all right for a bit. But I don't think we should waste any time.'

'Then tell me what to do.'

'Fetch Ben Fox,' Sarah told him. 'You can find the way, you went yesterday with Will. Tell him to come and help us – and he'll need to bring his chain saw for the tree.'

Fetch Ben Fox. Oliver gazed in horror at his sister. Fetch Ben Fox . . . go alone, up the hill, in the fog, to fetch Ben Fox. He wondered if she had any idea of what she was asking of him. But as he stood there, she pulled herself cautiously to her feet, placing her hands around the great curve of her abdomen, and he knew a strange surge of protectiveness, as though he were not a boy but a grown man.

He said, 'You'll be all right?'

'Yes. I'll maybe make a cup of tea and sit down for a bit.'

'I'll be as fast as I can. I'll run all the way.'

He thought of taking Will's sheepdog with him, but the sheepdog was a one-man animal and would not leave the farmyard, so he had to set off on his own, heading for the fields across which, yesterday, he and Will had made their way. Despite the fog, the first bit was not difficult, and without much delay he found the gap in the wall where they had fixed the makeshift fence, but once he had scrambled over this and into the tangle of undergrowth that lay beyond, he was in trouble. The wind up here seemed fiercer than ever, the rain even colder. It drove into his eyes, blinding him, and he could not find the path, could not see beyond the end of his nose. All sense of distance and direction were lost.

Brambles tripped him up, gorse tore at his legs, and more than once he slipped in the mud and fell, painfully bruising his knees. But somehow he struggled on, always climbing. He told himself that all he had to do was get to the top; after that it would be easy. he would find Ben Fox's house. He would find Ben Fox.

After what seemed like an eternity he realised that he had reached, at last, the base of the rocks. He put up his hands and leaned against the solid wall of granite, wet and cold and steep as a cliff. The path, yet again, had disappeared, and he knew that he had to find the gulley. But how? Out of breath, waist-deep in gorse, lost, he was all at once filled with a panic that was magnified by his own loneliness and hopeless sense of urgency, and he heard himself, like a baby, whimpering. He bit his lip, closed his eyes and thought hard, and then, keeping close to the rock, edged his way around its base. After a little, it began to curve inwards, and peering upwards, he saw the two flanks of the gulley rearing up towards the low, flying grey sky.

With a sob of relief he began to scramble, on all fours, up the steep track. He was dirty, muddy, bleeding, and wet, but he had found the way. He was on the summit and he could not see the house, but he knew that it was there. He began to run, stumbled, fell, got up and ran on. Then the dog began to bark, and out of the mist emerged the line of the roof, the chimney, the light in the window.

He was at the wall, the garden gate. As he struggled with the latch, the front door was opened, and light and the barking dog poured out towards him, and Ben Fox stood there.

'Who's that?'

He went up the path. 'It's me.'

'What's wrong?'

Incoherent, breathless, weak with relief, Oliver began to gabble.

'Now, take a deep breath. You're all right.' Holding

219

Oliver's shoulders, he squatted before him, so that their eyes were level. 'What's happened?'

Oliver took the deep breath and let it all out again, and told him. When he had finished, Ben Fox, surprisingly, did not leap immediately into action. he said, 'And you found your way up the hill?'

'I got lost. I kept getting lost, but I found the gulley and then I was all right.'

'Good boy.' He gave him a little pat and then stood up. 'I'll get a coat and the chain saw . . . '

The descent to the farm, hand in hand with Ben Fox, and with the black and white dog bounding down the hill before them, was so simple and quick, it was hard to believe that it had taken him so long to make the outward journey. In the farmhouse they found Sarah waiting for them, looking quite tranquil and recovered by the fire, and drinking tea. She had packed a suitcase, and this stood waiting by the door.

'Oh, Ben.'

'Are you all right?'

'Yes. I had another pain. I think they're coming every half hour.'

'We've time, then. I'll go and sort out that tree, and then get you to hospital.'

'I'm sorry.'

'Don't be sorry. Just be proud of that young brother of yours. He did well to find me.' He looked down at Oliver. 'Coming with me, or staying here?'

'I'll come with you.' Panic was forgotten, along with bleeding hands and bruised knees. 'I'll help.'

And so they worked together, Ben Fox demolishing the tangle of branches that had torn down the telephone wires, and, as they fell, Oliver hauling them aside, out of the way. It was a rough job that they did, but at last they had cleared a space between the road and the stream through which a car could conceivably make its way. When this was done, they went back to the farmhouse, collected Sarah and her suitcase, and all piled into her car.

When they reached the fallen tree, Sarah was horrified. 'You'll never get through there.'

'Well, we'll have a good try,' said Ben, and drove straight for the narrow gap, and there were the most terrible scratching and scraping sounds as they did so, but at least they were through.

'What's Will going to say when he sees what you've done to his car?'

'He'll have better things to worry about. Like a baby.'

'They won't be expecting me at the hospital, not for another two weeks.'

'That doesn't matter.'

' . . . and Will. I ought to telephone Will.'

'I'll get hold of Will. You just relax and hold tight, because we're going to drive like the hounds of hell. It's just a pity we haven't got a police siren.'

He did not drive like the hounds of hell because of the fog, but even so they made pretty good time, and before long had driven beneath the red brick arch and into the forecourt of the little country hospital.

Ben bundled Sarah and her suitcase out of the car. Oliver wanted to go too, but was told to stay and wait.

He did not want to be left alone. 'Why have I got to stay?'

'You do as you're told,' said Sarah, and reached in to kiss him goodbye. He clung to her, and when she had gone, sat back in the seat and felt tearful. Not simply because he was very tired, and because his knees and his hands had started to hurt again, but because there was a niggling anxiety inside him, which, on inspection, proved to be concern for his sister. Did it matter that the baby was going to arrive two weeks early? Would there be anything wrong with it? He imagined a shortage of toes, a swivelling eye. The rain still fell; the morning seemed to have lasted forever. He looked at his watch, and saw, with some amazement, that it was not yet noon. He wished that Ben Fox would come back.

He appeared at last, striding across the forecourt and looking more incongruous than ever in these neat hospital surroundings. He got back in behind the driving wheel, and slammed the door shut. For a long moment he said nothing. Oliver wondered if he was about to be told that Sarah was already dead.

He swallowed the lump in his throat. 'Did – did they mind her being early?' His own voice sounded strange and squeaky.

Ben ran his fingers through his thick red hair. 'No. They've got a bed for her, and she should be in the labour room by now. All very organised.'

'Why have you been so long?'

'I had to get hold of Will. I rang Truro market. It took some time to find him, but he's on his way.'

'Does . . . ?' It was impossible to talk to the back of a person's head. Oliver climbed through to the front seat. 'Does it matter, the baby being two weeks early? I mean, there won't be anything wrong with it?'

Ben turned to face Oliver, and Oliver saw that his strange eyes looked different, not flinty any longer but gentle, like the sky on a cool spring morning. He said, 'You been worrying about her?'

'A bit.'

'She'll be fine. She's a healthy girl, and nature's a wonderful thing.'

'I think,' Oliver said, 'I think it's frightening.'

Ben waited for him to enlarge on this, and suddenly, it was easy to confide, to say things to this man that he would have confessed to nobody, not even Will. 'It's cruel. I never lived in the country before. I never realised it. But the valley and the farm . . . they're full of foxes and hawks, all killing each other, and there was a dead rabbit on the road yesterday morning. And last night the wind was so wild, and I could hear the sea, and I kept thinking of drowned sailors and wrecked ships.

222

Why does it have to be like that? And then the tree falling down, and the baby coming early . . . '

'I told you. You mustn't worry about the baby. He's just a bit impatient, that's all.'

Oliver remained unconvinced. 'But how do you *know*?'

'I know,' was the quiet reply.

'Have *you* ever had a baby?'

The question was blurted out before he had time to think. As soon as he had said the words, he regretted them, for Ben Fox turned away from him, and Oliver could see only the sharp angle of his cheekbone, the lines about his eyes, the jut of his beard. A long silence lay between them, and it was as though the man had gone a long way away. At last Oliver could bear it no longer. '*Have* you?' he insisted.

'Yes,' Ben said. He turned back to Oliver. 'But he was stillborn, and I lost my wife as well, because she died soon after. But you see, she had never been strong. The doctors told her she should never have a child. I wouldn't have minded. I'd have settled for it, but she insisted on taking the risk. She said a marriage without children was only half a marriage, and I let her have her way.'

'Does Sarah know about this?'

Ben Fox shook is head. 'No. Nobody down here knows. We lived in Bristol. I was a Professor of English at the University. But after my wife died, I knew I couldn't stay. I threw up my job and sold my house and came here. I'd always worked with wood – it had been my hobby – and now I've made it my living. It's a good place to be, up there on the hill, and people are kind. They leave me alone. Respect my privacy.'

Oliver said, 'But wouldn't it help to have friends? To talk to people?'

'Maybe. One day.'

'You're talking to me.'

'We're talking to each other.'

'I thought you were running away from something.' He decided to make a clean breast. 'In fact I thought you

223

were hiding a secret, that the police were after you, or perhaps you'd murdered somebody. You were running away.'

'Only running away from myself.'

'Have you stopped running yet?'

'Maybe,' said Ben Fox. 'Maybe I have.' Suddenly, he smiled. It was the first time Oliver had ever seen him smile, and his eyes crinkled up, and his teeth were white and straight. He put out a massive hand and rumpled Oliver's hair. 'Maybe it's time to stop running. Just as it's time for you to come to terms with life. It's not easy. Just a long series of challenges, like hurdles in a race. And I suppose they keep coming until the day you die.'

'Yes,' said Oliver. 'Yes, I suppose they do.'

They sat for a little longer, in a comfortable and companionable silence, and then Ben Fox looked at his watch. 'What do you want to do, Oliver? Sit here and wait for Will, or come with me and we'll find a place to eat?'

Food sounded a good idea. 'What I'd really like would be a beefburger.'

'Me too.' He started the engine and they drove away from the hospital, under the arch, into the streets of the little town, and in search of a suitable pub.

'Besides,' Oliver pointed out, 'Will won't want us hanging around. He'll just want to be with Sarah.'

'Spoken like a man,' said Ben Fox. 'Spoken like a man.'

An Evening to Remember

Under the dryer, with her hair rolled and skewered to her head, Alison Stockman turned down the offer of magazines to read, and instead opened her handbag, took out the notepad with its attached pencil, and went through, for perhaps the fourteenth time, her List.

She was not a natural list-maker, being a fairly haphazard sort of person, and a cheerfully lighthearted housekeeper who frequently ran out of essentials like bread and butter and washing-up liquid, but still retained the ability to manage – for a day or so at any rate – by sheer improvisation, and the deep-seated conviction that it didn't much matter anyway.

It wasn't that she didn't sometimes make lists, it was because she made them on the spur of the moment, using any small scrap of paper that came to hand. Backs of envelopes, cheque stubs, old bills. This added a certain mystery to life. *Lampshade. How much?* she would find, scrawled on a receipt for coal delivered six months previously, and would spend several engrossed moments trying to recall what on earth this missive could have meant. Which lampshade? And how much had it cost?

Ever since they had moved out of London and into the country, she had been slowly trying to furnish and decorate their new house, but there never seemed to be enough time or money to spare – two small children used up almost all of these commodities – and there were still rooms with the wrong sort of wallpaper, or no carpets, or lamps without lampshades.

This list, however, was different. This list was for

tomorrow night, and so important was it that she had specially bought the little pad with pencil attached; and had written down, with the greatest concentration, every single thing that had to be bought, cooked, polished, cleaned, washed, ironed, or peeled.

Vacuum dining room, polish silver. She ticked that one off. *Lay table.* She ticked that as well. She had done it this morning while Larry was at playschool and Janey napping in her cot. 'Won't the glasses get dusty?' Henry had asked when she had told him her plans, but Alison assured him that they wouldn't, and anyway the meal would be eaten by candlelight, so if the glasses were dusty Mr and Mrs Fairhurst probably wouldn't be able to see far enough to notice. Besides, whoever had heard of a dusty wineglass?

Order fillet of beef. That got a tick as well. *Peel potatoes.* Another tick; they were in a bowl of water in the larder along with a small piece of coal. *Take prawns out of freezer.* That was tomorrow morning. *Make mayonnaise. Shred lettuce. Peel mushrooms. Make Mother's lemon soufflé. Buy cream.* She ticked off *Buy cream*, but the rest would have to wait until tomorrow.

She wrote, *Do flowers.* That meant picking the first shy daffodils that were beginning to bloom in the garden and arranging them with sprigs of flowering currant, which, hopefully, would not make the whole house smell of dirty cats.

She wrote, *Wash the best coffee cups.* These were a wedding present, and were kept in a corner cupboard in the sitting room. They would, without doubt, be dusty, even if the wineglasses weren't.

She wrote, *Have a bath.*

This was essential, even if she had it at two o'clock tomorrow afternoon. Preferably after she had brought in the coal and filled the log basket.

She wrote, *Mend chair.* This was one of the dining-room chairs, six little ballon-backs which Alison had bought at an auction sale. They had green velvet seats, edged with gold braid, but Larry's cat, called, brilliantly, Catkin, had used the chair as a useful claw-sharpener, and the braid had come unstuck and drooped, unkempt as a sagging petticoat. She would find the glue and a few tacks and put it together again. It didn't matter if it wasn't very well done. Just so that it didn't show.

She put the list back in her bag and sat and thought glumly about her dining room. The fact that they even had a dining room in this day and age was astonishing, but the truth was that it was such an unattractive, north-facing little box of a room that nobody wanted it for anything else. She had suggested it as a study for Henry, but Henry said it was too damned cold, and then she had said that Larry could keep his toy farm there, but Larry preferred to play with his toy farm on the kitchen floor. It wasn't as if they ever used it as a dining room, because they seemed to eat all their meals in the kitchen, or on the terrace in the warm weather, or even out in the garden when the summer sun was high and they could picnic, the four of them, beneath the shade of the sycamore tree.

Her thoughts, as usual, were flying off at tangents. The dining room. It was so gloomy they had decided that nothing could make it gloomier, and had papered it in dark green to match the velvet curtains that Alison's mother had produced from her copious attic. There was a gate-leg table, and the balloon-back chairs, and a Victorian sideboard that an aunt of Henry's had bequeathed to them. As well, there were two monstrous pictures. These were Henry's contribution. He had gone to an auction sale to buy a brass fender, only to find himself the possessor, as well, of these depressing paintings. One depicted a fox consuming a dead duck; the other a Highland cow standing in a pouring rainstorm.

'They'll fill the walls,' Henry had said, and hung them in the dining room. 'They'll do till I can afford to buy you an original Hockney, or a Renoir, or a Picasso, or whatever it is you happen to want.'

227

He came down from the top of the ladder and kissed his wife. He was in his shirt sleeves and there was a cobweb in his hair.

'I don't want those sort of things,' Alison told him.

'You should.' He kissed her again. 'I do.'

And he did. Not for himself, but for his wife and his children. For them he was ambitious. They had sold the flat in London, and bought this little house, because he wanted the children to live in the country and to know about cows and crops and trees and the seasons; and because of the mortgage they had vowed to do all the necessary painting and decorating themselves. This endless ploy took up all their weekends, and at first it had gone quite well because it was wintertime. But then the days lenghtened, and the summer came, and they abandoned the inside of the house and moved out of doors to try to create some semblance of order in the overgrown and neglected garden.

In London, they had had time to spend together; to get a baby-sitter for the children and go out for dinner; to sit and listen to music on the stereo, while Henry read the paper and Alison did her gros point. But now Henry left home at seven-thirty every morning and did not get back until nearly twelve hours later.

'Is it really worth it?' she asked him sometimes, but Henry was never discouraged.

'It won't be like this for always,' he promised her. 'You'll see.'

His job was with Fairhurst & Hanbury, an electrical engineering business, which, since Henry had first joined as a junior executive, had grown and modestly prospered, and now had a number of interesting irons in the fire, not the least of which was the manufacture of commmercial computers. Slowly, Henry had ascended the ladder of promotion, and now was possibly in line, or being considered for, the post of Export Director, the man who at present held this job having decided to retire early, move to Devonshire, and take up poultry farming.

In bed, which seemed to be nowadays the only place where they could find the peace and privacy to talk, Henry had assessed, for Alison, the possibilities of his getting this job. They did not seem to be very hopeful. He was, for one thing, the youngest of the candidates. His qualifications, although sound, were not brilliant, and the others were all more experienced.

'But what would you have to *do*?' Alison wanted to know.

'Well, that's it. I'd have to travel. Go to New York, Hong Kong, Japan. Rustle up new markets. I'd be away a lot. You'd be on your own even more than you are now. And then we'd have to reciprocate. I mean, if foreign buyers came to see us, we'd have to look after them, entertain . . . you know the sort of thing.'

She thought about this, lying warmly in his arms, in the dark, with the window open and the cool country air blowing in on her face. She said, 'I wouldn't like you being away a lot, but I could bear it. I wouldn't be lonely, because of having the children. And I'd know that you'd always come back to me.'

He kissed her. He said, 'Did I ever tell you I loved you?'

'Once or twice.'

He said, 'I want that job. I could do it. And I want to get this mortgage off our backs, and take the children to Brittany for their summer holidays, and maybe pay some man to dig that ruddy garden for us.'

'Don't say such things.' Alison laid her fingers against Henry's mouth. 'Don't talk about them. We mustn't count chickens.'

This nocturnal conversation had taken place a month or so before, and they hadn't talked about Henry's possible promotion again. But a week ago, Mr Fairhurst, who was Henry's chairman, had taken Henry out to lunch at his club. Henry found it hard to believe that Mr Fairhurst

229

was standing him this excellent meal simply for the pleasure of Henry's company, but they were eating delicious blue-veined Stilton and drinking a glass of port before Mr Fairhurst finally came to the point. He asked after Alison and the children. Henry told him they were very well.

'Good for children, living in the country. Does Alison like it there?'

'Yes. She's made a lot of friends in the village.'

'That's good. That's very good.' Thoughtfully, the older man helped himself to more Stilton. 'Never really met Alison.' He sounded as though he was ruminating to himself, not addressing any particular remark to Henry. 'Seen her, of course, at the office dance, but that scarcely counts. Like to see your new house . . .'

His voice trailed off. He looked up. Henry, across the starched tablecloth and gleaming silverware, met his eyes. He realised that Mr Fairhurst was angling for – indeed, expected – a social invitation.

He cleared his throat and said, 'Perhaps you and Mrs Fairhurst would come down and have dinner with us one evening?'

'Well,' said the chairman, looking surprised and delighted as if it had all been Henry's idea. 'How very nice. I'm sure Mrs Fairhurst would like that very much.'

'I'll . . . I'll tell Alison to give her a ring. They can fix a date.'

'We're being vetted, aren't we? For the new job,' said Alison, when he broke the news. 'For all the entertaining of those foreign clients. They want to know if I can cope, if I'm socially up to it.'

'Put like that, it sounds pretty soulless, but . . . yes, I suppose that is what it's all about.'

'Does it have to be terribly grand?'

'No.'

'But formal.'

'Well, he is the chairman.'

'Oh, dear.'

'Don't look like that. I can't bear it when you look like that.'

'Oh, Henry.' She wondered if she was going to cry, but he pulled her into his arms and hugged her and she found she wasn't going to cry after all. Over the top of her head, he said, 'Perhaps we are being vetted, but surely that's a good sign. It's better than being simply ignored.'

'Yes, I suppose so.' After a little, 'There's one good thing,' said Alison. 'At least we've got a dining room.'

The next morning she made the telephone call to Mrs Fairhurst, and, trying not to sound too nervous, duly asked Mrs Fairhurst and her husband for dinner. Oh, how very kind,' Mrs Fairhurst seemed genuinely surprised, as though this was the first she had heard of it.

'We . . . we thought either the sixth or the seventh of this month. Whichever suits you better.'

'Just a moment, I'll have to find my diary.' There followed a long wait. Alison's heart thumped. It was ridiculous to feel so anxious. At last Mrs Fairhurst came back on the line. 'The seventh would suit us very well.'

'About seven-thirty?'

'That would be perfect.'

'And I'll tell Henry to draw Mr Fairhurst a little map, so that you can find your way.'

'That would be an excellent idea. We have been known to get lost.'

They both laughed at this, said goodbye, and hung up. Instantly, Alison picked up the receiver again and dialled her mother's telephone number.

'Ma.'

'Darling.'

'A favour to ask. Could you have the children for the night next Friday?'

'Of course. Why?'

Alison explained. Her mother was instantly practical.

'I'll come over in the car and collect them, just after tea. And then they can spend the night. Such a good idea. Impossible to cook a dinner and put the children to bed at the same time, and if they know there's something going on they'll never go to sleep. Children are all the same. What are you going to give the Fairhursts to eat?'

Alison hadn't thought about this, but she thought about it now, and her mother made a few helpful suggestions and gave her the recipe for her own lemon soufflé. She asked after the children, imparted a few items of family news, and then rang off. Alison picked up the receiver yet again and made an appointment to have her hair done.

With all this accomplished, she felt capable and efficient, two sensations not usually familiar. Friday, the seventh. She left the telephone, went across the hall, and opened the door of the dining room. She surveyed it critically, and the dining room glowered back at her. With candles, she told herself, half-closing her eyes, and the curtains drawn, perhaps it won't look so bad.

Oh, please, God, don't let anything go wrong. Let me not let Henry down. For Henry's sake, let it be a success.

God helps those who help themselves. Alison closed the dining room door, put on her coat, walked down to the village, and there bought the little notepad with pencil attached.

Her hair was dry. She emerged from the dryer, sat at a mirror, and was duly combed out.

'Going somewhere tonight?' asked the young hairdresser, wielding a pair of brushes as though Alison's head was a drum.

'No. Not tonight. Tomorrow night. I've got some people coming for dinner.'

'That'll be nice. Want me to spray it for you?'

'Perhaps you'd better.'

He squirted her from all directions, held up a mirror so that she could admire the back, and then undid the

232

bow of the mauve nylon gown and helped Alison out of it.

'Thank you so much.'

'Have a good time tomorrow.'

Some hopes. She paid the bill, put on her coat, and went out into the street. It was getting dark. Next door to the hairdresser was a sweet shop, so she went in and bought two bars of chocolate for the children. She found her car and drove home, parked the car in the garage, and went into the house by the kitchen door. Here she found Evie giving the chidren their tea. Janey was in her high chair, they were eating fish fingers and chips, and the kitchen smelt fragrantly of baking.

'Well,' said Evie, looking at Alison's head, 'you are smart.'

Alison flopped into a chair and smiled at the three cheerful faces around the table 'I feel all boiled. Is there any tea left in that pot?'

'I'll make a fresh brew.'

'And you've been baking.'

'Well,' said Evie, 'I had a moment to spare, so I made a cake. Thought it might come in handy.'

Evie was one of the best things that had happened to Alison since coming to live in the country. She was a spinster of middle years, stout and energetic, and kept house for her bachelor brother, who farmed the land around Alison and Henry's house. Alison had first met her in the village grocer's. Evie had introduced herself and said that if Alison wanted free-range eggs, she could buy them from Evie. Evie kept her own hens, and supplied a few chosen families in the village. Alison accepted this offer gratefully, and took to walking the children down to the farmhouse in the afternoons to pick up the eggs.

Evie loved children. After a bit, 'Any time you need a sitter, just give me a ring,' said Evie, and from time to time Alison had taken her up on this. The children liked it when Evie came to take care of them. She always brought them sweets or little presents, taught Larry card games, and was deft and loving with Janey, liking to hold the baby on her knee, with Janey's round fair head pressed against the solid bolster of her formidable bosom.

Now, she bustled to the stove, filled a kettle, stooped to the oven to inspect her cake. 'Nearly done.'

'You are kind, Evie. But isn't it time you went home? Jack'll be wondering what's happened to his tea.'

'Oh, Jack went off to market today. Won't be back till all hours. If you like, I'll put the children to bed for you. I have to wait for the cake, anyway.' She beamed at Larry. 'You'd like that, wouldn't you, my duck? Have Evie bathing you. And Evie will show you how to make soap bubbles with your fingers.'

Larry put the last chip in his mouth. He was a thoughtful child, and did not commit himself readily to any impulsive scheme. He said, 'Will you read me my story as well? When I'm in bed?'

'If you like.'

'I want to read *Where's Spot?* There's a tortoise in it.'

'Well, Evie shall read you that.'

When tea was finished, the three of them went upstairs. Bath water could be heard running and Alison smelt her best bubble-bath. She cleared the tea and stacked the dishwasher and turned it on. Outside, the light was fading, so before it got dark, she went out and unpegged the morning's wash from the line, brought it indoors, folded it, stacked it in the airing cupboard. On her way downstairs, she collected a red engine, an eyeless teddy bear, a squeaking ball, and a selection of bricks. She put these in the toy basket that lived in the kitchen, laid the table for their breakfast, and a tray for the supper that she and Henry would eat by the fire.

This reminded her. She went through to the sitting room, put a match to the fire, and drew the curtains. The room looked bleak without flowers, but she planned to do flowers tomorrow. As she returned to the kitchen, Catkin put in an appearance, insinuating himself through his cat door, and announcing to Alison that it was long past his dinner time and he was hungry. She opened a tin of cat food and poured him some milk, and he settled himself into a neat eating position and tidily consumed the lot.

She thought about supper for herself and Henry. In the larder was a basket of brown eggs Evie had brought with her. They would have omelettes and a salad. There were six oranges in the fruit bowl and doubtless some scraps of cheese in the cheese dish. She collected lettuce and tomatoes, half a green pepper and a couple of sticks of celery, and began to make a salad. She was stirring the French dressing when she heard Henry's car come up the lane and pull into the garage. A moment later he appeared at the back door, looking tired and crumpled, carrying his bulging briefcase and the evening paper.

'Hi.'

'Hello, darling.' They kissed. 'Had a busy day?'

'Frantic.' He looked at the salad and ate a bit of lettuce. 'Is this for supper?'

'Yes, and an omelette.'

'Frugal fare.' he leaned against the table. 'I suppose we're saving up for tomorrow night?'

'Don't talk about it. Did you see Mr Fairhurst today?'

'No, he's been out of town. Where are the children?'

'Evie's bathing them. Can't you hear? She stayed on. She'd baked a cake for us and it's still in the oven. And Jack's at market.'

Henry yawned. 'I'll go up and tell her to leave the water in. I could do with a bath.'

Alison emptied the dishwasher and then went upstairs too. She felt, for some reason, exhausted. It was an unfamiliar treat to be able to potter around her bedroom, to feel peaceful and unhurried. She took off the clothes she had been wearing all day, opened her cupboard and

235

reached for the velvet housecoat that Henry had given her last Christmas. It was not a garment she had worn very often, there not being many occasions in her busy life when it seemed suitable. It was lined with silk, and had a comforting and luxurious feel about it. She did up the buttons, tied the sash, slipped her feet into flat gold slippers left over from some previous summer, and went across the landing to the children's room to say goodnight. Janey was in her cot, on the verge of sleep. Evie sat on the edge of Larry's bed, and was just about to finish the bedtime book. Larry's mouth was plugged with his thumb, his eyes drooped. Alison stooped to kiss him.

'See you in the morning,' she told him. He nodded, and his eyes went back to Evie. He wanted to hear the end of the story. Alison left them and went downstairs. She picked up Henry's evening paper and took it into the sitting room to see what was on television that evening. As she did this, she heard a car come up the lane from the main road. It turned in at their gate. Headlights flashed beyond the drawn curtains. Alison lowered the paper. Gravel crunched as the car stopped outside their front door. Then the bell rang. She dropped the newspaper onto the sofa and went to open the door.

Outside, parked on the gravel, was a large black Daimler. And on the doorstep, looking both expectant and festive, stood Mr and Mrs Fairhurst.

Her first instinct was to slam the door in their faces, scream, count to ten, and then open the door and find them gone.

But they were, undoubtedly, there. Mrs Fairhurst was smiling. Alison smiled, too. She could feel the smile, creasing her cheeks, like something that had been slapped on her face.

'I'm afraid,' said Mrs Fairhurst, 'that we're a little bit early. We were so afraid of losing the way.'

'No. Not a bit.' Alison's voice came out at least two octaves higher than it usually did. She'd got the date wrong. She'd told Mrs Fairhurst the wrong day. She'd made the most appalling, most ghastly mistake. 'Not a bit early.' She stood back, opening the door. 'Do come in.'

They did so, and Alison closed the door behind them. They began to shed their coats.

I can't tell them. Henry will have to tell them. He'll have to give them a drink and tell them that there isn't anything to eat because I thought they were coming tomorrow night.

Automatically, she went to help Mrs Fairhurst with her fur.

'Did . . . did you have a good drive?'

'Yes, very good,' said Mr Fairhurst. He wore a dark suit and a splendid tie. 'Henry gave me excellent instructions.'

'And of course there wasn't too much traffic.' Mrs Fairhurst smelt of Chanel No. 5. She adjusted the chiffon collar of her dress and touched her hair which had, like Alison's, been freshly done. It was silvery and elegant, and she wore diamond earrings and a beautiful brooch at the neck of her dress.

'What a charming house. How clever of you and Henry to find it.'

'Yes, we love it.' They were ready. They stood smiling at her. 'Do come in by the fire.'

She led the way, into her warm, firelit, but flowerless sitting room, swiftly gathered up the newspaper from the sofa and pushed it beneath a pile of magazines. She moved an armchair closer to the fire. 'Do sit down, Mrs Fairhurst. I'm afraid Henry was a little late back from the office. He'll be down in just a moment.'

She should offer them a drink, but the drinks were in the kitchen cupboard and it would seem both strange and rude to go out and leave them on their own. And supposing they asked for dry martinis? Henry always did the drinks, and Alison didn't know how to make a dry martini.

Mrs Fairhurst lowered herself comfortably into the

chair. She said, 'Jock had to go to Birmingham this
morning, so I don't suppose he's seen Henry today –
have you, dear?'

'No, I didn't get into the office.' He stood in front of
the fire and looked about him appreciatively. 'What a
pleasant room this is.'

'Oh, yes. Thank you.'

'Do you have a garden?'

'Yes. About an acre. It's really too big.' She looked
about her frantically, and her eyes lighted upon the
cigarette box. She picked it up and opened it. There were
four cigarettes inside. 'Would you like a cigarette?'

But Mrs Fairhurst did not smoke, and Mr Fairhurst
said that if Alison did not mind, he would smoke one of
his own cigars. Alison said that she did not mind at
all, and put the box back on the table. A number of
panic-stricken images flew through her mind. Henry,
still lolling in his bath; the tiny salad which was all that
she had made for supper; the dining room, icy cold and
inhospitable.

'Do you do the garden by yourselves?'

'Oh . . . oh, yes. We're trying. It was in rather a mess
when we bought the house.'

'And you have two little children?' This was Mrs
Fairhurst, gallantly keeping the ball of conversation
going.

'Yes. Yes, they're in bed. I have a friend – Evie. She's
the farmer's sister. She put them to bed for me.'

What else could one say? Mr Fairhurst had lighted
his cigar, and the room was filled with its expensive
fragrance. What else could one do? Alison took a deep
breath. 'I'm sure you'd both like a drink. What can I get
for you?'

'Oh, how lovely.' Mrs Fairhurst glanced about her,
and saw no evidence of either bottles or wineglasses,
but if she was put out by this, graciously gave no sign.
'I think a glass of sherry would be nice.'

'And you, Mr Fairhurst?'

'The same for me.'

She blessed them both silently for not asking for martinis. 'We . . . we've got a bottle of Tio Pepe . . . ?'

'What a treat!'

'The only thing is . . . would you mind very much if I left you on your own for a moment? Henry – he didn't have time to do a drink tray.'

'Don't worry about us,' she was assured. 'We're very happy by this lovely fire.'

Alison withdrew, closing the door gently behind her. It was all more awful than anything one could possibly have imagined. And they were so nice, darling people, which only made it all the more dreadful. They were behaving quite perfectly, and she had had neither the wit nor the intelligence to remember which night she had asked them for.

But there was no time to stand doing nothing but hate herself. Something had to be done. Silently, on slippered feet, she sped upstairs. The bathroom door stood open, as did their bedroom door. Beyond this, in a chaos of abandoned bathtowels, socks, shoes, and shirts, stood Henry, dressing himself with the speed of light.

'Henry, they're here.'

'I know.' He pulled a clean shirt over his head, stuffed it into his trousers, did up the zipper, and reached for a necktie. 'Saw them from the bathroom window.'

'It's the wrong night. I must have made a mistake.'

'I've already gathered that.' Sagging at the knees in order to level up with the mirror, he combed his hair.

'You'll have to tell them.'

'I can't tell them.'

'You mean, we've got to give them dinner?'

'Well, we've got to give them something.'

'What am I going to *do*?'

'Have they had a drink?'

'No.'

'Well, give them a drink right away, and we'll try to sort the rest of the evening out after that.'

239

They were talking in whispers. He wasn't even looking at her properly.

'Henry, I'm sorry.'

He was buttoning his waistcoat. 'It can't be helped. Just go down and give them a drink.'

She flew back downstairs, paused for a moment at the closed sitting-room door, and heard from behind it the companionable murmur of married chat. She blessed them once again for being the sort of people who always had things to say to each other, and made for the kitchen. There was the cake, fresh from the oven. There was the salad. And there was Evie, her hat on, her coat buttoned, and just about off. 'You've got visitors,' she remarked, looking pleased.

'They're not visitors. It's the Fairhursts. Henry's chairman and his wife.'

Evie stopped looking pleased. 'But they're coming tomorrow.'

'I've made some ghastly mistake. They've come tonight. And there's nothing to eat, Evie.' Her voice broke. 'Nothing.'

Evie considered. She recognised a crisis when she saw one. Crises were the stuff of life to Evie. Motherless lambs, egg-bound hens, smoking chimneys, moth in the church kneelers – in her time, she had dealt with them all. Nothing gave Evie more satisfaction than rising to the occasion. Now, she glanced at the clock, and then took off her hat. 'I'll stay,' she announced, 'and give you a hand.'

'Oh, Evie – will you *really*?'

'The children are asleep. That's one problem out of the way.' She unbuttoned her coat. 'Does Henry know?'

'Yes, he's nearly dressed.'

'What did he say?'

'He said, give them a drink.'

'Then what are we waiting for?' asked Evie.

They found a tray, some glasses, the bottle of Tio

Pepe. Evie manhandled ice out of the icetray. Alison found nuts.

'The dining room,' said Alison. 'I'd meant to light the fire. It's icy.'

'I'll get the little paraffin stove going. It smells a bit but it'll warm the room quicker than anything else. And I'll draw the curtains and switch on the hot plate.' She opened the kitchen door. 'Quick, now, in you go.'

Alison carried the tray across the hall, fixed a smile on her face, opened the door and made her entrance. The Fairhursts were sitting by the fire, looking relaxed and cheerful, but Mr Fairhurst got to his feet and came to help Alison, pulling forward a low table and taking the tray from her hands.

'We were just wishing,' said Mrs Fairhurst, 'that our daughter would follow your example and move out into the country. They've a dear little flat in the Fulham Road, but she's having her second baby in the summer, and I'm afraid it's going to be very cramped.'

'It's quite a step to take . . . ' Alison picked up the sherry bottle, but Mr Fairhurst said, 'Allow me,' and took it from her and poured the drinks himself, handing a glass to his wife. ' . . . But Henry . . . '

As she said his name, she heard his footsteps on the stair, the door opened, and there he was. She had expected him to burst into the room, out of breath, thoroughly fussed, and with some button or cuff-link missing. But his appearance was neat and immaculate – as though he had spent at least half an hour in getting changed instead of the inside of two minutes. Despite the nightmare of what was happening, Alison found time to be filled with admiration for her husband. He never ceased to surprise her, and his composure was astonishing. She began to feel, herself, a little calmer. It was, after all, Henry's future, his career, that was at stake. If he could take this evening in his stride, then surely Alison could do the same. Perhaps, together, they could carry it off.

241

Henry was charming. He apologised for his late appearance, made sure that his guests were comfortable, poured his own glass of sherry, and settled himself, quite at ease, in the middle of the sofa. He and the Fairhursts began to talk about Birmingham. Alison laid down her glass, murmured something about seeing to dinner, and slipped out of the room.

Across the hall, she could hear Evie struggling with the old paraffin heater. She went into the kitchen and tied on an apron. There was the salad. And what else? No time to unfreeze the prawns, deal with the fillet of beef, or make Mother's lemon soufflé. But there was the deep freeze, filled as usual with the sort of food her children would eat, and not much else. Fish fingers, frozen chips, ice cream. She opened its lid and peered inside. Saw a couple of rock-hard chickens, three loaves of sliced bread, two iced lollies on sticks.

Oh, God, please let me find something. please let there be something I can give the Fairhursts to eat.

She thought of all the panic-stricken prayers which in the course of her life she had sent winging upwards. Long ago, she had decided that somewhere, up in the wild blue yonder, there simply had to be a computer, otherwise how could God keep track of the millions of billions of requests for aid and assistance that had been coming at Him through all eternity?

Please let there be something for dinner.

Tring, tring, went the computer, and there was the answer. A plastic carton of Chile con Carne, which Alison had made and stored a couple of months ago. that wouldn't take more than fifteen minutes to unfreeze, stirred in a pot over the hot plate, and with it they could have boiled rice and the salad.

Investigation proved that there was no rice, only a half-empty packet of Tagliatelli. Chili con Carne and Tagliatelli with a crisp green salad. Said quickly, it didn't sound so bad.

And for starters . . . ? Soup. There was a single can

of consommé, not enough for four people. She searched her shelves for something to go with it, and came up with a jar of kangaroo tail soup that had been given to them as a joke two Christmases ago. She filled her arms with the carton, the packet, the tin, and the jar, closed the lid of the deep freeze, and put everything onto the kitchen table. Evie appeared, carrying the paraffin can, and with a sooty smudge on her nose.

'That's going fine,' she announced. 'Warmer already, that room is. You hadn't done any flowers, and the table looked a bit bare, so I put the fruit bowl with the oranges in the middle of the table. Doesn't look like much, but it's better than nothing.' She set down the can and looked at the strange assortment of goods on the table.

'What's all this, then?'

'Dinner,' said Alison from the saucepan cupboard where she was trying to find a pot large enough for the Chile con Carne. 'Clear soup – half of it kangaroo tail, but nobody needs to know that. Chile con Carne and Tagliatelli. Won't that be all right?'

Evie made a face. 'Doesn't sound much to me, but some people will eat anything.' She preferred plain food herself, none of this foreign nonsense. A nice bit of mutton with caper sauce, that's what Evie would have chosen.

'And pudding? What can I do for pudding?'

'There's ice cream in the freezer.'

'I can't just give them ice cream.'

'Make a sauce then. Hot chocolate's nice.'

Hot chocolate sauce. The best hot chocolate sauce was made by simply melting bars of chocolate, and Alison had bars of chocolate, because she'd bought two for the children and forgotten to give them to them. She found her handbag and the chocolate bars.

And then, coffee.

'I'll make the coffee,' said Evie.

'I haven't had time to wash the best cups and they're in the sitting-room cupboard.'

243

'Never mind, we'll give them tea cups. Most people like big cups anyway. I know I do. Can't be bothered with those demmy tassies.' Already she had the Chili con Carne out of its carton and into the saucepan. She stirred it, peering at it suspiciously. 'What are these little things, then?'

'Red kidney beans.'

'Smells funny.'

'That's the chile. It's Mexican food.'

'Only hope they like Mexican food.'

Alison hoped so too.

When she joined the others, Henry let a decent moment or two pass, and then got to his feet and excused himself, saying that he had to see to the wine.

'You really are wonderful, you young people,' said Mrs Fairhurst when he had gone. 'I used to dread having people for dinner when we were first married, *and* I had somebody to help me.'

'Evie's helping me this evening.'

'And I was such a hopeless cook!'

'Oh, come, dear,' her husband comforted her. 'That was a long time ago.'

It seemed a good time to say it. 'I do hope you can eat Chile con Carne. It's rather hot.'

'Is that what we're having for dinner tonight? What a treat. I haven't had it since Jock and I were in Texas. We went out there with a business convention.'

Mr Fairhurst enlarged on this. 'And when we went to India, she could eat a hotter curry than anybody else. I was in tears, and there she was, looking as cool as a cucumber.'

Henry returned to them. Alison, feeling as though they were engaged in some ludicrous game, withdrew once more. In the kitchen, Evie had everything under control, down to the last heated plate.

'Better get them in,' said Evie, 'and if the place reeks of paraffin, don't say anything. It's better to ignore these things.'

But Mrs Fairhurst said that she loved the smell of paraffin. It reminded her of country cottages when she was a child. And indeed, the dreaded dining room did not look too bad. Evie had lit the candles and left on only the small wall lights over the Victorian sideboard. They all took their places. Mr Fairhurst faced the Highland cow in the rain. 'Where on earth,' he wanted to know, as they started in on the soup, 'did you find that wonderful picture? People don't have pictures like that in their dining rooms any longer.'

Henry told him about the brass fender and the auction sale. Alison tried to decide whether the kangaroo tail soup tasted like kangaroo tails, but it didn't. It just tasted like soup.

'You've made the room like a Victorian set piece. So clever of you.'

'It wasn't really clever,' said Henry. 'It just happened.'

The decor of the dining room took them through the first course. Over the Chili con Carne, they talked about Texas, and America, and holidays, and children. 'We always used to take the children to Cornwall,' said Mrs Fairhurst, delicately winding her Tagliatelli onto her fork.

'I'd love to take ours to Britanny,' said Henry. 'I went there once when I was fourteen, and it always seemed to me the perfect place for children.'

Mr Fairhurst said that when he was a boy, he'd been taken every summer to the Isle of Wight. He'd had his own little dinghy. Sailing then became the topic of conversation, and Alison became so interested in this that she forgot about clearing the empty plates until Henry, coming to refill her wineglass, gave her a gentle kick under the table.

She gathered up the dishes and took them out to Evie. Evie said, 'How's it going?'

'All right. I think.'

Evie surveyed the empty plates. 'Well, they ate it, anyway. Come on now, get the rest in before the sauce goes solid, and I'll get on with the coffee.'

Alison said, 'I don't know what I'd have done without you, Evie. I simply don't know what I'd have done.'

'You take my advice,' said Evie, picking up the tray with the ice cream and the pudding bowls, and placing it heavily in Alison's hands. 'Buy yourself a little diary. Write everything down. Times like this are too important to leave to chance. That's what you should do. Buy yourself a little diary.'

'What I don't understand,' said Henry, 'is why you never wrote the date down.'

It was now midnight. The Fairhursts had departed at half-past eleven, full of grateful thanks, and hopes that Alison and Henry would, very soon, come and have dinner with them. They were charmed by the house, they said again, and had so enjoyed the delicious meal. It had indeed, Mrs Fairhurst reiterated, been a memorable evening.

They drove off, into the darkness. Henry closed the front door and Alison burst into tears.

It took quite a long time, and a glass of whisky, before she could be persuaded to stop. 'I'm hopeless,' she told Henry. 'I know I'm hopeless.'

'You did very well.'

'But it was such an extraordinary meal. Evie never thought they'd eat it! And the dining room wasn't warm at all, it just smelt . . .'

'It didn't smell bad.'

'And there weren't any flowers, just oranges, and I know you like having time to open your wine, and I was wearing a dressing gown.'

'It looked lovely.'

She refused to be comforted. 'But it was so important. It was so important for you. And I had it all planned. The fillet of beef and everything, and the flowers I was going to do. And I had a shopping list, and I'd written everything down.'

It was then that he said, 'What I don't understand is why you never wrote the date down.'

She tried to remember. She had stopped crying by now, and they were sitting together on the sofa in front of the dying fire. 'I don't think there was anything to write it down on. I can never find a bit of paper at the right moment. And she said the seventh. I'm sure she said the seventh. But she couldn't have,' she finished hopelessly.

'I gave you a diary for Christmas,' Henry reminded her.

'I know, but Larry borrowed it for drawing in and I haven't seen it since. Oh, Henry, you won't get that job, it'll be all my fault. I know that.'

'If I don't get the job, it's because I wasn't meant to. Now, don't let's talk about it any more. It's over and finished with. Let's go to bed.'

The next morning it rained. Henry went to work, and Larry was picked up by a neighbour and driven to nursery school. Janey was teething, unhappy and demanding endless attention. With the baby either in her arms or whining at her feet, Alison endeavoured to make beds, wash dishes, tidy the kitchen. Later, when she was feeling stronger, she would ring her mother and tell her that there was now no need for her to come and fetch the children and keep them for the night. If she did it now, she knew that she would dissolve into tears and weep down the telephone, and she didn't want to upset her mother.

When she had finally got Janey settled down for her morning sleep, she went into the dining room. It was dark and smelt stalely of cigar smoke and the last fumes of the old paraffin heater. She drew back the velvet curtains and the grey morning light shone in on the wreckage of crumpled napkins, wine-stained glasses, brimming ashtrays. She found a tray and began to collect the glasses. The telephone rang.

She thought it was probably Evie. 'Hello?'

'Alison.' It was Mrs Fairhurst. 'My dear child. What can I say?'

Alison frowned. What, indeed, could Mrs Fairhurst have to say? 'I'm sorry'?

'It was all my fault. I've just looked at my diary to check a Save the Children Fund meeting I have to go to, and I realise that it was *tonight* you asked us for dinner. Friday. You weren't expecting us last night, because we weren't meant to be there.'

Alison took a deep breath and then let it all out again in a trembling sigh of relief. She felt as though a great weight had been taken from her shoulders. It hadn't been her mistake. It had been Mrs Fairhurst's.

'Well . . . ' There was no point in telling a lie. She began to smile. 'No.'

'And you never said a word. You just behaved as though we were expected, and gave us that delicious dinner. And everything looked so pretty, and both of you so relaxed. I can't get over it. And I can't imagine how I was so stupid except that I couldn't find my glasses, and I obviously wrote it down on the wrong day. Will you ever forgive me?'

'But I was just as much to blame. I'm terribly vague on the telephone. In fact, I thought the mix-up was all my fault.'

'Well, you were so sweet. And Jock will be furious with me when I ring him up and tell him.'

'I'm sure he won't be.'

'Well, there it is, and I'm truly sorry. It must have been a nightmare opening your door and finding us there, all dressed up like Christmas trees! But you both came up trumps. Congratulations. And thank you for being so understanding to a silly old woman.'

'I don't think you're silly at all,' said Alison to her husband's chairman's wife. 'I think you're smashing.'

*   *   *

When Henry came home that evening, Alison was cooking the fillet of beef. It was too much for the two of them, but the children could eat the leftovers cold for lunch the next day. Henry was late. The children were in bed and asleep. The cat had been fed, the fire lighted. It was nearly a quarter past seven when she heard his car come up the lane and park in the garage. The engine was turned off, the garage door closed. Then the back door opened and Henry appeared, looking much as usual, except, along with his briefcase and his newspaper, he carried the biggest bunch of red roses Alison had ever seen.

With his foot, he shut the door behind him.

'Well,' he said.

'Well,' said Alison.

'They came on the wrong night.'

'Yes, I know. Mrs Fairhurst rang me. She'd written it down wrong in her diary.'

'They both think you're wonderful.'

'It doesn't matter what they think of me. It's what they think of you that counts.'

Henry smiled. He came towards her, holding the roses in front of him like an offering.

'Do you know who these are for?'

Alison considered. 'Evie, I should hope. If anyone deserves red roses, it's Evie.'

'I have already arranged for roses to be delivered to Evie. Pink ones, with lots of asparagus fern and a suitable card. Try again.'

'They're for Janey?'

'Wrong.'

'Larry? The cat?'

'Still wrong.'

'Give up.'

'They are,' said Henry, trying to sound portentous, but in point of fact looking bright-eyed as an expectant schoolboy, 'for the wife of the newly appointed Export Director of Fairhurst & Hanbury.'

249

'You got the job!'

He drew away from her and they looked at each other. Then Alison made a sound that was halfway between a sob and a shout of triumph and flung herself at him. He dropped briefcase, newspaper, and roses, and gathered her into his arms.

After a little, Catkin, disturbed by all this commotion, jumped down from his basket to inspect the roses, but when he realised that they were not edible, returned to his blanket and went back to sleep.

ROSAMUNDE PILCHER

THE SHELL SEEKERS

Artist's daughter Penelope Keeling can look back on a full
and varied life: a Bohemian childhood in London and
Cornwall, an unhappy wartime marriage, and the one
man she truly loved. She has brought up three children
– and learned to accept each of them as they are.

Yet she is far too energetic and independent to settle
sweetly into pensioned-off old-age. And when she dis-
covers that her most treasured possession, her father's
painting, *The Shell Seekers*, is now worth a small fortune,
it is Penelope who must make the decisions that will
determine whether her family can continue to survive as
a family, or be split apart.

'A deeply satisfying story written with love and confidence'
Maeve Binchy, in the *New York Times Book Review*

'A long, beguiling saga, typically English . . . splendid'
The Mail on Sunday

HODDER

ROSAMUNDE PILCHER

THE END OF SUMMER

Sitting on a California beach at summer's end, Jane Marsh thought back to her childhood at the estate called Elvie in a remote corner of Scotland. She remembered not only the heather-covered hills and lonesome loch, but her grand-mother . . . and, of course, Sinclair. She had secretly dreamed of marrying rakishly handsome Sinclair and settling at Elvie forever. Now an urgent visit from her grandmother's lawyer would become the catalyst for her return to Scotland . . . where waiting for her was passion, not gentle love, and the chilling realization that she might be ready to wed the wrong man.

HODDER

ROSAMUNDE PILCHER

ANOTHER VIEW

Emma Litton couldn't get on with her life until she found out just what place she'd had in her father's heart. Even after she met Robert Morrow, the handsome gallery owner, and rediscovered her stepbrother, Christo, she still felt compelled to probe into the truth about her past. But Emma might learn too late that it was the truth about herself she had to find and that letting go is the first step to keeping love.

HODDER

ROSAMUNDE PILCHER

SLEEPING TIGER

For the first time in her life, Selina Bruce wasn't sure what tomorrow would bring. She had impulsively left behind her lawyer fiancé in London and flown alone to a tiny island off the Spanish coast. She was searching for the father she'd never known, but exotic San Antonio offered Selina more than the penetrating brilliance of the noonday sun. It offered the mysterious George Dyer, who held the key not only to her past . . . but to her heart.

HODDER

ROSAMUNDE PILCHER

THE EMPTY HOUSE

Virgina Keile's secret dream was to have a second chance at loving the handsome Cornish farmer she had met – and foolishly lost – when she was a debutante. Life had taught her a great deal in twenty-seven years – about marrying a titled bachelor picked out by her mother, about a lonely marriage that ended in her husband's accidental death. Now she had come back to picturesque Cornwall to rent a battered seaside cottage for her children and herself . . . and to discover if this time she could fill an empty house with love.

HODDER

ROSAMUNDE PILCHER

SEPTEMBER

As spring comes to Scotland and the hills burst into life, a dance is planned for September. The invitations summon home the group of people Violet Aird has cared for most in her long life.

The oldest, strongest and wisest of them all, she sees Alexa, her vulnerable granddaughter, find love for the first time, while the decision to send her little grandson away to school is driving parents Edmund and Virginia even further apart. Far from them all is Pandora, the glamorous, exciting girl who ran away twenty years before. All will converge in Scotland this September.

'Wonderful, evocative and inviting'

Woman and Home

'Very special indeed'

Books

'Beautifully captures the magic of north-of-the-border country'

Sunday Telegraph

HODDER